T H E

KEEPER

NIKKI McCORMACK

ISBN-13: 978-0-9963196-8-3
First Edition 2016

Published by
Elysium Books
Seattle, WA

Written by Nikki McCormack (https://nikkimccormack.com/)
Cover Design by Heather Hudson (http://www.studiowondercabinet.com/)
Interior Design by Brian C. Short

*To Rick and Ann,
for your friendship, love,
and delightful conversations over many a
bottle of wine.*

rgus held a hand out behind her, signaling the other three to wait. She stepped back into the shadowed embrace of a massive steel I-beam, the hard surface radiating cold through her clothes, the smells of grease and metal thick in her nose.

Deynas, be silent, be strong. Keep the children quiet and calm.

They needed to hold their position until she signaled. The kids had done well so far, but if they experienced the same sensations she did, she wasn't sure they would be able to stand quiet this time. Her flesh prickled and her heart hammered in her chest like that of a child trapped in a night terror. She touched a finger first to her lips then lightly over her heart.

Undying Father, what comes that I should feel this much fear before I have even seen it?

She had encountered more than a few demons and crossbreeds in the process of leading others out of the overtaken city to the safety of the Endless tribe's training village in the desert. One fight left her with a shallow gash on her right shoulder and a trail of blood drying down that arm. None of those confrontations put her into the cold sweat that the approaching presence did. She was an Endless warrior, capable, quick and strong. The temporal caught in the assault depended on her.

She couldn't let herself be unsettled now.

It wasn't the first time demons had attacked this place. Back then, almost fourteen hundred years ago, it had been a small Endless city. The demons slaughtered that entire tribe. The remains of that city now lay beneath a towering metropolis run by a different Endless tribe, but home to a variety of human species and other creatures. The invading demons weren't looking to decimate the city this time, they were taking over. They were trying to eliminate the Endless tribe that ran the city, which meant they were being selective and there was time for escape. Time that was fast running out.

Keeping the one hand back to stay Deynas and the children and the other on the handle of the long dagger at her belt, she focused for a few seconds on slow and steady breathing. And silence. It wouldn't do to be heard.

She closed her eyes. The dark behind her lids was changed by whatever approached. Black and sinister, creeping. Soft footsteps shushed across the metal floor. She snapped her eyes open. A scent wafted around her, the too rich, sweet aroma of fallen rose petals crushed underfoot. She swallowed painful dryness. Whoever or whatever approached, they were now moving across the room behind the I-beam. She had to know what dread creatures gave off this foul aura, but she didn't dare step out of the deep shadows hiding her, not in physical form.

Of the three with her, only Deynas knew she was a spirit walker. He'd found out by accident. Somehow, when she moved her *umahk-ra*, her spirit form, apart from her body he could see it. He'd promised not to tell, promised on his late mother's god's blood pendant that he always wore under his shirt. It changed their relationship anyway. No matter how much she loved mentoring him, being around someone with such ability jeopardized her secret. Besides, their flirtatious banter was going to get them both into trouble eventually. She would tell Master Kochan what happened and ask him to place Deynas with a new mentor when they reached the village. First, she had to get them out of the city alive.

Glancing over her shoulder, she looked at Deynas, catching and holding his pale hazel eyes and gestured firmly for them to wait again, needing to know he would do so. He nodded, mouth set in a grim line, a hand on the shoulder of each child. She didn't look at the children. The future. Both might become Endless one day so long as they did not die here. It was her job to see that they survived.

She leaned against the cold metal, pressing her body into the corner for support, and closed her eyes again. Her hands relaxed to her sides. She stepped free of her body and drifted around into the open where she could see the walkway that passed behind them.

Tall. That was her first impression of the passing women. There were six of them moving in two rows of three, all wearing full-length, shapeless white dresses with red tubing along the seams and around the hemline. Disproportionately tiny feet in white slippers peeked out with every graceful sliding step making eerie whispers along the floor. High, rigid white collars elongated their necks and tilted the women's narrow chins up with a sharp point at the front in what looked to be an uncomfortable angle. Long, straight black hair contrasted the white paint over their faces. Their lips were painted a bright red and red eyes had been painted on their closed eyelids.

She drifted closer.

Two wires ran down either side of their collared necks emerging from the soft flesh on the underside of their jaws and disappearing down into the dress below the collarbone. A slow steady drip of red ran down each wire. Blood. The tubing on the dresses wasn't red, she realized, but clear, running red with the blood that dripped down those wires.

Argus felt her breath catch in her detached body. What were these women? Their features looked human, but they were exact copies of one another. They had to be some form of demon, though not one she'd encountered before.

The women stopped moving as one and began to hum, a resonant humming that turned her waiting flesh cold, making it shiver.

I should return to my body.

The humming reverberated through her spirit form, her *umahk-ra*, filling it with warmth that contrasted the chill consuming her flesh. The sensation was mesmerizing and terrifying. She'd never felt anything in this form, not the way she felt their haunting music. Her physical body heard the music and reacted with paralyzing fear, it didn't feel the electrifying resonance of the sound itself.

She drifted closer still, drawn by the music they made.

The women turned as if they stood on gears, rotating in place until they faced her *umahk-ra*. Then their eyes began to open, a ghastly pink light spearing from the sockets. The humming pinned her in place while the light washed over her hidden spirit form.

Six voices spoke in unison in her mind, awful sighing voices. *We see you.*

Their words preceded intense pain. Her spirit form arched back in the air, agony blazing through her, as if a boiling fluid flowed through her veins. Her physical body collapsed on the grated metal walkway. She could hear the breathing of her companions, the sound becoming so loud it hurt her suddenly hypersensitive ears. Her physical body was failing, the beat of her heart weak and faltering, but she couldn't go back. Their light held her prisoner. If she could have wept in this form, she would have, but even that release was denied her.

The women spoke again. *Your spirit is strong. Your flesh will become. Send the others away and we will not harm them.*

Their eyes closed then, cutting off the light, and her spirit form snapped back into her body, into blackness. She couldn't see. She couldn't move her arms or legs. Her chest felt heavy, each breath a struggle.

"Argus!"

A hand grabbed her shoulder and shook her.

Deynas? He forgets the honorific so often these days. I should have kissed him. I should have told him I wanted to.

She could feel them around her, Deynas and the two children, though she could not see them. For once in her life, she wanted to be selfish. She wanted to keep Deynas with her, to have him hold her the way he so obviously wanted to and tell her it would be all right.

Send them away.

"Deynas. Go. Now! Get Misa and Ren out of here."

"Argus, I won't leave you." His voice was strained, the despair in it tearing at her heart.

"Go! You have to save them. Please. I can't see. I can't move." *I can't even weep for myself. For you.* "They're your responsibility now. You have to lead them out of here." She could sense the women moving around the wall, coming closer, a sinister crimson presence in the blackness. "Go!"

A small sparkle of light dropped through the edge of the blackness, a tear, landing warm upon her cheek. Her heart split in two when his hand left her shoulder. She could hear their feet echoing upon the steel walkway as they ran away. The crimson forms moved to surround her, their voices reciting a chant both familiar and yet oddly changed.

That which is lost, you will find.
That which is forsaken, you will cherish.
That which is forgotten, you will remember.
That which is, you will keep.
The words burned through her flesh like fire. Argus screamed.

The sunlight was blistering. Deynas closed his eyes. Memories waited in the dark. Sweat trickled down the back of his neck. His hands were slick with it. He wiped them one at a time on his pants and gripped the staff.

Why?

He opened his eyes. Rage burst through him, a tidal wave of emotion battering a spirit scarred by years of such bombardment. He swept up the staff, catching the elder before him in the chin and sending him flying back. As soon as the end connected, he drew it back hard, catching the elder behind him with a jab to the gut. Then he spun, deflecting a third elder's attack and continued through, sweeping the staff around low to knock another elder's feet out from under them. He lunged after the falling elder, bringing the weapon up to strike a finishing blow. The elder hit the ground with an unmistakably feminine gasp.

Argus.

He hesitated. His vision blurred.

Green eyes, like precious stones set in a perfect face. Dark auburn hair, thick and glossy with health, with five delicate braids near the front to mark her five years as an Endless warrior. Five years that ended when he left her in the city to die.

Someone's feet planted solidly in his chest and sent

him flying. He hit the ground flat on his back with enough force that stars flashed before his eyes and another of the elders lunged in, stabbing him in the chest with a 'kill' blow.

"Deynas!"

Deynas cringed at the frustration in Master Kochan's voice. Even with padded armor, the blow hurt, but the pain blossoming in his chest wasn't entirely from the staff strike.

One of the elder fighters removed his facemask and offered Deynas a hand up. Before he could accept it, Kochan stepped in and struck the hand away.

"Let him pick himself up."

So much anger in that voice. There would be no ascendance to Endless this year if he didn't learn to silence his memories, but they persisted, quick to surface and as fresh as if he'd only left her there yesterday.

Deynas got to his feet alone and stood before the master, keeping his gaze downcast. He had shamed himself again.

"Leave us."

The other elders removed their protective masks and bowed to Kochan before exiting the sparring yard. Master Kochan didn't acknowledge the formal gestures. His steel gray eyes drilled into Deynas. His hard face bore many faint age lines and his many hundred long dark braids showed small hints of grey, a true testament to his advanced age. The eldest of the Endless in their tribe. It was a great honor to train under such a man and Deynas couldn't help wondering how much longer that honor would be granted him at this rate.

"Why do you train, Deynas? Why do you choose to be a warrior?"

Deynas blurted his answer. "I wish to fight to protect our people for as long as The Undying grants me breath to do so."

"Liar!" Master Kochan barked the accusation in his face. The big man's hawkish nose almost touched Deynas' bowed forehead. "You seek vengeance. Your mind is clouded with memory. Memory is meant to fade. Wounds to heal. This has only gotten worse with time. Even your *umahk-ra* resonates with her name. It has been five years since she died. Why do you cling to her?"

Kochan backed up several steps.

Deynas bowed his head more, the weight of truth heavy upon him. *Why? Undying Father, why can't I let her go?*

The whistle of a staff cutting the air warned him. The move was fast, so fast that he braced for the expected pain and was shocked when he got his own staff up in time to block the attack, the power of the master's strike jarring through his arms. He looked over their crossed staves into Kochan's eyes.

"Few Endless warriors could have blocked that strike. You waste yourself in remembrance." The master spun and began to walk away. "Go back to the ranks and fight with the temporal warriors. You are too broken to be Endless."

Deynas dropped to his knees with the sinking of his heart. It could not end this way. He shamed not only himself, but also the woman who had mentored him and died so that he and the others might live. "Master Kochan!"

Kochan stopped at the edge of the sparring yard. He didn't turn. His back was a wall, impenetrable and cold.

Deynas laid his staff on the ground and bowed before it. "Master Kochan, I fight to atone for my failure. I fight to honor the memory of Argus-ra. I want to be to the people the kind of warrior, the kind of hero, that she was. If this is a flawed ambition, then you are right, I cannot be Endless."

A shadow fell over him, shielding him from the intense desert sun. "Deynas." The hard edge was gone from the master's voice. "Yours was not a failure. You were the second oldest there. It was your duty to protect the children when Argus-ra fell. Had you not done so, had the children also fallen, then that would have been a failure."

Deynas stayed bowed. Tears stung his eyes and he bit his lip, fighting to hold them back. *Endless do not weep.*

Endless weep the same as anyone else.

Deynas stiffened. Though he'd never experienced such contact before, he recognized the light touch of the master's *umahk-ra* accompanying the words in his mind.

Kochan touched his shoulder. "You loved her."

A tear slipped free and a tiny puff of dust rose where it landed.

"Such passion and promise in one so young. Perhaps you have a place among the Endless yet. Come with me."

Deynas rose and followed Kochan into the temple. Inside, they both knelt on woven carpets and bowed before the towering statue of The Undying, the three-headed god of the Endless.

The head on the right, its features soft and undefined, represented the *umahk-ra*. The one on the left, the features strong and crisply defined, represented the mortal flesh. The center head was a blending of the two, a representation of the true Endless state achieved by no more than a third of those who carried the blood of The Undying, a perfect state of harmony between spirit and flesh.

It was this third head Deynas gazed up at as he stripped off his padded armor. Then he laid the armor on a bench and followed the master out of the soaring main chamber and into a small side chamber. Incense burned upon a shelf, its gentle spice filling the air with a soothing aroma. They knelt on either side of a low stone table and waited in silence until a servant brought tea in two plain stoneware cups. When they were alone again, Kochan sipped the tea then waited until Deynas had done the same before speaking.

The master turned the teacup so the handle pointed at his own torso, indicating his intent to speak.

Deynas set his tea down and turned the handle toward Kochan, indicating his willingness to hear the master's words. He waited.

"You have seen only twenty-three summers. You are but an infant to the ascended Endless." Kochan released a heavy exhale. "Argus-ra was also young. Barely twenty-three herself when she was lost in the city and already five years as an Endless warrior."

Deynas stared into the pale tea, watching tiny flakes of dried leaf that had slipped through the strainer sink to the bottom of the cup. Argus had become Endless at eighteen, something he had yet to achieve at twenty-three. He might have loved her, but she had been much too good for him. Was that what Kochan wanted him to realize? Did the master want him to see how much less he was than her?

"Her loss was felt deeply. She was *umahk-ra-en-mahde*." Kochan drank again and set the cup with the handle pointing to his right. "Do you know what that is?"

Deynas nodded. He left his cup as it was. He'd been given permission to speak, but this was Kochan's conversation to direct. "Yes. She was a spirit walker. One who can separate and move their *umahk-ra* apart from their physical self."

The incense wasn't strong enough to ward off the anxiety brought on by Kochan's shrewd gaze. Deynas focused on the rhythm of his own breathing and the beat of his heart, trying not to fret over what the master might be speculating.

"Spirit walking is a rare gift, yet you do not seem surprised to learn this of her."

How much to say? He could lie and say that Argus told him. Nothing he said could hurt her now, but the truth might hurt him. And yet...

He stared into those hard grey eyes. Ageless wisdom stared back at him.

How many braids did Kochan wear now? How many summers had he watched pass? How many hopefuls had he trained to Endless and how many had he watched fail to reach that lofty goal as Deynas himself seemed destined to do? How many loved ones had he seen die while he lived on? Did one dare keep secrets from the eldest of the Endless?

No, one didn't lie to such a man. "When we were working our way through the city that night, before we found Misa and Ren, she moved her *umahk-ra* apart to scout out an exposed crossing. I saw her spirit then and I saw it again before the Blooded Women crippled her." Anger crept into his voice when he spoke of the Blooded Women. He'd felt so helpless, forced to run away and leave her to them. They still knew almost nothing about those strange creatures.

Kochan took another sip of his tea. He stared into it, rotating the cup slowly in his fingers while he spoke this time. Leaving Deynas to wonder if the conversation dynamic was about to change again. "And you heard me when I spoke into your mind with my *umahk-ra* in the training yard, did you not?"

"Yes, Master."

"The problem you face makes more sense now. You are *umahk-ra-uden*. A spirit thief."

Deynas half-rose. "I am no thief."

Kochan held a hand out and motioned for him to sit. Deynas sank back to his knees.

"We no longer speak of such gifts because they are

often misunderstood by the temporal and because they make the bearer of such gifts a target for demons that collect or devour souls. There has not been a spirit thief in this tribe for over two-hundred years. The *umahk-ra-uden* is not a true spirit thief. Think of it as something more akin to the Keeper."

The Keeper? "But isn't the Keeper a demon?"

Kochan contemplated his cup. "We do not know what the Keeper truly is."

Deynas frowned. "And the Keeper doesn't collect just any spirits. Never those of the Endless nor those of mortal men."

"No. The Keeper collects only the spirits of certain creatures when they die, usually higher demon species that are nearly extinct or gods that are the only ones of their kind."

"What does she do with those spirits?"

"Preserves them. To what end, we do not know and for this discussion, it does not matter. Where the Keeper collects and preserves the full *umahk-ra* of the deceased, the spirit thief collects only a fragment of any *umahk-ra* that is revealed to them. Typically, this can only occur in the moment after death except in the rare case of a spirit walker. Just as a drawing of someone captures their physical image, the fragment a spirit thief captures holds an exact image of the person's spirit. I suspect that the fragment of her spirit you carry with you is the reason Argus continues to live so strongly in you."

"What does a spirit thief do with these fragments of *umahk-ra?*"

Kochan scratched his bearded chin. "I'm afraid I know little more of the gift than what I just told you. I do know the spirit thief is unusually sensitive to the *umahk-ra* of others and can sometimes hear thoughts directed at them as you did mine in the training circle. Your reaction confirmed what I had already begun to suspect about you. Why have you not spoken of your ability before?"

Deynas turned away, focusing on the lazy rise of smoke from the incense burner. "The first time it happened, I assumed others did the same thing I did. When I realized they didn't, I worried that something was wrong, that my *umahk-ra* had been corrupted somehow."

"If that had been true, you realize the ritual to become Endless would have stripped you of your *umahk-ra* and left you an empty shell?"

Deynas lifted his chin. "That was my risk to take."

Kochan shook his head, but he let the comment go without argument. "It would be best if we could find an elder *umahk-ra-uden* to work with you. I know of one who might be willing if he yet lives. He is the master of an eastern tribe who has seen even more summers than I have. I will send for him."

Deynas started to lean forward then stopped himself. It was disrespectful and immature to exhibit such impatience. "What do I do until we hear from this man?"

Kochan took a long drink of the cooling tea and Deynas deliberately did the same, trying to emulate the other man's composure. They both set their cups down, handles pointed to Kochan's right. "For now, Deynas, you will continue to train and seek what peace you can achieve on your own with the fragment of Argus-ra's spirit that resides within you."

He inhaled the incense in the air, steeling his nerves for the question he most wanted to ask. "Is there still a chance that I might ascend to Endless?"

Kochan smiled with uncommon gentleness. "It is no surprise that you and Argus were drawn together. The gifted are often drawn to like spirits." He tapped his fingers on the table then, pondering. "Argus-ra never went through the ritual to become Endless. The Undying chooses those among us who will bear such gifts and raises them without a proving. Because Argus was *umahk-ra-en-mahde* she became Endless when her spirit was ready. As *umahk-ra-uden*, it will be the same for you, though I fear this conflict within you has held you back. Know that you are destined to become Endless, Deynas. Nothing anyone says or does can change that. Now go. I must prepare a message."

Deynas rested his fingers on the edge of the low table and touched his forehead to them in a bow before rising. Master Kochan inclined his head in return, then called for a servant. Deynas left the room, but he did not leave the temple. He knelt before The Undying on a woven carpet and bowed his head, closing his eyes. The six eyes of the god gazed down heavy upon him.

The idea that something of Argus lived on in him brought him a sense of almost giddy joy, joy tempered by the dark certainty that he didn't deserve to carry any part of her within him. Kochan was right. It had been his duty as the second eldest to get the others to safety. The knowledge brought no peace. Most nights her screams, fading behind them as they ran away, haunted his dreams. They hadn't known what the Blooded Women were then. One of the few things they knew now was that the Blooded Women could see spirits. If they had understood what they faced, Argus would never have ventured out before them in spirit form. He'd seen her step out of her body and had crept forward to watch her. He could still see her *umahk-ra* convulsing in agony before the glowing eyes of the Blooded Women while her physical body collapsed beside him.

She never knew he loved her. He'd been afraid to tell her. Afraid she would laugh at him for being young and impetuous. She would not have laughed. He knew that now, perhaps because a part of her lived within him. But it was too late now. Much too late.

The Keeper felt the whisper of approaching death several minutes before the summons came and she disappeared. Once the flesh died, transfer had to come soon after. There was a small window of time, sometimes only a few minutes, sometimes longer, in which to collect the spirit of a being before it reabsorbed into the flow of energy that fueled all life. She had to be always ready for that moment, though, in this incarnation as in a few prior ones, she had learned to sense ripples in the flow that often preceded the death of a rare demon or a god as much as twenty minutes before their actual passing.

She appeared in a shadowed place, as she often did. This time it was at the edge of an indoor stadium, in an aisle between two sections of rising stone seats. The seating surrounded an immense dirt floored arena. The floor was dug down perhaps twenty feet below the lowest row of seating and high, spiked iron fences rose up twenty feet into the air, creating a barrier nearly forty feet high to separate the audience from the combatants. Towering gas torches, their stands molded into the shapes of several different greater gods, were set at intervals around the arena, adding drama to the setting with the dancing of flames.

She recognized the stadium. The call to keep had

brought her here before. It was in a restored part of the old Endless ruins carved into ground and now buried beneath the Undercity. She could feel the weight of life in the Undercity and the Old and New Cities above that pressing down.

The cheering of the crowd rose up loud and fierce, a bloodthirsty roar that filled the vast space with stifling sound pressure. She checked that her cloak—a dark silver and green woven material that moved in such a way as to make it nigh impossible to focus upon her at moments like this when she couldn't be completely invisible—hung far enough forward to shroud her face in impenetrable shadow. Then she walked down the aisle and up to the edge of the arena.

A hush started to fall in the seating nearest her. She touched the iron bars with her right hand and a section of the barrier rippled, melting down to reform itself into a ramp leading to the arena floor. The hush spread as she began to descend.

In the arena, dark greenish blood drenched the dirt, creating pools of foul smelling mud. A warrior stood in the center holding high a massive double bladed staff. He was part-man judging from his overall appearance, and at least a third demon judging from his considerable size, the backswept horns over his very human ears, and the blue cast of his skin. His weapon dripped thick globs of dark blood.

Before him lay a colossal creature, much like an octopus with its many limbs, but born to navigate the sands, not the sea. A greater mimic or shapechanger. It was a relatively simple-minded creature, but quite rare indeed, though not the absolute last of its kind. Not yet. A wood stake protruded from one eye, placed there to handicap the creature to 'balance' the competition. Aside from limiting the creature's vision, she could sense a poison in the wood to inhibit shape shifting, an increasingly rare poison given the scarcity of such demons.

The crossbreed warrior let out a roar of victory, trying to rouse the crowd again, but the hush falling over the audience finished its spread and a new sound began to take the place of the cheering. A soft chanting filled the air and many among the stands knelt, bowing their heads. Even in this den of vice, most revered the legend that was the Keeper. Their voices lifted, creating dark sorrowful harmony.

"*That which is lost, she will find.*"

The big warrior lowered his weapon. She was halfway across the arena now, close enough to smell the cloying scent of the dead demon's skin and the salty tang of sweat from the crossbreed.

"*That which is forsaken, she will cherish.*"

The warrior turned. His gaze lit upon the shadows of her hood and veered abruptly away. Many believed that to gaze into her hood was to bring death.

"*That which is forgotten, she will remember.*"

The warrior sank to his knees and set his weapon on the ground before him. He bowed his head.

"*That which is, she will keep.*"

The Keeper walked past him to the dead changer. Black roots, a physical manifestation of the power residing inside her, twined over the surface of her right arm, trailing down to taper off over her fingertips like long black nails, an ever-present indicator of her unique purpose. She placed this hand upon the demon's smooth purplish flesh. Swirling wind rose up in the arena, touching everything except her. Her cloak didn't move, but the watchers in the stands had to grab their hats, refreshments, and betting tickets to keep them from blowing away. Dirt lifted in that wind, obscuring the entire arena floor. The spirit of the dead changer moved up and out of the flesh that once contained it. It glowed before her eyes as brightly as the sun.

She lowered her gaze, bowing her head respectfully. *Come to me and you shall be remembered.*

No creature was so humble that it did not wish to live on in some way beyond death. At her words, the shapechanger's spirit swirled down, sinking into the roots that were a part of her flesh. With it came all of the pain of its death. The Keeper clenched her teeth and sucked back on a scream. It was always this way and she could not show weakness. She must hold the pain or risk losing the spirit. She had to accept it all, though it tore through her flesh as if the death had been her own. The long agony of the spike buried in the demon's eye, the pain of each strike of the warrior's blade splitting its flesh, all of it became her pain, compacted into almost a minute of anguish as the spirit flowed into her.

Then the wind stopped. The dirt fell wherever the wind had carried it, some showering down upon the crowd. The Keeper turned and faced the warrior. The spirit was kept, now there were punishments to deal out.

The warrior's head remained bowed as she approached. He began to tremble when she rested the fingers of her right hand upon his dust-coated brow. His physical strength could not protect him from this and he knew it.

"You have committed an unforgivable crime. Your life continues at the whim of greater powers, for death is not mine to deal, but you must pay in suffering."

"I must pay in suffering," the warrior repeated, a jaw full of oversized teeth garbling his words.

The poor creature wasn't much more than a malformed beast himself, handicapped by the mix of his blood and suited to little more than the life of a gladiator or thug. She pitied him, but that didn't stop her from passing the pain she'd absorbed briefly into him.

He let out a tortured howl and his body went rigid.

When she took her hand away, he fell to the floor, convulsing with the aftershocks of that agony.

The Keeper left him there, her business with him complete. Another deserved to feel that pain even more than the warrior did. This other had left the arena even before the end of the battle, but she didn't need to worry about finding him. The power within could sense him and it transported her, moving her from the torch lit stadium to the shadows of a dimly lit bedroom in an Undercity hotel.

A man was in the room, his back to her. He busily tucked clothing in a heavy pack that lay upon the neatly made bed. Ready to check out, it appeared. A short curved sword lay next to the pack, well within his reach. Black hair, generously run through with the silver of age, hung down to his shoulders. She walked up behind him. The man grabbed the sword and spun with startling speed. She caught the blade with her right hand, the black roots protecting her skin from its cutting edge. His eyes widened and he let go of the sword, dropping to one knee. He bowed his head.

"Forgive me, Keeper."

She stepped back from him and let the sword fall to the floor. The thud was the loudest sound for several heartbeats. She could sense the difference in his spirit, his *umahk-ra* she knew he would call it, that trace of something that made him a different breed from the thousands of humans still living in the city. In his veins ran the blood of The Undying. Few of his kind dared venture into the city now. Her left hand rose up under her hood seemingly of its own volition to touch the five braids in her hair.

Braids? Her hand sank back to her side.

"You are Endless?" The word stirred a deep unease in her as it passed her lips. She could see his shoulders tighten in discomfort or fear, but he kept his eyes downcast.

"I am."

"Where are your braids?"

He started to raise his eyes then caught himself and bowed his head lower than before. "I am *umahk-ra-uden*. I was never a warrior."

Umahk-ra-uden. The same as...as who? She struggled with the overwhelming familiarity of the term until he shifted and she pushed the feeling away.

"And yet you carry a sword?"

"I would be a fool to wander the Undercity unarmed."

That was true and irrelevant. She had a purpose to fulfill and only that purpose mattered. "You have committed an unforgivable crime. Your life continues at the whim of greater powers, for death is not mine to deal, but you must pay in suffering."

"I accept my punishment."

She rested her right hand on his head and let the pain flow briefly through. He stiffened, like the warrior, but didn't cry out or fall. He was stronger, not in flesh so much as in spirit. She turned her back on him, ready to depart. A soft yet insistent murmuring in the back of her mind compelled her to turn and face him again, and to say things she should not say.

"You needn't kneel before me. I am no god."

He didn't move, but there was fresh tension in his posture, an unvoiced anticipation flowing from him. "Then what are you?"

What am I? His question vexed her, as did his subservient pose. "Stand."

He rose with keen grace that spoke to considerable training and physical discipline. He still kept his gaze downcast. Tears ran silent down his cheeks. She raised her left hand and caught one upon her fingertips, bringing it to her lips. It tasted of sorrow, not pain.

"The warrior was merely a brute, paid to fight any

opponent brought before him. I understand how he came to this. You are no fool. You are Endless." *Umahk-ra-uden. Spirit thief. I remember.* "You cannot claim his ignorance. To bring an end to such a creature, one of the last of its kind, for mere sport. Why would you knowingly do this?"

"As you say, I am Endless. The Endless tribes were slaughtered or driven from this city by demon-kind. Perhaps the procurement of such rarities for the arenas is the only way I can sate my hunger for vengeance."

"If that is true, then why do you weep for its death?"

The muscles in his jaw twitched. The question made him uncomfortable, but he was quick to turn it back. "Is not any death sufficient cause for mourning?"

He answers me with such a question. She felt a strange twisting in her chest. Why had she spoken to him at all? What made her linger here? She turned away again.

"Wait."

She waited, still as a statue, knowing she should be gone and relishing, in some part of her being, that she was pushing boundaries, even if she wasn't sure who had laid those boundaries to begin with or why.

"Where do you go now, Keeper?"

She stared into the shadows of the doorway. It was none of his business. *Endless. Umahk-ra-uden. Have I known another like him?* "I go wherever I wish until I am needed again."

"I am Naago-ra. Travel with me for a time."

The Keeper turned to search his face. Was he serious? Did he realize how absurdly inappropriate the request was? "Why?"

He looked into her hood, peering against the un-natural darkness that shielded her features from curious eyes. He didn't fear it, or perhaps he didn't care enough to fear.

"If you are no god, then you are alone, as I am. For

a short time, mightn't we appreciate the company of one another?"

Such presumption. And curiosity. Hers as much as his. The twining roots felt tight upon her arm and shoulder. Warning or anticipation? She looked into his deep blue eyes. They were very old, those eyes. "Be quick then. I do not wish to linger here."

That was true. Something or someone in the Undercity, in this hotel in particular, beckoned her. Not in the sense of spirit that needed keeping, but something else, at once familiar and strange. Whatever it was, it made her uneasy and she dreaded coming here.

Was that a smirk she saw before he turned back to his packing?

The glimpses of a manner that bordered on disrespect didn't reconcile with the reverence he'd shown her at first. Perhaps she should have let him continue to regard her as a god, but, for reasons she didn't understand, she didn't like to see him kneeling before her. That was why she agreed to travel with him, out of mere curiosity. Besides, the Blooded Women did not care where she wandered, so long as she was there when a spirit needed keeping. Wandering the world unseen and alone had lost its novelty many incarnations ago.

Naago closed his pack. He tucked the sword into a sheath at his belt then pulled on a long brown leather duster and matching hat, both scuffed, faded and scarred with hard use. After scanning the room once, he threw the pack over one shoulder and pulled the hat down so the brim shadowed his face.

"Shall we." He gestured to the door.

She didn't move. This was wrong somehow and yet somehow comfortable. "I will follow you."

He shrugged and moved past, picking up a hard case that sat in the shadows near the door on his way out. "If you like."

She followed him from the room and out into the dark streets of the Undercity. Those streets smelled of blood, old and fresh. Some of it came from the meat processing plant at the east edge of the district, but most came from the many fighting rings. There were twenty-five registered rings and another fifteen or so operating without permits. She had been called to keep in several of them. The city's enforcers raided the illegals and put in a token effort at shutting them down on occasion, but the self-titled warlords who ran the Undercity were always a step ahead. They hired people to pose as vagrants among the thousands living on those dark streets and give warning whenever enforcers started a sweep.

They were out there now among the beggars, petty criminals, and thrill seekers; men and women who watched for the warlords, risking punishments much worse than death for the ability to feed themselves and their families. There was a certain shrewdness in their eyes when they thought no one was watching that gave them away, and they never knew when she was watching. They gave Naago measuring looks, but only him. Their eyes slid past her as if she were not there.

The Endless man was attentive enough to notice the behavior before they'd walked more than half a block. "Why don't they look at you?"

"It is the cloak. It lets me be seen only when I choose to be seen by whom I choose to let see me. When I keep, I must be seen because all should know when a spirit worthy of keeping has passed. The rest of the time, it is my choice to be seen or not."

A battered flyer buzzed loudly past, the breeze that rose in its wake blowing back Naago's duster. Her cloak didn't move. He noticed this too.

"Damn. It's as if you aren't even there. I could use a cloak like that."

"To them, I am not here."

He glanced around at the eyes of the many humans, demons, and crossbreeds roaming the street and his expression soured. "Oh. That's nice. So they think I'm talking to myself?"

A rare thrill of amusement spread warm through her chest and brought a slight curve to her lips. "I imagine they do."

Someone rang the singing stone outside his hut. The warm, rich tone of the stone's song drew Deynas up from a restless sleep. He sat on the edge of the stone slab that served as his bed. The bedding needed refreshing. It had for some time now. Because of that, his body ached as if he'd slept the night with nothing between him and the hard stone.

"Deynas."

Misa.

He stared at his bare feet, toes curling on loose strands in the rough woven carpet alongside the bed. Yesterday's clothes lay in a heap on one corner of the carpet. It was time to do some washing. When Argus was around, he'd learned to find ways of keeping up with those mundane chores. She teased him about the state of his room when he let it go and made him work twice as hard in training. Without her, old habits crept back in. Maybe, if he let it get bad enough, her spirit would come back to chastise him.

A soft, weary chuckle slipped between his lips at the thought.

"Come on, Deynas. Master Kochan said you would take us to chase the wind today. He needs a message sent."

His hands tightened on the edge of the stone slab.

Why give him such a task when he had training to do? Plenty of temporal warriors in the village at the base of the cliff were capable enough flyer pilots to chase the wind. Was Kochan trying to distract him from his troubles? Or perhaps the Endless master meant to show him that he was sending the message to the other master with haste to reassure him. Either way, sending him out with Misa and her younger brother was far from the most effective way to get his mind off Argus. They were the two children he'd led out of the city the night Argus died. They were the reasons he couldn't stay and save her… or die trying.

"Deynas? Are you in there?" Misa was starting to sound uncertain.

He rubbed his eyes and stood. "I'll be right out."

Perhaps this was a test of his flying skills. He would have to take out one of the bigger flyers to accommodate his passengers. He hadn't flown one of those since his early training days and then only a couple of times. They weren't as agile as the smaller birds like his.

There was nothing suitable for flying in the folded stack of clean clothes on the shelf, so he dug through the piles on the floor until he found a one piece training uniform that didn't make him feel woozy when he sniffed it. It was the appropriate grey and blue of a flying suit at least, which meant it must have been on the floor for over a month. Long enough for the stench of sweat to dissipate. Unbidden memories crept in while he stepped into the suit.

He was fastening the last button on the front of the uniform when the door swung open and Argus stepped in, backlit by bright sunlight, auburn locks tossed by a gentle breeze. The four small Endless braids, soon to be five, hung heavier than the rest.

Her intense gaze swept around his room. Disapproval stiffened her posture. "Look at this disaster."

He gaped at her for a moment, still half-asleep, then he glanced around at the messy room. His cheeks grew hot. "Training's been keeping me so busy. I..."

She laughed, her posture relaxing and a sudden smile bringing the sunlight into the room. Then she stepped around him and put a hand in his back, pushing him toward the door. "Don't think I'm going to lighten up on you so you can keep up with your chores. You'll have to sleep less."

He stepped through the door and glanced over his shoulder at her, wanting to catch another glimpse of her smile.

"Come along, tenderfoot." She winked. "Let's fly."

His whole body warmed in response to her teasing, a burst of fresh energy flowing through him.

Tears stung his eyes. One hand balled into a fist and he swung out, connecting with the unyielding stone wall. Pain and regret rewarded the action.

"Son-of-a-bitch!" He curled over his hand and gritted his teeth against blossoming pain. He was lucky he hadn't broken it. As it was, he'd split the skin over two knuckles.

"Deynas? You all right?"

"Yep, fine. One more minute."

"Alright."

After rinsing the blood away in the basin, he wrapped the knuckles with a strip of cloth and ran a comb through his hair. Still no braids for the teeth to catch upon. What he wouldn't give to have that to complain about.

A song crept into the room, the deep tones, rising and falling, carefully drummed out on the singing stone. Misa was getting restless. Adolescent impatience played out on the stone. He listened a moment, letting the neatly crafted tune eat away at his melancholy until he could muster a smile again. Then he tucked his mother's pendant under his shirt and jerked open the door.

Misa startled, jumping back and stumbling over her own feet. She looked up at him with wide brown eyes that narrowed quickly.

"You did that on purpose."

He grinned. "Yes, I did. Where's Ren?"

"He ran to get some seed bread."

"Not even going to let me sit down for breakfast in the hall first?"

She smiled, a sparkle of excitement gleaming in her eyes. "Nope. We're going up." One finger pointed to the bright morning sky. "Besides, Master Kochan said you'd be in a hurry to get this message off."

He looked up. There was almost no breeze and a few wispy clouds lay white across the blue sky like paintbrush strokes. Going up this early would avoid the heat of the day, but there would be very few wind spirits active in that tranquil sky.

"What happened to your hand?"

"Nothing." His knuckles throbbed in disagreement. He looked at her. "You have the message?"

"Of course." She tapped the pocket sewn into the arm of her flight suit for carrying such message vials. "What's in it?"

Her sly sideways glance had an edge of sultry in it that threw him off for a few seconds. He gave himself a mental shake and turned to look up the road toward where the landing pad waited. "Shall we go pick out our flyer?"

"Yes." There was a hint of a pout on her lips before she bounded ahead of him, her youthful energy burning through his lingering fog of sleep.

She had already picked out a newer pale grey and lavender flyer and was fiddling with the harness straps in the inset passenger seat when Ren caught up carrying a small basket containing several slices of seed bread slathered in honey butter and three small cups. The cups were for the teapot dangling from two fingers under the basket. The ungainliness of his age making it all look far more precarious than it probably was. Deynas took the basket and the teapot. They sat upon the deck of the craft and made quick work of the meal. Then Ren set the dishes on a workbench and hopped into the seat.

Misa followed him and they strapped themselves in, checking one another's buckles before pulling on their goggles. They were both enthusiastic and attentive students. Misa was old enough that her brunette hair hung down to her shoulders to show that she had begun training to join the Endless ranks. Long enough to braid if she ascended, but restricted to exactly that length until she either ascended or was denied a place among The Undying's chosen. Ren, his short-cropped hair a shade lighter than his sister's, had less than a year to go before he could officially declare whether he would try for Endless or be satisfied with the status and life expectancy of a temporal tribesman.

Becoming Endless required years of rigorous training and sacrifice, and there was no guarantee of ascendance no matter how hard one worked for it. Those who did ascend were sworn to protect the rest of the tribe in times of danger. Many people chose to forego the possibility of extraordinary longevity in favor of enjoying the more certain temporal life free from the burden of martial service and constant training expected of the Endless. It took a special fire in one's spirit to earn a place as one of The Undying's favored children. Misa had that fire. Ren didn't seem to, not yet, but there was still time.

Deynas rechecked their straps himself and took the message vial from Misa, tucking it into the pocket on his suit before he walked to the fore of the craft. He buckled his feet down into the insets on the deck of the flyer and adjusted the pedals so that he could reach them with his toes. Then he stood straight, resting his back against the support stand and buckled on the harness that would hold him upright against it. He faced forward over the pointed beak of the craft and adjusted the independent hand control rods to the right height. When he was satisfied, he put on his goggles and twisted the key to turn on the flyer.

With a low whistle and a sharp hissing noise, the craft came to life and rose to hover about three feet above the stone landing pad. The landing legs whirred as they retracted up into small compartments in the bottom. It wobbled when he adjusted his balance. He shifted from side to side to get a feel for its responsiveness, rocking the craft back and forth until the tips of the long wings gently tapped the stone. Precision was crucial to flying. The smallest movement could have significant impact upon the craft in the air. When he felt comfortable, he gave it more fuel with the thumb throttle and pulled the hand levers back enough to get a nice, gradual lift.

As soon as they were clear of the landing area and high enough to avoid striking the tail on the ground, he plunged his thumb down on the throttle and pulled back hard. The flyer surged upward on a steep ascent. Misa's delighted squeal brought a grin to his lips.

Warm air whipped around them, creating a wind of their own. Deynas took his thumb off the throttle, letting the craft hang in the air for a second before it began to drop. His long black hair blew into his face. Then he pushed the levers forward to different degrees and hit the throttle again, surging into a long, banking right turn that swept his hair back again. From there, he straightened the craft then dove, pulling up hard again several feet above the red stone of the temple spire.

Misa giggled in delight again. Ren's laugh sounded strained.

Deynas nodded to himself. The big flyer wasn't as agile as his was, but he had it well under control. He took them up then, waving at a few patrol flyers running watch circuits on the way past, and holding a gradual ascent until they were high enough to run with the wind spirits. He flipped a switch on the control rod with his right hand. The craft began to emit a long high note as it went along, a sound that would draw wind spirits to them. He settled into a steady cruising speed and waited.

A wind spirit appeared almost five minutes later, a rippling misty form that looked much like the wispy clouds, its sentient nature given away by deliberate movements and vivid blue eyes that watched them while it darted around the craft, sizing them up.

Deynas began to turn the craft, working to get into position without alarming the spirit. It rarely worked that way, however, and this time was no exception. The wind spirit sped away and Deynas punched the throttle, giving chase. The spirit led them down and around at such a speed that the bigger flyer was hard pressed to keep up. Then the spirit stopped and turned, charging at them.

Despite his surprise, Deynas reacted in an instant, dropping the left wing and going into a big barrel roll that swept them out and around the spirit. The spirit twisted in the air and charged them again. He gunned the throttle. This time, the spirit caught the tip of the wing and rocked them hard enough that the engine stuttered and his passengers both cried out. He kept the craft moving away from the hostile spirit, twisting to glance over his shoulder. The spirit hovered a ways behind them, big blue eyes watching them flee. He might have tried to catch it, if not for his passengers. As it was, he would need to report the incident to Master Kochan. That kind of aggression wasn't normal in a wind spirit.

A short distance ahead, he spotted another wind spirit. Pushing aside his rattled nerves, he focused on this new quarry and gave chase. They raced through the sky, diving, spiraling, rolling and rising like birds in a mating dance. This was how it usually worked. The moment he got a clean shot, he pressed the button to release the spirit net. It sparkled silver in the sunlight as it jetted out and wrapped around the spirit, giving its inconstant shape a more solid border for an instant before the net disintegrated, falling away in a rain of silver dust. The wind spirit waited for them where the net had caught it. The game was won.

Deynas pulled up the craft next to it.

The great blue eyes blinked slowly at him. Its voice, when it spoke, was like a whisper on a breeze, sometimes dropping almost below his ability to hear it. "You chase well, Deynas-ra."

No matter how many times he dealt with the wind spirits, it unnerved him that they always knew his name, though this one erred by including the honorific. Deynas inclined his head. "Thank you, Wind Lord, but I am not true Endless."

"Not in this moment, perhaps." The spirit blinked twice, its form rippling in the air. "What favor do you seek?"

Deynas drew the vial out of the pocket. "A message."

"I will honor our covenant and deliver this message."

"Thank you, Wind Lord."

Deynas dumped the contents of the vial, the message dust, out on his palm. The wind spirit swirled around him, drawing the dust into itself, then it sped away. Deynas tucked the empty vial back into the pocket and twisted to look back at his passengers.

"Mission accomplished. You want to drive back, Misa?"

"I do." Misa had her harness detached before she finished answering and started to move quickly over the flyer's deck.

Deynas opened his mouth to tell her to clip on her safety line, but she was already almost to him, her stance low and well balanced. Later, he could reprimand her. For now, he needed to focus on getting her in place and buckled in. He reached a hand back to her. Her fingertips touched his, then the craft lurched, tipping steeply to one side. Time stopped for an instant as he stared into Misa's wide eyes, then she was toppling, falling out of his reach over the side of the flyer.

"Misa!"

Ren's cry tore through him, full of an anguish that Deynas knew too well. It haunted his nights when he dreamed of Argus. He turned and grabbed the controls, catching a glimpse of the wind spirit that had struck the flyer. The same one they'd had trouble with earlier. It had followed them. He pushed the levers and gunned the throttle, diving hard and spinning to get a visual on Misa. He spotted her fast, slender legs and arms spread wide to slow her descent. Every tribe member learned how to fall before they were allowed to go up on a flyer. She'd learned that lesson well.

Deynas pulled up level to get a target lock on her. Too high. The two patrol flyers they'd seen earlier were speeding their direction. He dove again and pulled up well below her, steadying the craft and holding a finger over the trigger for the rescue net. When Misa was a few feet above their altitude, he hit the trigger. The net wrapped around her. The line reeled out more and stretched to slow her descent without jerking her too hard. When it finally pulled tight, the craft tipped and Deynas shifted his weight hard to counterbalance. As soon as it steadied, he flipped the switch to start reeling her up.

A massive knot of tension unwound in his chest, allowing him to breathe again. He closed his eyes for a second, the image of Misa falling burned into his mind.

He exhaled and leaned back, letting the support stand and harness hold his weight for a moment. A shifting of the craft drew his attention to his other passenger. Ren was working at the buckles on his harness.

"Don't," he ordered. "Stay there. I'll get her."

Not wanting to risk another incident, he scanned around for the rogue spirit. The other flyers were pulling up alongside them now. The spirit was nowhere in sight. He clipped a safety to the support stand before unbuckling his harness from it and moved to the edge where the line was bringing up their catch. As soon as she was in reach, he grabbed her and pulled her up, releasing the bands on the net. It fell away and retracted into the craft.

Misa wrapped her arms around his neck and clung to him, her grip almost strangling. She was shaking.

"Are you all right?"

He pushed her back, holding tight to her arms, and looked her in the eyes. There were tears on her cheeks, but she nodded, a fire of shame coloring her face.

"I'm an idiot." Her voice shook.

"You let enthusiasm and overconfidence override caution. No matter how sure you are on your feet, clipping on the safety needs to be your first action any time you move around on a flyer." He wiped away a tear running down her cheek and forced a smile. "But you fell very well, Misa. You kept your head and used your body to slow your fall."

She nodded and wiped away another tear with one trembling hand, staring into his eyes with an intense admiration that made him feel suddenly awkward holding her. "I knew you would catch me. You've always protected us."

The words twisted like a dagger in his chest, stealing his breath away.

She didn't seem to notice. Instead, she shifted her

weight against him and reached toward the pilot support stand.

He found his voice again. "What are you doing?"

She gave him a puzzled look. "Driving."

"I suppose I did offer." He nodded approval when she clipped in her safety. "You could have died. If you make another mistake like that, I will have to recommend that you be grounded."

Satisfied with the look of abject horror on her face at his words, he stood and moved back to the pillar, attaching his harness to it before securing her harness to his. She wasn't yet approved to fly solo so it was tandem or nothing.

One of the other craft sank down alongside theirs.

"You three all right?"

Deynas nodded. "We're all right, though it looks like we've got a corrupted wind spirit. I'll report it to Master Kochan after we land."

The pilot nodded. "I expect we'll see you on the hunt then. Fly strong."

Deynas nodded in return. Misa settled herself against him, refreshing that awkward feeling from moments ago. Forcing himself to ignore it, he gave her the go ahead to move them out.

•

"You did well today, Deynas."

Deynas knelt before Kochan and lowered his gaze. "I almost got Misa killed."

"Her overconfidence and a corrupt spirit almost got her killed," he countered. "You are too quick to assign guilt to yourself. This once I will tell you kindly to stop doing so. Next time, I will take a staff and use it to pound this foolishness out of your head. Understood?"

It was remarkable how the man could threaten

bodily harm and sound so benevolent doing so. "Yes, Master."

"You did precisely what was expected of you. We must all mentor the young. When something went wrong, you kept your wits about you and dealt with it as well as any true Endless warrior would have." Kochan paced in front of him, striding back and forth before the bare feet of The Undying with his hands clasped behind his back. There was an uneasy air about him. "The important thing at the moment is that we have a corrupted wind spirit to deal with. Though I hate to do so, we must hunt it. As you are familiar with the spirit now, I would ask you to lead that hunt."

"Yes, Master."

"I also ask that you to take over mentoring Misa in her flying and begin her combat training. Be careful with her though. She is taken with you."

Deynas forced back the memory of those awkward moments on the flyer. "She's seven years younger than me?"

"She is sixteen now and she looks up to you. Young hearts are easily won and even more easily broken."

"Then why assign her to me?"

Kochan shrugged as if the answer were obvious. "Because she will try harder for you. I have seen that her spirit is ready. She is strong like your Argus-ra was."

My Argus. "Then it will be my honor to mentor her." Deynas started to rise then hesitated. "Is that why you assigned me to Argus?"

Kochan smirked. "You may go."

Swallowing frustration, he rose and turned to leave.

"Deynas, I would know how the Wind Lord addressed you today?"

He turned to stare back at Kochan, puzzled. The master was gazing up at the three faces of The Undying high above them.

"By my name."

"Just Deynas?"

He thought back to the encounter and shook his head. "No. It called me Deynas-ra. I corrected it."

Kochan smirked up at the statue as if his answer were a subtle joke shared between the two of them. "Did you?"

"Of course." Deynas had to struggle to keep his tone respectful. Nothing had changed. He was still not Endless. Why did they insist on taunting him with it?

Kochan waved a hand toward the door then. "Go now. Hunt well."

Deynas bobbed his head in a quick bow and stalked from the temple.

There was something fitting in the fact that Naago left the city on foot. The image he presented, in his worn duster and hat, trekking along the desert road with a pack on his back and the hard case in one hand, simply looked right. Were all the Endless like that? Did they all fit whatever place they were as if they always belonged there?

He claimed to prefer travelling afoot. It let him see the world in greater detail and gave him time to think about things, he claimed, though the Keeper didn't notice him staying silent long enough to contemplate much of anything since they left the confines of the towering metropolis. If he typically travelled alone, then perhaps he had built up a backlog of things to say, though she always travelled alone and did not share his proclivity for conversation.

"You don't talk much, do you?"

The question almost made it seem as if he were party to her thoughts. But no, he was bound to notice the one-sidedness of the conversation eventually. "Of what would you have me speak?"

"I don't know. If I already knew what you might have to say, I wouldn't need you to say it."

There was a certain logic to the statement.

A heavily laden wagon driven by an old part-demon

with dark blue skin, sagging jowls, and a piggish nose was rolling past, drawn by a plodding eyeless beast with six burly legs and two long trunks that waved ahead, seeing with touch and smell in place of sight. The young human boy sitting on the seat next to the blue-skinned crossbreed was staring openly at Naago.

"Do not stare, boy," the crossbreed rumbled. "A man's madness is his own affair."

She laughed under her breath at the sound of Naago grinding his teeth beside her. He held his tongue until the wagon was well out of earshot.

"I'm glad my humiliation can be a source of amusement for you, Keeper."

She smiled. It was an odd thing to smile so much. The expression served very little purpose and yet it was pleasant somehow. "Does the pride of an Endless man increase with his age?"

"Not so much. I believe it has been rather the opposite for me."

He sounded sad when he said those words, though his stolid expression didn't change. A gust of wind blew dust around them. He turned his face away from it and put his free hand on his hat to keep it in place. The power of her cloak also shielded her from such petty annoyances.

"What do you do when you are not keeping spirits?" he asked after the gust died down.

Nothing like this. "Sometimes I rest and wait in the Halls of the Blooded. Sometimes I roam alone and watch the passing of time."

"That's a start. Where do you go when you roam?"

Why did this meaningless talk matter to him? Perhaps she would come to understand if she indulged him. At the very least, there was a touch less grimness to his expression now that she was talking. Reason enough to humor him for now.

"Wherever I am inclined to go."

He shook his head and looked up, squinting his eyes against the bright sunshine. "You must have seen many incredible things in your time. Tell me about some of those things."

"I do not understand. What things?"

He gave her an odd look. "Things that have made an impression on you."

"I still don't understand what you're asking for."

Another gust came up and he turned away from the stinging dust, waiting patiently for it to pass before speaking again. "What's your favorite place to go?"

She looked at him, almost wishing he could see her face. Would the extra input of her expressions be enough to salvage what felt like a hopeless rift in communication?

It didn't matter. She wasn't supposed to be seen like that. "What makes one place better than any other?"

His lips pressed into a tight line and he faced forward, sinking into a brooding silence. They walked on the road that way for a while, passing two sweepers busily dusting sand off the road with their myriad tentacles and a travelling merchant with whom Naago bartered to replenish their water stores and acquire more food since he hadn't packed for two. He stopped them late in the afternoon to stand and watch a pod of sand dolphins diving through the dunes off to one side of the road. She watched him watching them, intrigued by the soft smile and the childish delight that lit his eyes.

Even a day's walk away, the towering city brought an early dusk over them as the sun sank behind it and he found them a sheltered spot within the dunes that now crept in at the very edge of the road. He gave her his pack to lean on while they sat in the sand and, when they had both settled, he passed her one of the meal bars he carried.

"Do you ever take that thing off?" He gestured to her cloak with a half-eaten meal bar.

"Not where I can be seen."

"Why n…" His words trailed off and he stood, turning his intense gaze out into the distance like a predator sighting for prey.

The Keeper closed her eyes and followed his gaze with her spirit eyes, quickly spotting the approaching blue glow. A wind spirit. She opened her eyes and stood beside him. The spirit swept low over the dunes, sending up a fine spray of sand to either side like water before the bow of a ship. Its big blue eyes shone bright in the deepening darkness. It drew up before Naago, but its eyes locked on her while its form rippled back and forth, to and fro.

"Wind Lord." Naago bowed his head in respect.

"If I had known delivering this message would bring me before the Keeper, I would have begged the man to let me carry it rather than delay this moment with the chase." There was something akin to awe in its whispering melodic voice. "It is a great honor to exist in your presence, *Umahk-ra-sehndo.*"

True spirits bound to roam forever in this world, the wind spirits could see through all her protections. It was their right, for she was more a part of their world in many ways than she was the world of men, demons, and gods.

She inclined her head. "Thank you, Wind Lord. You are most gracious."

The blue eyes blinked once and it gazed upon her for a moment longer in silence before turning to Naago.

"Naago-ra, I bring a message."

"I am grateful to you." The Endless man held out his palm.

The spirit swirled around him and a pile of red dust appeared upon his palm. Then the spirit settled into its rippling motion once more, its eyes turning to her again as if unable to resist gazing upon her.

"I have completed this task to satisfaction?"

Naago closed his hand. "Yes, Wind Lord. The contract between our races is venerated by your efforts."

The wind spirit blinked once more then left, spraying sand over Naago as it sped away.

Indifferent to yet one more sand bath, Naago turned to her, giving her a long, scrutinizing look. His pale eyes strained to see into her hood. Her hands itched with the desire to reach up and ensure that the hood hadn't shifted. She made them stay still at her sides.

"Is something wrong?"

"It called you *Umahk-ra-sehndo*. A title spoken in the Voice of The Undying. One I've never heard before."

There was a nervous squirming in her gut. The black roots pulled tight upon her skin as they had when she made the decision to go with him. "I know nothing of this."

He continued to stare as if determined to read the answers he sought in the dark shadows of her hood. He still held up his hand, the fingers closed over the red dust.

She gestured to the hand. "Your message?"

He glanced down with a look of mild surprise. "Yes."

He moved around her and she stepped to one side, watching while he crouched down and dug into a front panel on his pack with one hand. For a second she considered offering to help, but this man was accustomed to functioning alone. She remained still and quiet. He pulled out a thin slab of red stone about twice the length of his hand. This he held up flat in front of him. She took a step closer now, watching with interest.

"A reading stone?"

"Yes."

He let the message dust trickle out onto the face of the stone while he moved his hand in a smooth spiraling motion above it until the surface was covered in a fine film. Then he blew upon it and the dust cleared off in a puff. Beneath it, the blank stone now had characters marked upon it in the written language of the Endless tribes.

She read over his shoulder. "You have been summoned to the Temple of The Undying in Valbra."

He gave her another long look, his brow furrowing. "You can read this?"

Her stomach squirmed again and she took several steps back from him. "Yes."

"Then you have no demon in your blood. If you are neither god nor demon, what are you?"

She turned away and stared up at the darker form of the distant city looming in the night. "Will you answer the summons?"

"I will, though I do not imagine I will find much welcome."

She glanced back at him. "Why not?"

He poured a sparing trickle of water over the stone and the characters vanished. When he had the stone put away again, he stood and gave her a hard look. The good-natured curiosity had vanished from his eyes.

"We all have our secrets, don't we?"

•

Though she woke often in the night with the thought of leaving, morning found them walking together again. Naago's apparent irritation with her had faded overnight. He was more distant than he had been, his mood contemplative and perhaps a bit sullen as he stared ahead on the road, but not angry as he had seemed when he'd put his back to her to sleep. Soon after the sun began to rise, casting a gold and orange glow over the landscape, she pointed out another pod of sand dolphins, hoping to better his temper.

He stopped as he had the day before, only this time she saw the shine of tears in his eyes while he watched them. She stood watching him once again, feeling the air around them begin to warm up from the chill of the night. Through the black roots, she could feel the spirits of the sand dolphins. She could feel his spirit as well, strong and very old though his face bore no more age than that of a human man in his early forties at most.

"Have you a name other than the Keeper?"

She turned to watch the last member of the pod disappearing in the distance, the early sunlight turning the graceful creatures' tan skin gold. "Not that I am aware of."

They began to walk again. He kept silent while a group of seven young crossbreeds on flyers sped past, several of them looking down on him with disdain. The red-skinned leader went so far as to bare his pointed teeth and toss his mane of flaming locks as he tipped the flyer just enough to shoot up a spray of fine sand at Naago.

The crossbreeds often thought themselves better than men because they were stronger and faster. They weren't likely to recognize the Endless man for what he really was, which was probably for the best. His kind was of a different blood than common men and their inherent ability alone made them an easy match for any crossbreed. A young, hotheaded bunch like this might be tempted by such a challenge.

When they were out of sight, he took off his hat and shook the sand off the brim. "How did you become what you are?"

She glanced at him, hoping to understand without

asking more questions, but it was no good. His face told her nothing. "What do you mean?"

"Were you born the way you are now, with the powers and responsibilities you have?"

"I am the Keeper. I have always been this way."

He gave her a look full of sympathy, which only served to confuse her more. "Even as a child?"

Why did he ask such questions? Her chest tightened with inexplicable sorrow. "I do not remember a childhood."

"How old are you?"

"I do not know. How old are you?" She snapped the question back at him. His questions were vexing. Perhaps this was why she always travelled alone.

Her irritation didn't deter him however. "I stopped counting my summers when I stopped adding braids."

"You told me you were never a warrior."

"I did, didn't I?" For someone caught out in a lie, his expression was distinctly lacking any hint of shame. "I cut the ends of the braids off and set them on the steps of the temple the night I left my village."

Her fingers started to come up, seeking the braids in her hair. She stopped herself and lowered her hand back to her side. Why were they there? Had they always been? She couldn't recall.

His question from the prior night played back in her mind. *If you are neither god nor demon, what are you?*

He chuckled wryly to himself then glanced sideways at her. "Isn't it somewhat ironic?"

"Isn't what ironic?"

"That the Keeper, the one whose purpose it is to remember, has forgotten herself."

The sound of engines gave her something else to focus on. The flyers that had passed only moments ago were coming back around. She stopped and closed her eyes, watching their spirits approach. There was a malicious intent in them. They had decided the lone traveler was worth some sport after all.

"You should leave the road." She opened her eyes.

Naago had set down his hard case at the edge of the road and was putting his pack down next to it. "There is nowhere to hide here."

She glanced around. The dunes had receded away from the road and the small patches of desert grass offered no solace. There truly was nowhere to go.

The flyers sped up to them and spun to a stop, forcing Naago to shield his eyes with one hand from the spraying sand.

He must be growing weary of that.

The red-skinned youth sneered down at him, open disdain in his gleaming gold eyes. He was the absolute opposite of the brute crossbreed warrior she had punished in the arena. He was strong, but lean rather than bulky, and his pointed teeth weren't oversized enough to interfere with his speech. His long mane rippled like liquid fire. It was no wonder arrogance flowed off him. He was beautiful, an example of crossbreeding gone right.

"It is a long road to travel alone, stranger."

Naago gave a slight nod. "That it is, friend."

The red youth snorted and a few of his companions snickered. "I am no friend, but I'll make you a friendly wager."

Naago held his silence, watching the youth, alert, but calm.

"Defeat me in single combat and I'll give you my flyer to speed your journey."

"And if I lose?"

The gold eyes flashed and he grinned, showing off his teeth. "You're free to continue, if you're still in a condition to do so."

"If I refuse to fight?"

"You also die."

Naago heaved a weary sigh and pulled off his hat and jacket, adding them to the pile at the edge of the road. The crossbreed hopped down from his flyer, leaving it hovering, and drew a long, graceful curved sword from a sheath strapped to one wing. He stood no less than a foot taller than the Endless man. At the very least, his reach would be superior.

He nodded to the sword at Naago's hip. "You prefer the blade?"

Naago drew his sword. It was half as long as the red youth's blade, exacerbating the reach imbalance. "I do."

"Be careful," the Keeper murmured, stepping back from them still unseen.

Naago gave an almost imperceptible nod and moved toward his opponent. The crossbreed swirled his blade in a showy circle. Naago swept in without warning, his speed forcing the youth to make a hasty block and spring back out of reach. The other crossbreeds called out teasing jeers at their companion, but the gleam of amusement in the red youth's eyes had changed to something more sinister. The mane of flame darkened a shade.

He sprang at Naago then, sweeping his blade with unnatural speed up and into Naago's chest, only the Endless wasn't there when the point thrust forward. He had twisted to one side and brought his blade around, catching the crossbreed with a shallow cut along his ribs. The youth let out a roar of fury. His opponent had drawn first blood. That very clearly wasn't how he envisioned the fight going.

They engaged again, blades flashing with speed no normal man could hope to follow, coming together with the bone-chilling clash of steel on steel. The others had fallen silent, captivated by the intensity of the combat. A line of red appeared across Naago's shoulder, a shallow wound. There were two more cuts along the youth's ribs now, a trio of identical slashes bleeding down his side. The two were well matched in speed and strength, but the Endless man had more refinement and skill. The crossbreed was also falling victim to his own temper. He made a reckless dash in and came away with a fourth slash opened in his side of an equal length and depth to the other three.

They faced one another, the crossbreed breathing hard.

"Do not insult me!"

Naago looked almost relaxed, still holding his sword as if it weighed nothing. "Don't be so eager to die."

It was much too late for reason. The agile youth sprang in fast, his blade sliding harmlessly past as Naago dodged. Then Naago twisted around to strike the crossbreed in the back of the head with the pommel and kick his feet out from under him when he staggered before the blow. The crossbreed hit the ground with a grunt and rolled over. He got up on one knee and wavered there, shaking his head as if to clear it. Dark blood streamed through his mane from a wound on the back of his head. He reached for his sword where it had landed next to him, but stopped when the point of Naago's blade touched his chin.

"I will kill you if you come at me again."

The youth moved his clawed hand away from the weapon.

"Good." Naago turned his back on the crossbreed and walked over to gather his things.

The Keeper moved closer to the youth, watching the burn of hatred in his gold eyes. When Naago walked past him toward the flyer, the youth snatched up his sword and lunged. She grabbed the blade with her right hand, becoming visible to them, and the fine metal snapped in two, half of it falling to the ground. Naago, who had spun to block the attack, his weapon again in hand, looked down in surprise at the half of the blade now lying between them.

The crossbreed looked down at it too, then at her. Tears welled in his gold eyes. He dropped the remains of the weapon and knelt, bowing his head. His companions were already knelt where they stood upon the decks of their flyers, their eyes to the ground.

"Forgive me, Keeper," the youth blurted.

Why had she intervened? It was not her place to meddle in such things, though there was something very familiar about the youth kneeling there, almost as if she had not only seen him before, but in this very pose. She said nothing. There was no precedent for the circumstances.

Naago sheathed his sword. "Shall we go?"

Again, she said nothing, following him silently to the hovering flyer. He hopped up and offered her a hand. She shied away from it, stepping up on her own. The flyer was a new expensive model with a support stand for the pilot and another that pulled up out of a compartment behind it for a passenger or instructor. The body was painted red with gold flames upon the wings and black stripes down the center, a custom job designed to complement its striking crossbreed pilot.

Naago tucked his things into a small cargo hold in the back then locked the secondary stand into place, moving with efficient haste. They buckled in and he pressed in the throttle hard, leaving the crossbreed and his companions behind in a cloud of sand.

The wind parted around her, blocked away by the barrier of the cloak. She closed her eyes, imagining that wind running through her hair. While he drove, she felt each subtle shift in body position, change in throttle pressure, and movement of the steering rods as if she piloted the craft herself. The anxiety brought on by her inappropriate intervention faded and a smile curved her lips. She flew.

They made much better time with the flyer, and the lack of conversation forced on them by the wind gave the Keeper a reprieve from the questions she knew he would ask. It didn't save her from the questions going through her own head though. Not the least of which was, if she truly dreaded his questioning so much, why didn't she leave? What kept her there with him? She'd never travelled with someone else before, not in this incarnation or, as far as she knew, in any others. Why do so now?

When they finally stopped at a traveler's haven a little after dusk, she sat on the wing of the flyer and waited while he went to pay for a cabin. There were many such places in the desert and, with a swift means of travel like the flyer, one could jump between several of them in the course of a day.

When he returned, she moved back to the center and sat there while he glided the flyer over to park in front of the rented cabin. He smiled as he unlocked the door and held it open for her. She liked his smile, it made her feel less alone, not that she'd ever noticed her aloneness bothering her before he pointed it out.

He went about lighting a fire in the fireplace to keep away the chill of the desert night. They sat in chairs before the fire, eating a scant meal in silence. Afterwards, he brought out the case he had been carrying and began to release the latches. She looked on, curious to know what waited within.

"You did not break my sword when I turned it on you at the hotel." He didn't look up from the case while he spoke. "Why not?"

Now the questions came. He'd held off longer than she expected, though she would have been happier if he skipped it altogether. "You were defending yourself against an intruder. It would have been wrong to deny you your weapon because of that. The crossbreed used his blade with corrupt intent. Had he killed you with that strike, it would have polluted his spirit."

Naago gave a derisive snort. "I suspect your intervention comes a little too late for that one."

"Not entirely. His spirit dances on an edge. There is still time for him to change his path." Why had the crossbreed seemed so familiar? What good was a memory that retained nothing but dead spirits and their pain? She shook her head, pressing her hands to her thighs to keep them from curling into fists.

"So that was why you stopped him, to protect his spirit."

"No."

He gave her a thoughtful glance, perhaps expecting her to expound upon that answer. When she didn't speak, he gave a small shake of his head and opened the case.

"A violin?"

He smiled lovingly at the polished wood instrument as he lifted it from the case with careful hands. "Your tone says you expected something else. A weapon perhaps?"

She had in fact expected a weapon. It was rare that she misread someone that completely.

For several minutes, he turned single-minded attention to the instrument, looking it over and polishing the dark wood with a soft cloth he pulled out of the case. When he was satisfied with its condition, he began to pick at the strings and adjust the pegs to tune it.

"You are the only one of your kind, correct?"

"I am." She sat back in her chair and gazed into the fire, listening to the sounds of the strings. Where would this line of questioning lead them? It was like a game in a way, one she wasn't sure she liked playing.

"So what happens when you die?"

"I do not die."

The angry sound of a string picked too hard reverberated through the cabin. He pressed his palm over the strings to quiet it. "Even gods can die."

She relaxed a little, pleased that she now understood what he was asking. "You wish to know what happens when this host, this body, dies. When that happens, another host will be chosen to take its place."

Even knowing he couldn't see her face within the protection of the cloak his cold stare gave her that uncomfortable squirm in her gut again.

"Are you saying the body you wear is not your own?"

The brief comfort of understanding whisked away. She sensed that their conversation was heading to dangerous places without comprehending exactly why. Was there some way to answer the question without increasing the distress she sensed growing in him? She tried to pick her words with care. "I would say that it is mine, for I wear it."

"But you didn't always wear it? It belonged to another?"

The reality of the situation wasn't that simple. The body still belonged to its original wearer and it belonged to the Keeper. In a way, the Keeper also belonged to it, for she couldn't function properly without it. It would be hard to explain that to him in a way he would understand.

For simplicity's sake, she settled for answering exactly the question he had asked. "Yes. It belonged to another."

"Who did it belong to?"

She shifted in the seat and her right sleeve slid back, revealing the hand with the black roots woven around it. His gaze moved to that hand. Her hands were all he had ever seen, hands that would look human if not for the roots upon the right one. She resisted the urge to cover it up. "It belonged to another."

He turned back to his instrument and continued tuning. When he was satisfied, he drew the bow and began to play. A slow lament filled the cabin. She closed her eyes and watched the notes in violet and blue, rising from the wooden instrument and swirling around them. The spirit within her flesh—*umahk-ra*, Naago would call it—stirred, responding to the sweet mournful music. That spirit was often restless and she let it go now as she sometimes did, giving it freedom to join the dance of light. It moved apart from the body, its bright glow drifting out into the mixing of light that was his music, carrying a portion of her awareness with it.

The music screeched to a jarring stop. The spirit snapped back into her and her eyes opened.

Naago was standing, glaring warily at her, the bow and violin hanging forgotten in his hands. "Let me see you."

Umahk-ra-uden. Spirit thief. She was a fool. This man could see spirits and he had seen the form of the one she carried within her.

He set the instrument on the chair and stepped closer. "Let me see your face."

She rose and started to back away, but he grabbed her arm, his grip tight enough to cause pain. There were many ways she could make him suffer for that. It would take little more than a thought and the powers that resided in the black roots would give him the pain of all those she had kept. That much pain all at once would almost certainly kill him. It would, at the very least, drive him mad. A mere thought to put him in his place.

And yet, his anger, his distress with her... This was something new. Something she hadn't experienced before and some part of her sparked to life in response, compelling her to wait and see how this moment played out.

She stood motionless, her breath trapped in her throat. He released her arm. "Let me see."

It was more an insistent plea than a demand this time. She lifted her hands. Flickers of pain swept through her arm and shoulder, racing down the right side of her back and up to her right temple. Everywhere the roots touched her skin there was a flash of pain. She had endured much greater pain fulfilling her purpose as Keeper. The warning was easy to ignore. She drew back the hood.

His gaze took her in, her eyes, her face, the tendril of root that peeked out of her hair at the temple, the five braids. Outrage stormed up in his spirit so strong that she almost cowered from it, but she would not allow herself such weakness. She was the Keeper.

His expression darkened. "You took the body of an Endless warrior."

The resentment in his voice made her chest ache. "No. As the Keeper, I do not choose my host body. It is given to me... or rather, I to it. I can only accept what the Blooded Women choose. They tend to take Endless warriors if they can because the body lives long and the spirit of ascended Endless is not as susceptible to the corruptions that can afflict the spirits of other beings."

His anger still flared around her, hotter than the fire, though he was hesitant now. Unsure where to direct his emotions if she were not to blame. "Who did this body belong to?"

Her hand rose up to touch the ends of the braids. Five braids. Five years as an ascended Endless warrior. A word came to mind in the Endless tongue. "*Umahk-ra-en-mahde.*"

"She was a spirit walker."

"Yes I... she... was." *Is.* Her thoughts became cluttered, as if too many were trying to come to the fore at once. Some of those thoughts tasted strange, as if they came from someone else. Something more than merely the spirit of the host stirred within her now.

"I know her *umahk-ra* still lives in this body. I could see it just now while I played. What became of her thoughts and memories?"

"All of that exists still. Within." She put a hand to her chest. *She is part of the Keeper or the Keeper is part of her.* "The same way her spirit..." *umahk-ra.* She stumbled on the mental correction, losing her place for a moment. Meeting his eyes, full of anger and yet still yearning to understand, she found her place again. "The same way her spirit still exists within this body."

He closed his eyes. The muscles in his jaw worked almost convulsively with the chaos of emotion that rent the air around them. After a moment, he returned to his chair and picked up the violin, positioning it under his chin. The bow touched the strings and another lament filed the cabin, this one not sweet as the first, but despairing. Still standing, she closed her eyes again and watched the notes move around them in darker colors, watched the diamond-like sparkle of slow tears moving down his cheeks. She stood still, keeping the spirit leashed inside this time. The tears stopped seconds before the song did. She watched the glow of his spirit as he set down the bow and walked over to her again.

"She was beautiful." His voice was soft, sorrowful.

She opened her eyes to see his hand rising toward her face. Did he actually mean to touch her?

A familiar sensation nagged in the back of her mind and she tried to push it away.

No. Not now.

Part of her wanted to make him understand. Another, more analytical part found the encounter fascinating and yearned to see where it would lead.

"Five years as an Endless warrior." His fingers brushed the braids in her hair. "The color?"

How strange it must look to him? Her hair and the irises of her eyes were both a lustrous silvery black, not a color natural to his kind. "The color always changes to this. It is a physical manifestation of the Keeper, like the roots that weave upon this skin."

His pale eyes met hers, then shifted to the tendril of root at her temple. When his fingers moved toward it, she drew back a little and he touched her cheek instead, a soft caress that burned bittersweet upon her skin and left her breathless.

Had anyone ever touched her that way? There was no such moment within the Keeper's memory, though that memory had no beginning and no comprehensive sense of time. There was a glimmer of something from the mind within the host, however, even though those memories were supposed to remain dormant.

She held still, reluctant to do anything that might end the contact. His gaze moved down, watching with a troubled fascination as his thumb lightly traced her lower lip.

The call became undeniable then. A spirit needed keeping. She opened her mouth to explain and disappeared.

Deynas sucked in a breath and willed himself to keep his hands on the support rails. Misa had taken them into this dive. He needed to stand steady and trust her to pull them out of it on her own.

She moved them into a spiral, the wind whipping past while the landing pad below grew larger by the second. Calm and deliberate, she shifted her weight and hands so they pulled out of the drop long enough to shoot out and dive over the cliff down towards the village at its base where the temporal, those who had never ascended to true Endless or who were still too young to begin training, lived. The ascended Endless now lived up on the higher cliffs near the temple and along the road leading up to it along with the instructors and Endless hopefuls.

Misa pulled out of the dive a few yards above the stone council hall and banked around, red stone huts flashing beneath them. Then she turned up and rose to a cruising altitude, easing back on the throttle.

The sound of her laughter made him smile and shake his head.

"All right, you've shown that you can maneuver this thing, let's see if you can land it."

She poked him with an elbow. "Of course I can."

If only Argus could see the invincible *umahk-ra*

of this girl they had saved. Misa was easily as fiery and determined as Argus had been, though she still needed to learn some restraint.

You would be proud of her, Argus-ra.

He touched the small lump of the pendant that hung under his shirt. A glossy black stone shaped like a teardrop. It was the hardened blood of a god. The god had given the pendant to his mother to thank her for coming to its aid against a group of men hoping to profit from its flesh and organs in the illegal Undercity medicine markets. She had in turn placed the pendant in Deynas's hand before she died and tried to say something, but death had stolen the words from her lips. He would never know what she meant to say, but he always wore the pendant even though it caused him distress for years wondering why her spirit didn't haunt him the way Argus's did. Had he not loved her enough?

Now he knew it was because he had never seen her spirit, so he did not carry a piece of her in him the way he did Argus. It was at least a small consolation.

He had sworn upon that god's blood pendant to keep secret Argus's spirit walking ability, not that it really mattered now. The rare Endless gifts were kept as secret as possible because they made one more of a target for certain forms of demon who collected or fed upon spirits. The temporal warriors of the tribes also tended to be uneasy working with ascended Endless who had such gifts, so it was prudent not to speak of them.

Gifts like mine.

Misa pressed back against him as she brought them to a halt above the landing pad and started to drop slowly down. The craft wobbled a little as she leaned out to one side and then the other to make sure she was clear of the other flyers. He looked too, though his height allowed him to do so without moving as much, and tried not to wonder if she were trying to flirt with him with the press of her body against his. The craft bumped down a little hard when she finally cut the engines and she cringed.

He put a hand on her shoulder and gave it a reassuring squeeze. "You did well. I think you're ready to try a supervised solo flight."

She popped her buckles and twisted around to look at him, her face glowing. "Really!"

I shouldn't have touched her. He held back his smile and began to free the buckles of his harness. "Yes. Though you need to keep practicing those landings or you'll never get your own flyer."

She flushed and handed him the key to the craft. "I know."

Did her fingers linger too long upon his when she gave him the key? Was this what it was like for Argus working with him? At least he had been closer to her age. He hoped that made it less awkward for her than this was for him.

He turned quickly away and hopped down from the flyer.

She followed close behind. "Deynas?"

The tentative tone drew his attention. "Yes."

"Was it our fault?"

He searched her eyes. "What?"

"Argus-ra. You had to leave her because of us. If we hadn't been there—"

"Stop." There was a painful spasm in his chest. He stared into her eyes, noticing the way her lips remained parted with unspoken words. He could say yes. Could dump the blame on them. Part of him wanted to, but he knew it was wrong. "What happened was the fault of the demons who took the city. She was Endless. It was her duty to protect all of us. She did that. You and Ren were never at fault."

"So you don't hold it against me...I mean us?"

"Of course not."

"That makes me glad, because I..." Her cheeks flared pink and she dropped her gaze.

"Deynas-ra." Ren called, running over to them.

Thank The Undying. "I'm still not Endless, Ren," Deynas reminded him, so pleased at the interruption that the improperly assigned honorific didn't irritate him this time.

The youth waved a dismissive hand at him. He'd been using the honorific ever since the wind spirit had addressed Deynas that way. "You will be soon."

"Perhaps." *Keep it secret.* It felt a little like cheating to know he wouldn't have to go through the ritual to ascend to Endless, but then Argus hadn't either and he didn't think it made her any less worthy.

"Come look at this fantastic flyer." Ren grabbed his hand and pulled, leaning his weight into it as if he might have a hope of dragging Deynas along by force.

When he didn't budge, the boy turned around and took hold with both hands, pitching his lanky frame back ineffectually. He gave up after a moment and glowered up at Deynas.

"You win. I won't call you Deynas-ra until its proper."

Deynas glanced at Misa to see if she'd recovered from their candid conversation and hoping she wouldn't try to finish whatever she'd been about to say.

Her lips pressed together in a regretful line for a few seconds then she shrugged. "I guess we better follow him before the excitement kills him."

Deynas grinned, relief easing the tightness in his chest. "I guess so."

Another flyer took off and passed over them. The pilot tipped it to one side at the edge of the landing pad nearest the temple to admire what was certainly the object of Ren's enthusiasm. A fancy new tandem flyer sat parked there. It was a flashy deep red with gold flame upon the backswept wings and black racing lines down the center of the back. It sported two more jets than on any other flyer in the village. The support stands had black leather over thick padding along the spine and shoulders and the grips had wraps of similar supple black leather. The machine was as well-appointed as any light craft built for speed could hope to be.

The little boy in Deynas wanted to dash about the flyer and exclaim gleefully as Ren did. To avoid embarrassing himself, he settled for an admiring grin as he traced one finger along the edge of a glossy wing.

"I bet this thing can spin like crazy," Misa murmured, her voice thick with awe.

A man strode out of the temple toward them. He was no one Deynas had seen before. His shoulder-length hair hung loose, free of braids, so he wasn't an Endless warrior. Deynas gestured with a wave of his hand for Misa and Ren to step away from the flyer, which they did with sour looks.

The man walked up and opened the small storage compartment in the rear of the craft, not acknowledging them in any way.

Rude, but then, he did look rather unhappy.

"It's a beautiful flyer," Deynas ventured in an effort to break the ice.

The man still didn't look at him, but he did respond, if somewhat curtly. "I won it in a wager. I'd prefer something less conspicuous."

Not a great start, but perhaps it was worth another try. He mustered a grin. "You can have mine."

He'd meant it as a joke, but the man looked up, his pale blue eyes locking on Deynas. They were ageless eyes. He must be Endless then, but...

"Where is it?"

Mystified, Deynas pointed at his flyer. "Right over there."

The man pulled a pack and a hard case out of the hatch, then locked it and tossed the key to Deynas who shut his gaping mouth and snatched it out of the air. They key was painted the same deep red as the flyer.

"You're serious?"

The man walked up to him and looked him steadily in the eyes. "I am."

They stood of an equal height and, as Deynas met his gaze, something about the man stirred a feeling of recognition in him. "Do I know you?"

"No."

"You're the one Master Kochan sent for."

"Deynas." Kochan stood in the doorway of the temple, his face storming with black emotion. "I would speak with you immediately."

The strange man held out his hand, eyes boring into Deynas.

Deynas dug into his pocket and held the key to his flyer out to Misa. "Can you show this man to my flyer? Get my emergency kit and anything else out of the back before he departs."

"I'm on it." Misa took the key. "Follow me."

The man gave a nod and strode after her without another word.

It was hard not to follow him. There were so many questions Deynas wanted to ask, but he would have to hope Kochan was willing to answer them. From the look on the master's face, he wasn't in the mood to wait. As soon as he started toward the temple, Kochan turned and vanished inside. Deynas broke into a jog and hurried inside after him. As he entered the temple, he heard his flyer starting up behind him and glanced down at the red key still in his hand.

Odd. He tucked it into a pocket.

Inside, he searched around until he found Kochan back in one of the private chambers, kneeling before a low table. There were two cups of tea upon the table, both untouched. Kochan stared at the one farthest away as if he hoped to shatter it with his gaze.

"That man was the one you sent for," Deynas blurted, discarding proper ceremony. "Why is he leaving?"

"I sent him away," Kochan snapped. His hands gripped the edge of the table tight.

Deynas stared. There was a sinking sensation in his chest. "I don't understand, Master. I thought he was going to help me to work with my ability."

Kochan's nostrils flared as he drew in a deep breath. "Naago has abandoned his tribe and temple. He is not welcome here."

Ageless eyes and a sword at his hip. Hair lightened with more silvery-gray than Kochan's, but with no braids to mark his years. The man was a deserter. And yet…

"What about—"

"I will find someone else." Kochan pounded a fist down on the table, spilling the tea in front of him.

Deynas had never seen the master this openly angry. He bowed his head and backed out through the door that way, then turned and strode from the temple. Outside, he stopped beside the red flyer for a minute, watching the way the setting sun set the gold flames ablaze. Then he strode to the cliff at the far edge of the landing pad and looked down. The lamplighters were moving through the temporal village below, lighting the many street lamps. It got dark much faster down there than it did up at the level of the temple.

Not so long ago, the entire village housed only the Endless trainees and their trainers. Now they shared it with the temporal and the Endless warriors. That all of them could live there without overcrowding said dark things about how many were lost when the demons took over the city. Somehow, temporal and Endless still didn't live together. The children who were too young to worry about such things didn't seem to notice the separation, but the Endless kept themselves mostly apart from their shorter-lived kin. Or perhaps it was those below who encouraged the division. It didn't matter. He had no family down there.

He peered out into the desert. Somewhere out there, his flyer was speeding away above the sand, his chance to understand and manage his ability vanishing in the sunset on its back.

He put his hand in his pocket and tightened it around the red key until the edges bit into his palm. He pulled the key out and opened his hand, staring at it. The red flyer was his now. He would gladly trade it for the knowledge that the estranged master could have given him.

Deserter. He looked up again. The red flyer was his now and it was a lot faster than the one Naago was flying.

Deynas ran back to the red flyer and folded the rear stand down into its compartment to reduce wind drag. Then he leapt up and strapped himself in, positioning the goggles that still hung around his neck. When he turned the key, the craft purred to life, the sound of the engine no louder than that of the parking stands sliding smoothly back into their casings. The grips were soft as a woman's skin.

He grasped them gently and took the flyer up to get it clear of other craft. Then he gunned the throttle and almost inverted it when the unexpected surge of power threw him off balance. He recovered quickly, easing back on the throttle and regaining stability before he accelerated again, less aggressively this time.

It took less than fifteen minutes for him to catch up with the other craft skimming away across the desert. When he brought the flyer up alongside Naago, the man gave him a sour look and came to an abrupt stop. Deynas eased his craft into a smooth arc, coming around to stop near his former flyer. He was already getting the hang of the more sensitive controls.

"What do you want, Deynas-ra? Is the craft not to your liking?"

"I need your help, Master Naago."

Naago stared into the distance, his lips pressed tightly together for a moment. "I gave up my right to that title years ago."

"And I am not Endless."

Naago looked at him then, his light eyes glowing in the fading light. "You are *umahk-ra-uden*. The Undying has given you a free pass into his inner circle. That change is nearly upon you. Can't you feel it?"

A chill of dread and excitement spread through Deynas. He did his best to shrug it off. "Help me. I need to understand the way my ability works. I'm haunted by the spirit fragment of someone who died and it's holding me back."

Naago's nose wrinkled as if he'd smelled something foul. "Go back to your tribe. I can't help you."

"Where are you running away to?"

Naago revved the flyers engine, his lip curling in a silent snarl. "To the Undercity, where all the unwanted creatures go."

Deynas ground his teeth, fighting to hold back his frustration. It was a losing battle. He could see that in the set of the other man's jaw, but he couldn't let it go. "You're an Endless warrior and *umahk-ra-uden*. How can you stand to lie down beneath a blanket of self-pity in the filth of the Undercity?"

Naago's hand sank to his sword hilt. "You know nothing of me. Go back to your village, Deynas-ra, or I will send you there in pieces."

Deynas started to reach to his belt and remembered that he'd brought no weapons. "You're right. You don't deserve to be called master."

With those cutting words, Deynas gunned the flyer, barely managing to keep his balance this time. He left Naago in a cloud of sand and didn't look back.

The cooling night air nipped at his skin as he sped away. The flyer responded to every tiny shift of weight like a perfect extension of his body, barreling up into the sky and diving down again at speeds that left him gasping for air. He flew for a long while, tearing up the sky and the dunes in turns until his frustration had faded and a poignant sorrow taken its place. By then he was shivering in the cold night. He took the flyer home.

Sleep was slow in coming, not helped by the fact that he still hadn't refreshed the padding on his bed. He tossed and turned for hours, then finally slipped into restless slumber and strange dreams.

In the dream, his *umahk-ra* parted from his flesh like that of a spirit walker, a bright presence moving out of his body. Once free, it turned and embraced him, a comforting warmth enfolding him. Then it was Argus's *umahk-ra* that embraced him, a brightly glowing form wearing her face, her indomitable smile. Pain burned through his flesh like the scalding of a high fever and he wept in his sleep, trembling while her *umahk-ra* held him. She stroked his hair and murmured to him in words he couldn't quite understand.

The pain and trembling grew worse and worse. Her words became clear.

"Welcome, Deynas-ra."

She spoke those words repeatedly, her form expanding, her voice changing and separating until it echoed all around him, sexless, beautiful, and terrifying all at once. He looked up at her and found the three faces of The Undying gazing down at him.

"Welcome, Deynas-ra."

He woke covered in sweat and shaking. Pain swept through him, putting every muscle into spasm as the ascendance changed him. Master Kochan was right, he would not have to endure the ritual to become Endless, but he would still endure the agony of ascendance. After what could have been several hours or a scant few minutes, the spasms stopped. He threw up on the woven mat by his bed and lay there, chilled with cooling sweat, too fatigued to clean up the mess.

The Halls of the Blooded were always brightly lit, even in the middle of the night. The Blooded Women never slept, or perhaps they never really woke. Steel walls, steel floors, and steel ceilings all painted pearlescent white and blood red where they weren't left silver. The Halls felt colder than the Keeper remembered, colder and lonelier. She'd returned eight long days ago after keeping another spirit and hadn't had a moment of peace since.

Sometimes months passed without the call to keep. Sometimes it came several times in a day. She couldn't decide if the timing of the last call had been inconvenient or fortuitous, snatching her away from Naago's disconcerting attentions. That she arrived at the origin of the call with the hood of her cloak down wasn't a problem. The cloak didn't have to cover her fully to shield her form from sight when she needed not to be seen. That she hadn't been able to erase the sensation of his touch from her mind since leaving him was more of an issue. The *umahk-ra* that belonged to this host stirred, more restless than ever, refusing to fall silent again.

Six Blooded Women moved down the hall, their eyes closed so the red eyes painted upon their eyelids showed. They didn't use their physical eyes to see. They moved with a smooth, sliding step, their white silk slippers whispering upon the metal. Their hands, painted white like their expressionless faces with bright red nails, remained crossed in front of their stomachs. Straight black hair hung down, never shifting like the long white dresses they wore, the matching white collars forcing their chins high. Blood trickled in an endless stream down the wires running from under their jaws down into the collars of the dresses, feeding the tubing that ran along the seams.

The Keeper stepped to one side and lowered her gaze while they flowed past. The Blooded Women were always aware of her presence, but they rarely acknowledged her. There was rarely a need to interact beyond the process of transferring her into a new host when such was necessary. They were her handlers. Nothing more.

Did they know the things she had done? Did they know she'd interfered in an affair that had nothing to do with keeping, possibly changing the intended outcome of the fight between Naago and the crossbreed? Did they know she had traveled with the Endless man? Did they know she had let her face been seen and touched by him? Would they care if they did?

When they were gone, she stood still for a moment in the shadow of a massive I-beam support. She looked down at her hands. They were shaking. That was new.

She normally paid as little attention to the Blooded Women as they did to her. They were the ones who chose her host and somehow accomplished the task of moving the Keeper out of one host into another. There was no recollection of how these things worked. No memories existed of the different bodies that had hosted the Keeper. All the Keeper ever truly remembered was the spirits she kept, centuries of spirits and the pain of each death. Those things stayed with her forever. It was her purpose to remember them.

"The Keeper, the one whose purpose it is to remember, has forgotten herself."

She had been heading for her quarters within the Halls when his words in her head stalled her. The idea of going there, of being alone in a chamber of cold steel, made her eyes sting and her chest ache. Where could she go? Naago was the only one she'd spoken with beyond the expected words that preceded punishment. Had she broken something within herself with that unprecedented action? Was it truly unprecedented or had such things happened before, lost in the memory of prior hosts now forgotten?

There was a nagging sensation in the back of her mind and she breathed easier. Despite the pain she would have to endure, the process of keeping was something she understood absolutely. Something expected, with rules that never changed. Completing the task she existed for would put off her troubling thoughts and free her from the man whose words haunted her, at least for a short time.

She exhaled, releasing a heavy weight of worry with her breath, and put up her hood as she disappeared.

•

She reappeared in the narrow mouth of a small canyon collapsed at one end. It served as a natural trap for the two-headed dog-like beast that lay near the back wall, its black blood oozing out around the myriad spears driven into its flesh. The three men who had slain it were now creeping in close to its corpse. They were normal men, not of Endless blood. The star-branded butchering knives they drew from their belts as they congratulated one another on the kill marked them as hunters for a particular group of illegal medicinal and delicacy shops in the Undercity. That a warlord was comfortable enough to brand his men's equipment in such a way spoke volumes to how much control they had in the city.

One of the men turned to speak to his companion who was raising his blade to chop into the fresh kill. His words died on his lips when he saw her approaching and he dropped to one knee, bowing his head. The other two turned. The raised butcher knife fell to the sand with a soft thud. The other men also knelt and two of them took up the chant in low, shaking voices. The third trembled in silence, a man who thought he could handle the risks until the moment he faced true punishment.

"That which is lost, she will find.
That which is forsaken, she will cherish.
That which is forgotten, she will remember.
That which is, she will keep."

She stopped beside the creature and sank her right hand into its matted wiry brown fur. Wind rose up and filled the canyon with swirling sand. The beast had incisors as long as her arm, one of which was cracked down the center, and it smelled like a month old bloated corpse, but that didn't make its death any less tragic. This unpleasant creature was a low god. The men probably thought it a demon. They tended to make such assumptions based on appearance and this god was a mangy looking thing. Its spirit, however, rose up and out of the expired flesh, glowing with a pale gold brilliance, beautiful and precious. Such a shame that the men couldn't see that aspect of the beast.

She braced her mind for the coming pain and bowed her head respectfully. *Come to me and you shall be remembered.*

The spirit moved into her without hesitation, bringing the pain of its death in every minute detail. The fear, the rage, the agony of each spear ripping through its thick hide and puncturing organs within, all of it more crisp and powerful because it had been a god. She clenched her teeth, her hand closing into a fist on a handful of coarse fur.

When the pain finally passed, she turned to the nearest man and placed her hand upon his head. His spirit was familiar. She had punished him before.

"You have committed an unforgivable crime. Your life continues at the whim of greater powers, for death is not mine to deal, but you must pay in suffering."

"It is as you say," he murmured.

His courage didn't keep him from screaming when the pain rushed through him. The second man trembled at her touch. He accepted his punishment in a flood of guilty tears. When she turned to the third man, he jumped to his feet and ran. There were always some who tried to escape their sentence. The Keeper couldn't allow that. She disappeared and reappeared beside him, grabbing his arm. The power within her stopped him in his tracks. He squirmed pathetically in her unyielding grip and fell to his knees, pleading for mercy. These hunters would drive him out of their guild after this. Even among the lowest criminals, there was a code of honor.

"You have committed an unforgivable crime." She held him in place not with physical strength, but with the inevitability of her purpose. "Your life continues at the whim of greater powers, for death is not mine to deal, but you must pay in suffering."

He collapsed when she passed the pain into him and she left him writhing in the sand. This task wasn't complete. Another required punishment.

She vanished and reappeared in a hut up above the canyon. A figure stood, silhouetted in the light coming through one window. Then the figure turned from the window and knelt before her, bowing his head.

Naago.

Emotions she couldn't recall ever feeling with such potency twisted inside her at the sight of him like some malignant being come to life within her chest. Hurt and rage so powerful they made her vision darken.

Her voice shook when she spoke the words that preceded punishment.

He spoke softly, responding with same words he had said the first time she punished him. "I accept my punishment."

She placed her hand upon his cheek and passed the pain and fear into him, not the brief flash that she usually gave, but the full crisp clarity that she had suffered upon receiving the spirit along with a taste of the betrayal that twisted within her chest. His body arched backward and he cried out. His agonized wail tore through her, bringing a flicker of satisfaction before regret chased it away. His spirit and flesh weren't fortified to cope with such pain the way the Keeper was. She took a few steps back and watched him fall forward onto his hands, trembling and breathing hard.

She drew back her hood. "Why did you do this?"

He didn't look at her. His voice came out strained and unsteady, interrupted by ragged breathing. "I didn't know...how else...to find you."

She turned her back to him. Right then, she couldn't bear to look at him. She closed her eyes. "When I keep a spirit, I must endure every agony of their last moments, every wretched emotion and physical hurt. The pain I gave you just now is the pain I suffered when I kept that spirit. You lured it into their trap. Was that suffering worth whatever they paid you?"

"I'm sorry. I never would have done it if I realized it would hurt you like that."

"You would apologize for hurting me, not for bringing death to a low god?"

His silence held great weight. Even he hadn't understood what the beast was.

The uncomfortable turmoil of emotion in her chest broke upon his silence, leaving a hollow feeling inside her. "Is your hatred so great?"

"When the demons drove us from the city they were without mercy. The first attack came at night. I was in one of the temples of The Undying when it happened." There was a tremor of misery in his voice. "I rushed back to my apartments, but I was too late. Nara, my *ra'sen*, was sleeping when they came. They'd torn her apart. Our bedroom was painted with her blood. Yes, my hatred is so great. Great enough that I knew I was no longer fit to be master of the tribe, so I cut my braids and left my tribe."

His *ra'sen* or *umahk-ra'sen*. His spirit match.

She didn't know how to respond to that. Grief flowed from his spirit like water from a river in flood. After a long moment in silence, she turned. He stood facing her, his face etched with sorrow, his eyes full of tormented loathing for the demons that had taken everything from him.

She looked into those eyes, searching for answers. "Does trading in the lives of demons bring you peace, Naago-ra?"

He turned his face away, shame in the hang of his shoulders. "No."

She brought her normal hand up and placed it against his cheek, turning his face back to her with light pressure. His skin was warm and rough with stubble. "Then why do you do it?"

"I have to do something to keep this loathing, this anguish, from tearing me apart." He met her eyes again and his hand came up, pressing over the top of hers on his cheek, holding it there.

"Did you really do this just to find me?"

He nodded. "I felt alive for the first time in years when you were with me."

"I am the Keeper. I don't belong with you. I don't belong with anyone."

"I don't care."

A tightening sensation in the black roots preceded what was likely to be another bad decision. "I don't wish to remain here, not knowing what they're doing in that canyon."

"Then we'll leave."

He wrapped his fingers around her hand and kept it, leading her toward the door. With her right hand, she pulled up the hood as she followed him out. A flyer waited in front of the hut, an older model much inferior to the one he had taken from the crossbreed.

She stopped, pulling her hand away. "That isn't made for two."

"Nonsense. The Endless tribes use them for tandem training all the time. You can ride behind me against the support stand and I'll buckle into your harness while I drive."

He dug into the small hatch and tossed her a harness. While she strapped it on, she eyed the flyer controls. An unfamiliar yearning swelled inside her. He hopped up on the wing and held a hand down to her. She took it this time and let him draw her up. When he gestured to the support stand, she shook her head.

"I want to drive."

He drew back, giving her a startled look. "Do you even know how?"

"I believe this host does."

For a few seconds, he looked resistant. Then he shrugged and stepped around the stand to buckle himself in. She moved in front of him and buckled her feet into the insets, moving with a memory that belonged to her and yet was not hers. When she stood, he buckled her harness to his, forcing her to stand close enough that his body warmed her back. He offered his goggles up to her and she waved them away. The cloak would shield her.

She started the craft and it lifted to a low hover, drawing up the parking stands with a soft squeal of metal rubbing metal. It tilted with every movement she made while she raised it up a little higher. She rocked back and forth a few times, tipping each wing to the sand and finding her balance. Then she pushed the throttle down and it sped forward, rising with a gradual pull on the levers.

She smiled, settling into the muscle memory that grew stronger and more certain with every passing second. The Keeper had never driven such a craft before, but this host could fly.

The craft bucked with her surprised jerk when Naago slid his arms around her waist and pulled her back snug against him. The host knew that wasn't necessary and yet she didn't feel the need to correct him. After a few startled heartbeats, she leveled out again and shot across the desert.

Deynas-ra."

He cringed inwardly. Damned Misa. She seemed to take his mentoring her as permission to meddle in all his affairs. Or perhaps he hadn't discouraged her attentions sufficiently.

"Misa, what are you doing out here this late?"

"Spying on you." She smiled a little too fondly, emboldened perhaps by the dark and their lack of audience. "I have been all week."

At least she was honest. "And what have you seen?"

He finished adjusting the items in the red flyer's hatch for the best weight balance before securing them in place. The process helped mask the way his nerves danced with apprehension, anticipating the complications that might arise depending on her response.

She stepped up beside him, leaning out over the flyer in an effort to look him in the eyes. He needlessly adjusted a few things in the opposite corner to avoid her gaze and the warmth of her nearness.

"I've seen you sneaking out here at odd hours and stashing things in the hatch. Suspicious things. Things you'd need for a long trip somewhere."

He started to slam the hatch shut and caught himself at the last second. The noise would alert someone else to their presence and further expose his already jeopardized clandestine activities. So far, it appeared that only Misa had caught on that he was planning something, unless she'd already told someone else.

With gentle pressure, he clicked the hatch shut and locked it, then turned to stare at her in the dark, standing tall in an attempt to intimidate her with his superior height. "And what do you plan to do with this information?"

She met his eyes, defiance in the straightening of her own posture. "I haven't told anyone yet, and I won't," she reached out to touch his hand, her expression softening, "as long as you take me with you."

"No." He spun on his heel and started stalking down the road that curved along the cliff toward the main part of the village below. Huts belonging to Endless and Endless hopefuls were set along the cliff face on the inside edge of the road. His was less than halfway down.

She trotted after him. "You're going after that man, aren't you? The one who traded you that flyer?"

Perceptive little monster. Although she was making his life more difficult, he found it hard to fight back a fond smile, which would be the worst possible response just then. "It doesn't matter where I'm going. You aren't coming with me."

"Why? Is it dangerous?"

Dangerous and probably pointless. He stopped and drew in a deep breath, seeking to calm his nerves. Then he turned, put a hand on each of her shoulders, and stared her in the eyes, hoping she would see in his face how serious this was to him. Her shoulders felt small and fragile under his hands, reinforcing his decision.

"Misa, this is something I need to do. I can't put you at risk. It could be dangerous and I'll be lucky if Master Kochan doesn't banish me for it. Do you want that?"

Her big eyes grew moist. "No! I don't want you banished."

He chuckled and took his hands away before she could read too much into the contact. "I meant for you. You don't want to risk being banished, do you?"

"If you are."

Deynas exhaled and looked up. The sky was bright with stars and a steady light wind brought out a number of wind spirits, their vivid blue eyes adding to the glorious display. It would be a good night to fly.

There was a hollow feeling in his chest. Even now that he was truly one of the Endless, he felt the loss of Argus eating away at his spirit. That was why he had to try to find Naago again. The Endless deserter was the only one who might know how to quiet her presence within him so he could move on.

"I'm sorry, Misa. I can't let you come with me. Master Kochan would banish me for certain if I put you in danger. Tell someone if you must. It won't change my decision."

"Deynas, please don't leave me."

There was something in her pleading tone that brought to mind the night Argus died. He steeled himself against the fresh ache breaking through him and walked away from her, heading down to get the last of his things from his hut. She didn't follow him. When he came back up a short time later, she was nowhere around. That he had won the argument so easily was almost disappointing. Fighting it out a little longer would have delayed that moment of no turning back. It might have even drawn someone else out who could have talked sense into him.

His gut writhed with a nest of nervous knots as he tucked the last few things into the hatch and stood staring at the collection of supplies.

What would he do if Kochan did banish him?

The master refused to speak more of Naago, but he'd sent wind spirits to several of the other tribes the day after the man left and had already received discouraging replies from most of them. The masters of those tribes were aware of no *umahk-ra-uden* within their villages and knew little of how the gift worked. It made no sense to wait on the responses from the last few tribes when he already knew of someone who could help him if he could just talk the stubborn bastard into it.

He closed and locked the hatch, then climbed up on the flyer and buckled in. For what felt like hours, though he suspected it hadn't been more than a few minutes, he stood staring down the road that curved down and out of sight toward the village.

Could he really fly away from all this? Could he face the prospect of not be allowed to come back?

Giving himself a little shake, he turned to the waiting night. When his goggles were in place, he turned the flyer on. It came to life with the soft purr of an affectionate kitten. He had considered taking a less attention grabbing craft, but the quiet engine reduced the risk of detection on the way out and the superior speed would allow him to outrun patrol flyers if they chose to question his unusual nocturnal outing. The latter wasn't likely to be a problem though. He knew the patrol routes, so he knew how to avoid them.

Keeping low so he barely cleared the stands on the other flyers, he accelerated toward the opposite cliff, away from the village, and dove over, letting the craft plummet down the side. At the last second, he pulled up and punched the throttle, speeding away from the village and keeping low over the dunes without dropping close enough to make the dust billow. By morning, he would be well out of patrol range.

•

"You think you're ready to really fly, tenderfoot?"

Deynas hesitated, staring at the insets where he would strap in his feet. He might be almost five years younger, but he stood several inches taller so Argus was up on a slightly elevated platform attached at the foot of the support stand just behind those insets.

Did they truly expect him to stand so close in front of her?

Swallowing his nerves, he climbed up and bent over to buckle his feet into the insets in front of her. When he stood straight, she attached his harness to hers and leaned in so that her lips were next to his ear. All thought of flying vanished, pushed out by indecent fantasies involving the body pressing up against his back. The uncomfortable stirring in his groin made him glad she wasn't the one in front.

"Are you blushing, Deynas?" Her breath caressed his skin.

He was, fiercely. "No."

She only laughed and leaned back again. "Then what are you waiting for, tenderfoot. Get this thing off the ground."

By the time dawn spilled over the landscape, he was far enough from the village to drop down and skim the dunes, playing casually with the spraying of sand the way he and Argus had when they started flying individual crafts together. He'd graduated out of tandem flying very quickly and had almost regretted not having her body close behind him anymore, but being able to look over and see her dazzling smile as they raced through the sky had been worth the separation.

Sand dolphins joined him, jumping up alongside the craft, their muscular bodies arcing through the air. He grinned and eased up on the throttle a little, encouraging them to stay and play. Argus would search them out during flight training and challenge him to mimic their movements.

"Try it, Deynas. Learn from them. In the right hands, a flyer can be just as agile as a sand dolphin, though never as beautiful."

Hers had been the right hands and he wanted to argue that, with her on its back, the flyer was more beautiful than any sand dolphin, but he'd felt too much like a little boy reaching to catch a star. His doubts had kept the words locked inside.

A dolphin twisted alongside him as it leapt through the air and he mimicked it, doing a barrel roll in the valley between two dunes. There was something about the creatures, in their unassuming beauty and the joy they took in these simple games, that lifted his mood. He jumped with them, bringing the ship up and down in graceful arcs that he pulled up just before the nose tipped the sand.

After a time, the dolphins turned off deeper into the dunes and he continued alone, his better mood departing with them. He forced himself to continue through the day and up until dusk, by which time his eyes were struggling to stay open and his speed and balance had both grown erratic. Then he found a place well away from the main road to make camp before his weariness could plant him and the craft nose down in the sand.

He slept in some the next morning. The closer he got to the city, the less he could afford to be tired and inattentive. When he felt suitably refreshed, he took off again, angling toward the road that would take him to the massive black tower looming ahead. At the speed he was traveling, he would reach the city before evening.

By late afternoon, he could see the varied service and pleasure craft flying amidst the towering buildings of the New city at the top of the massive structure. Rather than use the crowded ground level entrances, he ascended and got into the queue to enter through a portal at the uppermost level of the Old city. He hadn't been

Endless long enough to wear any braids in his hair, but even without them, it seemed best to avoid the tighter security of the New city higher up and there were no legal entrances into the Undercity from the outside.

The winged demon tucked into the box at the entrance barely looked at him when it asked his business. He claimed to be a tourist coming from Ginakwa, the city to the north that supplied water to the tower city through a run of three massive pipes stretched across the desert like a leash. The portal iris opened and the demon waved Deynas through with a clawed hand the size of his head. Once through the portal, he found it hard not to stare.

When the city had belonged to the Endless tribes, there had been few demons in the Old and New city levels. Some gained entrance, if they proved trustworthy in their dealings, and spirits and gods often moved freely through the city levels. Now the Old city looked much like the Undercity, with demons of all types walking the streets among the human inhabitants, most of whom looked nervous, darting glances over their shoulders as if they expected an assault to come at every corner or from within every doorway. Even with bright lighting powered by the many generators within the tower, it felt like there were more deep shadows in the streets than when he had called the city home. More trash as well. A lot more.

Deynas could almost feel sorry for the people there, but those not of the Endless tribes, men and women who didn't have the blood of The Undying in their lines, had turned the tribes away when the demons overran the city, locking them out of their homes and businesses. They deserved their unhappiness.

He schooled the contempt from his expression and cruised slowly through the city, watching the signs like a tourist would in case the locals or, worse yet, the city enforcers, took an interest in him.

A howler, one of the big dog-like beasts the demons used to sound alerts in the city, lifted its long head when he passed, gazing at him through myriad amber eyes. It lost interest after a few seconds and returned to resting at the end of the chain that bound it to one of the massive steel columns supporting the levels of the city.

He made his way down the ramps leading deeper into the Old city. On the lowest two levels above the Undercity, he spotted a few shifty looking shops in the darker streets, places that likely dealt in drugs or illegal remedies. He also saw demon and crossbreed whores walking openly in the streets among those of the impoverished who were fortunate enough to afford life in the bottom of the Old city. In the deepest darkest reaches of the Undercity, one could always buy any kind of pleasure or punishment they were brave enough to seek out. Now that element was seeping upward, as if the Undercity overflowed its boundaries.

The scant number of human prostitutes who had peddled their flesh on low levels of the Old city when the Endless tribes had kept the demon element restricted below had vanished. Only a truly desperate woman would dare sell herself when possible customers included the most base and degenerate varieties of demon. Human flesh was never meant to stand up to the depravities such creatures enjoyed. Not all demons were that way, of course, but he didn't see any down here he would care to meet alone in the dark.

Dropping down into the Undercity was easy. Any adult could go down at their own risk. It had always been that way. Children going down and anyone coming up had to go through a checkpoint, though the guards weren't taking their job too seriously given the state of the streets above.

Deynas struggled to keep judgment from his face as he pulled up next to a guard box. The guard, this one human with a girth so great he almost didn't fit in the confines of the box, turned his glazed eyes to Deynas. He sat chewing, staring in silence until he spit a blue substance on the ground, just missing the wing of the red flyer.

"Need somethin'?"

The man smelled like soured milk. Deynas swallowed against the press of nausea in the back of his throat.

"I had hoped to find lodging with secure storage for my flyer."

The guard smirked at the fancy craft. "Yer goin' down?"

Deynas nodded.

"Best ye'll do is Kato's hotel next to The Firelight. He'll make ye pay fer it though."

"Right." Deynas grimaced. He didn't have a lot of currency, but he'd worry about those details later. There were some things in the hatch he could trade if the need arose. Ideally, he wouldn't stay long enough for the need to arise.

The big man chuckled. "Spent all yer money on yer toy, did ye?"

Deynas didn't answer. He sped away from the box and plunged into the heart of the Undercity.

The streets here were always dark, the lights far overhead coated over with years of grime that no one cared to clean up, creating an unending state of deep dusk that favored its unsavory inhabitants. At one time, those inhabitants had at least been monitored and held to some degree of accountability. Now, although he spotted two greater demon enforcers, he saw no evidence that they had any interest in anything beyond the pair of crossbreed whores they were fondling alongside one of the shabbier gambling dens.

He kept his speed up and avoided eye contact, making a quick run for the hotel. He'd never spent much time in the Undercity, but he knew its layout. Every child in the tribes studied maps of the city levels before they were old enough to begin training as Endless. When the Endless still lived in the city, The Firelight had been one of the few gambling dens frequented by residents from the Old and New city levels. He could only hope it retained some of that dubious prestige.

The Firelight came into view, impossible to miss for the clever trickery that made its black metal walls look like they were perpetually on fire. The smell of molten metal filled the air along with a slight undertone of sulfur. The den hadn't lost its dramatic flair and, judging from the more affluent looking crowd in front of the building, it still had a draw that reached beyond the denizens of the Undercity.

He angled in to the valet round before the hotel next to The Firelight, a little surprised to find that it was still in operation. Such amenities seemed out of place down in the darkest part of the city.

Two men and a young crossbreed were on duty at the stand. The men hung back and let the crossbreed approach. Other than his eyes, in which even the whites were inky black, the youth looked almost human and, when Deynas stepped down from the craft, he turned out to be several inches shorter, unusual for a crossbreed.

Deynas hesitated a moment. He didn't really want to stay in the city, especially down here, but it seemed unlikely that he would find Naago fast enough to leave before nightfall.

He retrieved a pack from the hatch then handed the crossbreed the key. The youth inserted the key into a short metal tube then pressed the pointed tip of the tube to the inside of his arm. An encoded mark appeared there at the end of a long row of several similar marks running up to his elbow. He then pointed the tip at Deynas who held out his wrist so the youth could print a matching mark there. There was a tiny spark of pain, almost more like a sharp itch, with the printing. The crossbreed broke off the marking tip and handed it to Deynas. He slipped it into a pocket. No one without that mark would be able to open the tube and access the key. The mark itself would fade away within a week and need to be renewed if he was still here. He didn't intend to stay half that long.

He left the flyer in the youth's care along with a tip of three stones, then entered through the door one of the men held open for him.

The inside of the hotel looked and smelled like the outside of The Firelight. Imaged fire flickered upon the interior walls and the polished black stone floor tiles reflected the flames. The overall effect made him a touch dizzy as he walked to the front desk. A crossbreed woman stood watching him from behind the desk, her plump lips painted a deep crimson and her very full breasts pushed up by a corset that didn't entirely cover her red nipples. When she smiled the corners of her mouth angled up, creating a peculiar symmetry with her sharply angled eyes and the pointed ears that peeked out through a luscious mane of raven hair.

For all that he tried not to notice, her shapely body and scant attire caused a stirring in his groin and he had to work hard to keep his focus on her eyes. She flicked her long tail up onto the desk and his gaze inadvertently shifted to follow the movement, catching on her breasts on the way back up. He forced his attention to her face.

She laughed, a deep throaty sound that whispered of secret pleasures and sweat soaked bodies. "Can I help you?" Her hands dropped to her hips leaving the front of her body open for full viewing.

"I… ah."

He set a hand on the desk to give himself a sense of stability. The women in the village weren't like this. Knowing she was probably paid to dress and behave that way didn't make it any less distracting.

She leaned her elbows on the desk, squeezing her breasts forward between her arms so that they threatened to pop free of the corset, and ran a finger over the back of his hand, the pointed nail brushing the skin in a light caress.

"We've got rooms. They come with and without company, though most come faster with."

He cleared his throat. "Let's start without."

She pushed her lip out in a spectacular pout and stood up straight. "You're no fun."

He smiled despite himself. "Sorry. This trip isn't for pleasure."

When she walked to the back of the booth to get a room key, he tried hard not to watch the way her hips swayed or to stare at her pert ass as her tail moved up, lifting the edge of the short skirt to reveal more smooth flesh. She turned suddenly and he snapped his gaze up, but not before she noticed and grinned. Swaying her hips provocatively, she walked back and leaned on the desk again. She dangled the room key between them, licking her crimson lips and making a show of looking him over.

"You look a little feverish, Love. You sure you don't need someone to take care of you?"

He took the key. "Maybe later." He turned and started to walk away.

"You know where to find me," she called after him.

Deynas stopped. She had his heart racing and he did feel a bit feverish, more than a bit actually, but this was business. Business that she just might be able to help him with. He steeled his nerves and walked back.

She was still leaning on the desk. Her eyes sparked with a gleam of victory. "Change your mind?"

The obstinate willpower that should have kept him from giving in to such temptation was beginning to desert him. "You are persistent."

"And very flexible." She reached out one finger, tracing his jaw with a soft caress, the fingernail just barely touching the skin to hint at a possibility for more aggressive pleasures.

Business. He gave himself a mental kick. "I don't doubt that, but I came back to ask you a question. Do you know a man by the name of Naago?"

He didn't really expect her to have any information. If he were to be honest, he'd asked mostly because he wanted to look a minute longer, since she didn't seem to mind him doing so. She seemed to enjoy it in fact.

The fond smile that touched her lips then was strikingly sincere and even more disconcerting for that. "Now that's a man who knows how to please a woman. If you're that good, I might consider coming up once for free."

So Naago's city life wasn't all suffering and misery. "I think he might have a few more years of experience."

"Never hurts to practice." She gave him a playful wink.

He inhaled, trying to clear his head and noticed the dusky sweet fragrance of her under the other smells in the room. That didn't help in the least. What would it be like to bed a crossbreed like her, someone schooled in the arts of pleasure?

"Is he around here?"

"Not right now, but he keeps a room upstairs. He's never away for long." She batted her thick lashes, giving him a seductive smile. "If you're going to wait, why wait alone?"

He searched for the words to turn her down again, his vocabulary failing him.

One arm came toward him suddenly and she slipped

her fingers into his hair, pulling him closer. She leaned further over the counter, her peeking nipples brushing the smooth surface. Her lips closed on his and her tongue dove into his mouth. Searing lust and the passionate promise in her kiss hammered down the last traces of resistance. He slid a hand around the back of her neck and kissed her back hard. She tasted faintly of cinnamon and chocolate and the deeper he kissed her the more he wanted to taste.

Perhaps she had the right of it after all. Why wait alone?

It was almost noon before Deynas untangled himself from Kaira. The crossbreed woman succeeded in making him forget just about everything with her seemingly boundless knowledge of how to please a man. There wasn't much of anything to dislike about her body and her playful attitude kept him from brooding. While he didn't have much reason to leave the room, he did get hungry eventually and decided it might be better to go to the food and take a chance to clear his head rather than have the food brought to them.

She went to check in with the front desk while he ate alone in the hotel dining room and wondered if he had anything he could trade in order to buy her company for another night. Alone he would only brood after all.

The meal was uninspiring, but it served its purpose. No longer distracted by hunger or Kaira, he decided to venture through the open wall between the bar and The Firelight to check out the gambling den. It was a gaudier, louder version of the hotel inside. The lights were turned low even in the daytime and imaged flames flickered high up the walls. Like the hotel, the floor was a reflective glossy black, only in the casino the high ceiling was the same, giving the visual effect of walking into a furnace. They kept it warm inside, to enhance the atmosphere, and a selection of scantily clad, primarily crossbreed women danced provocatively to loud music in glass-floored cages suspended above walkways woven through the numerous bars and gaming tables.

Most of the tables were busy, as were the bars. Deynas avoided eye contact with dealers at the tables and the serving women carrying around precarious platters of drinks or emptied glasses. He wasn't interested in joining the games or drinking just now. More than anything, he was curious and he needed to kill some time.

He shifted out of the way of a crossbreed woman carrying empties and someone bumped into him from behind. He twisted around.

The man behind him slapped a hand on his shoulder and shoved him back. "Watch where you're going, asshole!"

The rude individual appeared to be human, though his two burly companions looked like they had a shallow mix of some low demon in their blood. They grinned, confident in their superior size, and Deynas smirked back at them.

"Perhaps you and your mongrels should take some of that advice." Kochan would be so ashamed of him for that taunting remark, but Kochan wasn't there and he was itching for something to ease the restlessness that had crept back in the absence of Kaira's pleasant distractions.

The man responded with a sneer and Deynas did a quick mental inventory of the position of his hands, the set of his legs, and the nearness of his two companions. When he threw the punch, Deynas was ready. He ducked to one side and grabbed the man's wrist. One of the two crossbreed thugs lunged at him and he spun, swinging the man's arm up over his head and around, twisting it in and up behind his back. The man cried out, bending forward and shrinking down in an effort to escape the pain.

With a quick sidekick to the knee, Deynas took the first thug down. Then he swung back around, using the man for extra leverage to land a precise kick to the second crossbreed's jaw, dropping him like a rock. As soon as both feet touched the ground again, he jabbed behind the man's ear with a solid elbow strike. The impact rang out hollow and Deynas released him, letting him fall unconscious on top of his companions.

Activity had ceased at the closest bar and surrounding game tables while the brief altercation was going on. As soon as it ended, most of them turned back to their business. A couple of bouncers were moving across the room toward them, grinning in a way that Deynas suspected meant they were either going to enjoy throwing him out or they were about to congratulate him.

"Warlord Kato would like to speak with you."

Deynas spun toward the guttural voice. It had come from the fat centipede-looking creature now looming behind him. Its reddish pulsating flesh was semi-transparent, giving a glimpse of the shadows of organs within. Its many limbs and the various intimidating appendages around its mouth moved unceasingly. From looking, it was hard to tell just how the creature managed human speech at all, though he made a point not to look long. The demon was of a form commonly called hypnotists because their constant motion had hypnotic qualities that could mesmerize most any man. He didn't care to find out how that worked first hand.

Keeping his gaze turned to one side, he said, "I'm not sure I want to speak with him."

"Follow me."

The demon didn't wait for him. It shifted around in a wave of nauseating motion and started toward the back of the gambling den, its myriad legs undulating along its thick sides. Deynas tossed a glance over his shoulder and one of the bouncers now standing over his downed opponents gestured toward the retreating demon with a jutting of his chin.

"Ain't never done no one no good to make Kato wait."

One fight for the day was probably enough. He glanced down on the three figures with the slightest twinge of guilt and then nodded and followed the hypnotist. The creature led him down a hallway at the back and up a long flight of stairs. At the top, they emerged in a big room made entirely of the polished black stone, only here the floor was transparent, giving a view of the tables and bars below. There was a bar along one wall and a long curved desk in the center, both gleaming black.

A creature lay stretched across the top of the desk, vaguely cat-like at first glance, though covered in pointed scales rather than fur. Colors—red, orange, yellow and gold, even a glimmer of bronze—rippled along those scales when it breathed.

Deynas stepped closer, captivated by the dancing colors. He was aware of the hypnotist heading back down the stairs behind him. Then the beast got up off the desk with feline grace, rising up tall on its hind legs to gaze down on him. It had wings, wings that lay camouflaged against its skin until it stretched them, spreading them out over half the width of the big room. The sharply angled gold eyes and pointed ears reminded him faintly of Kaira. It rolled its neck, audibly popping several vertebrae. When it stopped moving, the color of the scales settled to a burnished maroon.

It grinned at Deynas. At least he hoped it was grinning, otherwise he was probably about to be eaten.

"I am Warlord Kato." The demon had a deep, disarmingly soothing voice with a hint of a purr in it. "It pleases me to make your acquaintance." He offered a slight bow of his head.

A demon who believed in social graces? Then again, Kato had ruled over part of the Undercity for as long as Deynas could remember. He was a warlord whose name had been whispered with awe and respect even back when the Endless required some level of compliance with the laws from the Undercity residents. This demon knew how to play at politics, something to keep in mind when dealing with him.

Deynas gave a slight nod in return. "I don't mean to be disrespectful, Warlord Kato, but I can't say if meeting you pleases me yet or not."

The demon chuckled. "Caution is never amiss in the Undercity. I asked you here because recent evidence suggests that you are capable of handling yourself in a fight and I am freshly short one guard."

Asked him there? It hadn't come across as a request. "I'm not planning to stay long in the city."

The demon shrugged, color rippling through the scales along its muscular shoulders. "Work for me for as long as you are here and your room and board will be provided free of charge. It's less risky than wandering the streets and will give you a way to burn off excess energy while you wait for Naago."

Deynas felt the muscles pull tight up his spine and across his shoulders. "You know why I'm here?"

"I know everything that transpires within my walls."

Kato walked toward the black bar. The ripple of color that moved through the scales over his legs and his long tail held Deynas rapt for a moment. Many people asserted that true demons were always ugly, crude beasts and he might have been inclined to agree before now. Kato was magnificent.

"Would you care for a drink?"

No. It wouldn't be right to let this creature to serve him. He couldn't allow it.

He took a step toward the bar, intending to suggest

that he do the serving, then he noticed a faint scent in the air, sweet and savory, like a favorite meal. So soothing, like Kato's voice and the play of colors...

He shook his head hard to try to clear it and stepped back. "You're manipulating me."

Kato chuckled and began to pour himself something. His long clawed hands moved with remarkable dexterity. "Good. You have some sense. You will do fine. I would like you to start by carrying out a personal favor for me. If you do so, I will also send Kaira to warm your bed again tonight."

Kaira. He grew hard at the thought and realized with a flush that the warlord was manipulating him in a multitude of ways. Still, it would solve the dilemma of how to pay her for another night. "What favor?"

Kato reached under the bar and brought up a small package wrapped in unmarked gray paper. He set a clear message film on top of it. "Deliver this package and message to Dokkon's rooms down in the ruin level. Go down the stairs across from those you came up to get here and turn left at the arena. Dokkon's door is the last one on the right. He won't be there right now, but you can walk in and leave the items on his desk."

"That doesn't sound so hard." Deynas walked up and took the package and message film, trying not to watch Kato's colors dance as he raised his drink to his lips and downed it in one quick swallow.

"I suggest you keep your weapons close down there." Kato gestured with one long finger to the blade and the staff grip at his belt. "Some of the fighters haven't learned to save their aggression for the arena."

The words sent a chill through him. It was one thing to take on a trio of overconfident bullies. Getting into a conflict with an arena fighter was more trouble than he needed. He touched the two weapons for reassurance as he left. Working for an Undercity warlord didn't appeal to him, but Kato was right, it was probably a lot safer than wandering the Undercity streets in search of distraction and it wasn't going to be for long.

There was another set of stairs going down across the hall as Kato said. Deynas descended, moving his hand away from his weapons to avoid provoking anyone. At the bottom, he came to the back edge of the seats surrounding the ruin-level stadium. There was no one nearby, so he sidetracked through to the edge of the unlit arena and gazed across to where the far reaches disappeared in blackness. The arena was enormous. How many lives were thrown away upon that vast dirt floor?

He shook his head and went back to the hall. Another hypnotist, or perhaps the same one, undulated down the hall. It bobbed its long neck in what appeared to be a greeting and continued on its way. A doorway on the left opened to a small sparring ring where two crossbreeds were fighting with staves. Deynas itched to join them, but he had a task and he meant to get it done with quickly.

At the last door on the right, he turned the knob and walked in. The door, poorly balanced on its hinges, swung lazily closed behind him. The main room itself was simple with bare stone walls, floor, and ceiling like the huts in the village. An Endless tribe had built their settlement here ages before the city above had been so much as a thought in someone's head. Some parts of that ruin, like the arena itself, were still in use beneath the Undercity. The furnishings here were modern and offensive to the eyes in garish bright red, violet and gold. A loud multicolored carpet lay upon the floor beneath the legs of a violet couch and a gold table. A matching gold desk sat by one wall with a red chair behind it.

He walked over to the desk and set the package down. His gaze moved up to the wall where three gold arena champion trophies hung. Fighting ability and design sense apparently didn't go together. Certainly not in this case.

There was a soft hush of cautious footsteps moving up behind him. He spun around.

A hulking crossbreed had entered from an adjacent room carrying a heavy axe in one hand. He had blue tinted skin and backswept horns above a blocky, but mostly human face. His jaw was oversized and teeth that didn't quite fit in a human head garbled his voice when he spoke.

"No one enters Dokkon's rooms."

The arena champion might not be the brightest, but he still wasn't someone with whom Deynas cared to pick a fight. He snatched the message film off the package and held it out to the glowering warrior.

"I was told to bring this to you."

Dokkon narrowed his eyes, but he snatched the film and held it over a brand on his wrist. The corner of the film flashed in recognition and words appeared. The warrior leaned away, holding his axe blade up between them so Deynas couldn't read the film. After a second, his lip lifted in a snarl. He let go of the film and it disintegrated before it hit the floor.

Dokkon hefted his axe and swung it at Deynas. Despite his surprise, he managed to leap clear and the heavy blade cleaved the desk in two.

"Wait."

The warrior twisted, swinging his axe about and Deynas leapt back over the gold table. He landed on his ass on the violet couch and shoved the table with his feet, sending it into Dokkon's shins. The big crossbreed merely grunted and lunged into his path when he made a sprint for the door.

Deynas held up his hands and backed away. "There's been some misunderstanding."

Dokkon swept out with his other hand and Deynas caught the flash of a dagger at the last second. He leapt back. The tip cut shallow gash over his heart. Pain focused him. No more playing nice. This was about survival now.

He drew his sword as he ducked another swing of the heavy axe. Then he lunged in before the swing was complete and thrust the blade deep in Dokkon's chest, feeling the friction of the razor edge scraping bone. The axe and dagger both clattered to the floor. The warrior looked down at the blade in his chest and then at Deynas who met his eyes.

"That's how it's supposed to be done."

He jerked the blade free and Dokkon fell over backwards. Someone threw the door open. The two he'd seen practicing stalled in the doorway, staring down wide-eyed at the fallen champion. Over their heads, the swaying head of the hypnotist rose up. It glanced down at Dokkon, then at Deynas. The insectile face was impossible to read.

"The bastard tried to kill me." Deynas stated, gesturing to the corpse with the point of his blade. "I only came to deliver a package."

The hypnotist bobbed its head. "Come. We must report this to Kato." The two crossbreeds stepped back to let Deynas pass and the demon moved in, lowering its head to look each in the eye. "See that this door remains shut until I return."

They nodded and Deynas stepped between them to follow the hypnotist back up the stairs to Kato's office, his nerves on fire with the burst of adrenaline and the fear of how the warlord would react to the loss of his champion.

Kato waited with his back to the door. The hypnotist left Deynas there without a word. As soon as he was gone, the warlord turned in an elegant motion accentuated by the dance of color upon his scales. His gold eyes considered the sword Deynas still held, its blade streaked with Dokkon's blood. Then he looked up at Deynas and smiled.

"Is there a problem?"

There was little point in hedging. "I'm afraid I killed your champion."

"Did you leave the package in the room?"

Not the response he expected. "Yes. Dokkon was there. He read your message and promptly tried to kill me. I want to know what the hell is going on."

"I am pleased. The message served its intended purpose. I told Dokkon that his skills were no longer needed and that I sent you to kill him."

Deynas stared at him. The cut over his heart stung, the blood soaking into his shirt. The hand holding the sword hilt twitched.

"This was the favor I required, for you to free me of Dokkon. I acknowledge that I wasn't particularly up front about the details."

"You bastard," Deynas breathed, fully aware that he might be taking on more than he could handle by insulting the demon warlord, but far too outraged to hold his tongue.

Kato gestured to the bar. "Would you care for a drink now?"

Deynas tightened his grip on the sword hilt. "I would care for an explanation."

"Dokkon was difficult to manage and the audience was bored with him. I offered him generous compensation to throw a fight and step down as champion, but he would not take it. When my guards find the package of performance enhancing illegals you delivered, they'll assume he got paranoid and attacked you out of fear that his drug use had been found out. Everyone will believe he was using the enhancers in the arena because how else could a normal man like you defeat Dokkon the Unstoppable. After a few months, they'll even begin to say they knew it all along. Now I am free to initiate competition for a new champion. That will draw the bigger crowds back. It all works out quite satisfactorily."

"If he was such a great warrior, what made you think I could defeat him?"

Kato smiled slyly, flashing the tips of his pointed incisors. "Because I knew that he, like most everyone else, would mistake you for a normal man, and you are no normal man, Endless."

Deynas knew he should deny it, but something in the shrewd demon's gold eyes told him it would be pointless. "How did you know?"

"I always watch the men Kaira takes an interest in. Her mother was attuned to the spirits of others. She was an Endless woman with the gift I believe your kind call spirit reading, *umahk-ra-inra*. Kaira possesses some of trace that gift and, because of it, she is attracted to stronger spirits like a moth to a flame. I found Naago out through her instant fascination with him. It was much the same with you."

"If you know about Naago, why didn't you have him get rid of Dokkon for you?"

"Because Naago and I have a special working arrangement. Having him perform this service would have drawn unwanted attention to that arrangement."

Kato strode over to the bar and Deynas watched him. The strange enchantment of the demon's color-changing scales and the scent he emitted commanded his full attention, soothing away his anger. Deynas was aware of it. He didn't try to fight it. In this situation, his anger would only get him killed. The sooner he let it go, the better.

"The sword is not your weapon of choice?"

Deynas touched the staff grip. "No."

Kato reached behind the bar again and pulled out

a cloth. He tossed it to Deynas who caught it easily and used it to wipe the blood from his blade. Then he sheathed the weapon and tossed the bloodied cloth back to Kato. The big demon sniffed at the blood and smiled before setting it down on the black bar.

"It would be grand to watch Endless fight in my arena again. It is a shame your kind have been banished."

"I won't argue that."

"The offer to work for me while you are here still stands. I can always use an additional guard downstairs. I will provide you room and board and keep your secret. In exchange for the service you've done me today, I will also give you Kaira to warm your bed each night you are here. A generous offer, don't you agree?"

He wanted to hate Kato for using him, but he couldn't. The demon was clever. He knew his business well and he used his uncanny glamour to his advantage in a way that Deynas couldn't entirely resist.

"I will work for you, but I will hate you for lying to me."

Kato turned, dropping to all fours. He looked as natural there as he did upright. His muscles bunched and he launched himself toward his desk. Deynas caught his breath at the stunning play of color that swept along his impressive form. He landed on the glossy black desk top as lightly as if he weighed nothing.

Kato chuckled and stretched out upon the desk. "On the contrary, Deynas-ra, you will love me because you cannot help it. Go to your rooms now. I will send Kaira up to stitch that wound and tend any other sore spots that might need attention."

Deynas stared at him. There were so many questions he still wanted to ask. Ultimately, however, it was wiser to let his curiosity go unsatisfied and leave the warlord's presence while he retained enough will to do so.

He bowed his head once and walked away.

For three days, the Keeper let Naago show her his favorite places in the desert, or rather, let him direct her to them. She insisted on piloting the flyer. The arrangement was risky given that she could be called to keep at any time, but there was usually enough warning that she would have time to take the flyer down before she disappeared. It wasn't clear to her what he saw in the vast canyons and towering rock formations he took her to, but something about flying from place to place put her at peace with the host body. The more she flew, the easier it became to let the host and its memories guide her movements.

Dusk of the third day found them parked on top of the tallest dune for miles around, sitting on the peak next to the flyer. They'd finished eating and the Keeper was content to wait, letting the light breeze blow through her hair while Naago held his silence, watching the setting sun. The fading light reflected off a pod of sand dolphins passing nearby and he stood. She stood with him, watching him, the wistful smile that played across his lips, the shimmer of sorrow in his eyes.

When the pod passed out of sight, he turned to her. "You never watch them."

"Should I?"

"Nara loved to watch them."

"Your *umahk-ra'sen?*"

He nodded. "You don't find them beautiful?"

Frustration tightened her jaw. She gazed past him toward where the pod had been. "I don't know that my spirit recognizes beauty the way yours does."

He took a step closer and her attention shifted back to him. One of his hands came up to touch her cheek. "I recognize a great deal of beauty in you."

Despite the obviousness of the flattery, she couldn't stop a smile. Even if the flesh she wore hadn't always been hers, there was something nice about his complimenting it. Or perhaps it was because of this host and its memories that his words affected her.

A nervous flutter rose in her stomach when he moved another step closer. She turned toward the flyer, fleeing his touch. "You said there was a travel haven nearby."

"Yes. Do you want to pilot again?"

The thought brought another smile to her lips, which was all the answer he needed. He hopped up to buckle himself in against the stand. She climbed up and fastened her feet into the insets. When he had her harness secured to his, she reached to turn on the craft then hesitated, the deepening dark bringing a twinge of uncertainty. She twisted to look over her shoulder at him.

"I haven't tried flying in the dark and I don't know the way. Perhaps you should pilot this time."

He reached his arms around her and took her hands, placing them on the control grips. His hands rested over the top of hers, his body pressed warm against her back.

"I'll guide you," he murmured in her ear.

At first, it was hard not to resist him when he adjusted her hands to change their trajectory. By the time they reached the *travel haven,* they were moving together easily, even playing with the sand and performing some simple maneuvers in harmony. It was what she imagined dancing would be like had she ever done it. The mind within the host was silent on the matter.

She pulled her hood up and followed him to get a cabin from the caretaker, watching his hands as he swapped currency for the key. They were strong hands that could wield a sword with frightening expertise, yet they could touch with such gentleness. Fascinating.

They moved the flyer to the cabin and he led her to the door, unlocking it and stepping to one side to open it for her.

Something slammed into her chest, throwing her back from the doorway. She hit the ground hard enough to knock much of the air from her lungs. The beast that struck her landed alongside her head and skidded in the sand. It spun around to snarl at the now empty doorway then hissed at Naago, who already had his sword out and poised to strike.

She surged to her feet and threw a hand up to stay his blade. "Don't. It's only a desert cat. Since it can't see me, it's probably rather confused and frightened right now."

The cat's ears lay flat against its head and it cowered low to the sand, its teeth bared. The Keeper let herself be seen and the animal started, bounding sideways in surprise. It hissed once more, then bolted into the night.

Naago sheathed his sword. "Are you all right?"

She put a hand to her chest, feeling the strong fast beat of the heart there. "Startled mostly."

He turned to eye the cabin. "Cruel trick, locking that beast in there."

"Yes." She wondered if he meant it was a cruel trick to play on the person opening the door or if he meant a cruel trick to play on the animal, as she did. Probably the former from what she knew of him, though he had surprised her before.

The cabin reeked of urine and every inch of available fabric was shredded. She waited while Naago went back to trade the key for one to a cabin that hadn't been subjected to the temper of an angry desert cat. This time he insisted on entering ahead of her, just to be sure. He lit the two lanterns hanging on the wall. She watched while he started a fire to keep the nighttime chill away. When he finished and turned to face her, his gaze focused in on her neck, his brow furrowing.

"You're bleeding."

She hadn't even noticed the sting until he said something. "I'm sure it's just a scratch."

"I should check it. No sense taking chances." He walked over and brushed her hair out of the way, his fingertips tracing across the skin of her neck. "It's not bad. You're right. Just a scratch."

She sensed a change in his intent then and became aware of how close he stood, the warmth of his body heating the scant inches between them. His fingers slid up the side of her neck, his gaze following them along the curve of her jaw and on to her lips. She didn't notice his other hand moving until it released the clasp on her cloak. The cloak dropped to the floor with a soft rustle of fabric. When she opened her mouth to object, he leaned in, silencing her with his lips on hers.

She stiffened, frozen by surprise and a powerful lack of context to pull upon for this situation.

He moved his lips away enough to murmur, "Trust me."

Trust him? She had no idea how to respond to his attentions. Once again, the Keeper's restricted memories had no guidance to offer.

His hand moved back down the side of her neck, fingers gliding over the black roots twined upon her skin and under the shoulder of her simple black dress, moving the fabric off her shoulder.

The Keeper's pulse sped up then and her body warmed. The host body and the mind of the woman buried within it knew how to respond to him. The Keeper retreated to a back corner of their shared mind and let that presence guide her the same way she had with the flying.

When he kissed her again, she closed her eyes and kissed him back, letting him draw the sleeves of her dress down over her arms. Once her hands were free of the fabric, they moved up to begin undoing his shirt.

He unfastened the loose hanging belt at her waist, letting it fall on the soft cushion of her cloak. With that gone, he moved his hands down her body, sliding the dress over her hips so that it joined the rest on the floor. Then his hands began to move freely over her skin, exploring her curves with his gentle caresses. The host moaned into his mouth, pressing her body into his touch. Sensations swelled in her breasts, along the curve of her waist, over her hips, between her thighs, everywhere his fingers and lips touched.

The Keeper hung back, staying present enough to feel his touch upon the host, discovering what pleased it and how it pleased him. There was no confusion, only pleasure and the touching and joining of flesh. So new and yet familiar.

•

After Naago found the satisfaction he craved from her host body, he got up and went to sit in a chair before the fire, leaving her lying naked on the bed. The other within that flesh was quiet now, perhaps also contented.

He pulled out his violin case as he had every night and began to open the buckles. "When I told you to trust me, I didn't expect such a willing response."

She got up and began to dress, suddenly wary of

the possibility of being called to keep while in this state. The cloak couldn't hide her if she wasn't even in contact with it. "Were you disappointed?"

"Not in the least." He smiled at her, watching her with open appreciation while she pulled on the dress.

She adjusted the belt, aware that he seemed to expect some reaction to his words, but unsure what that reaction should be.

"And you don't even blush a little."

"I wear the body of an Endless woman. That does not mean I am one."

"What are you?"

She glanced at him, feeling a prickling of frustration. "You have asked this before."

"And you didn't give me an answer," he countered, his tenacity apparently as endless as his blood.

She picked up the cloak from the floor and flung it around her shoulders. "I am not an Endless woman."

"You figured out how to respond like one fast enough."

"In that, you are wrong. I didn't know how to respond to you, but she did, so I let her."

His brows pinched together as he watched her now, troubled. "Is it always that way? You can share control with the one whose body you inhabit?"

She fastened the clasp on the cloak, feeling measurably safer in its embrace. "No. I know it isn't supposed to be this way. She should be silent. Dormant within this body."

He was still for a time, his pensive look offering her none of the reassurance she suddenly longed for. The memory of the Keeper might have its limits, but that knowledge was certain. The host body was never more than a silent shroud of flesh controlled by the Keeper. Why was it different this time? Was it because the woman had been *umahk-ra-en-mahde*? Was it something Naago had awakened? He was *umahk-ra-uden* after all. Both were favored by The Undying. Perhaps bringing them together had disrupted something.

She went to sit in the other chair beside him. A few minutes passed in silence, then he pulled out the violin.

"If I play, will you let her *umahk-ra* come out again?"

"If you play, I will listen. Beyond that, I cannot say."

He positioned the violin and took a moment to check the tuning. Then the bow sang across the strings. He closed his eyes and filled the cabin with a beautiful music. She closed her eyes as well, watching the light of the music dance in the darkness. This time it danced through the room in contented gold and romantic rose tones, a warmer, brighter song than any he'd played before.

She smiled. The *umahk-ra* within the flesh stirred and she let it move apart to flow with the music. There seemed little reason to hide it from him now. The spirit thief had already seen it once. He had stolen his fragment.

•

They left early the next morning, finally heading back to the city. He let her fly again, content to ride along. On occasion, he would start moving his hands over her body through the cloak until she would snap at him not to distract her from driving. Then he would laugh and tell her to focus. With the Endless woman's presence actively helping her fly, it was especially hard to ignore his touch and he enjoyed teasing her.

They reached the city that evening and he took them in through one of the ever-changing illegal portals the sand demons controlled into the Undercity. He knew the demons on both ends of the portal they used well enough that they hailed him by name. She stayed unseen on the way in, standing still in front of him with her feet on the surface of the flyer and her hands clasped before her. The cloak worked to hide her harness, though a careful eye might have noticed the periodic shifting of his harness at the attachment points.

The uncomfortable beckoning sensation returned the moment they entered the Undercity, intensifying when they went in through the backdoor of the hotel she'd first met him in. The crossbreed guard also hailed Naago by name and opened the door to let him in. It wasn't easy to become this well-known and regarded in the Undercity. Such notoriety came from dealings with the Undercity warlords who ran the fighting rings and the illegal medicine shops, businesses that were contrary to the very nature of the Keeper. For a time, she had managed to forget the circumstances that brought them together. Now his crimes began to weigh heavy on her again.

She followed him out to the lobby of the hotel, hanging back unseen, curious to watch him in the hostile environment he had made his own, a world that would tear him apart if it knew what he really was.

He strode across to the front desk, behind which a very tall, svelte blue-skinned crossbreed woman waited. In place of hair, she had a mane of dark blue feathers that hung down past her waist and was about all that covered her. She moved up to the desk, her body swaying like a stalk of grass before a soft breeze, and batted her long lashes over bright sapphire eyes.

"Welcome back, Naago."

He smiled tightly and glanced about as if looking for someone. "Is Kaira around?"

There was a wicked gleam behind the crossbreeds smile. "She's been warming the new guard's bed the last several nights."

"Has she? He must be something."

The Keeper noticed a trace of tension in Naago's voice. Interesting.

"Oh, he is." The woman grinned and batted her long lashes. "What's the matter, Honey? Jealous? I can distract you from you're woes."

"I don't need company right now," he replied a little too sharply.

Perhaps the crossbreed had read him right. He was jealous.

"I'm busy anyway," the woman answered just as sharply, her sullen pout belying the sentiment.

"Any messages?"

She reached a hand under the desk and brought up two envelopes that she handed over to him, then she turned her back on him and started to fiddle with the keys hanging on the wall.

Naago opened the first envelope and glanced inside. A thick bundle of high denomination slips nestled within. He pulled a blank message film out and closed the envelope, tucking it under his arm. He held the film over a small code printed on his left palm and a blue dot in the corner of the film flashed once. Text appeared on the clear surface.

The Keeper read over his shoulder, a flash of anger tightening her shoulders. The bundle was a bonus for helping the hunters take down a lesser god. There were unique organs in a god's body that brought a very high price on illegal markets. The warlord who employed those hunters was sharing a small percentage of expected profits with Naago for luring the beast into their trap.

He tucked that message in a pocket and pulled another film out of the second envelope. This was from Kato, the demon warlord who owned the hotel, The Firelight gambling den, and the fighting ring in the ruins beneath it along with several other properties in the Undercity. The message informed Naago that the current champion had 'the good graces to finally die' and offered the 'usual compensation' if he were interested in rounding up some challenges for the new round of hopefuls.

Naago pocketed that message as well and turned around, heading for the elevators without acknowledging her. He was growing accustomed to that aspect of their relationship at least.

A rowdy bunch of smartly-accessorized, overindulged New City crossbreeds stormed through the entrance and took up a lively banter with the part-demon woman behind the counter. The Keeper followed Naago into an elevator, happy to leave the noisy group behind.

They went to the same room he'd been in when she first met him, likely a long-term rental given the kind of work he did for Kato. Naago tossed his things on the couch then turned, reaching for her with open desire in his eyes.

She took a quick step back from him.

He stared at her, the desire giving way to confusion. The lines in his brown deepened. "What's wrong?"

"Have you no respect for life at all?"

"More than you could know."

He turned away and stalked to a credenza along the wall. A well-stocked array of bottled alcohols waited within. Glass clinked loudly as he shoved the bottles around, finally drawing out an unmarked, dark bottle tucked toward the back. He poured himself a glass then glanced back at her, holding the bottle up.

"Do you want some?"

She shook her head. There was no way to know how this body would respond to alcohol. None had passed its lips since it had become her host.

He shoved the bottle back in and kicked the door shut. With glass in hand, he sank down in a wide chair and took a long drink, grimacing as he swallowed. He'd barely settled when someone rapped on the door in a playful cadence.

Naago scowled into his glass. "Not now, Kaira."

"I know you're in there. I just need a minute."

Naago smacked the glass down on a table. He stood and stormed to the door. The Keeper stepped back against the wall, intrigued by both his anger with her and by his response to the visitor. The very well-endowed crossbreed woman standing outside when he opened the door smiled and leapt into him. Her hand came up to run through his hair and she pressed her hips forward into his groin.

He turned his face away from her attempted kiss and gave her a firm push away, though it wasn't hard enough to be more than a mild discouragement. "I'm not in the mood."

"Fine." She gave a sultry pout and pushed herself further away from him with a quick shove against his chest. "Now isn't a good time anyway. I brought some-one who needs to talk to you. I'll leave you boys alone."

With that, the crossbreed spun on her rather sub-stantial heels and sashayed from the room.

Someone else stepped into the doorway, a younger man with long black hair and dark blue eyes that carried sadness beyond his years. His features were strong and yet refined enough to give a softening beauty to his masculinity.

It wasn't his attractiveness, however, that made her catch her breath at the sight of him. It wasn't anything she could name. Her chest tightened when he stepped into the doorway and she felt dizzy. She moved silently across to a hard chair in the corner where no one was likely to notice the change in weight upon the seat and sat down.

"Deynas-ra." There was a harshness to Naago's tone, but she spotted a glimmer of something more like respect in his eyes. "I'm a little surprised to see you here."

The man, Deynas, strode into the room, not waiting for an invitation. His eyes skimmed the surroundings then came back to Naago, his gaze sharpened with an edge of contempt.

"I see life in the Undercity has been a trial for you."

Naago glanced back toward the still open door, quickly connecting the dots. "A little judgmental coming from someone who has spent his time here playing guard for Kato and enjoying Kaira's pleasures."

"As I'm sure you already know, Kato can be very persuasive." Deynas bumped the door shut with his heel, making it clear he didn't intend to leave without whatever he'd come for. "At least I didn't abandon my tribe to come here."

Naago stepped toward him, his frame rigid with aggression. "Didn't you? I'd bet my life you didn't get Master Kochan's approval for this adventure. What do you think he will do when he finds out where you are? Go back to your village now, while you still have a tribe to return to."

Deynas's voice changed, a whisper of some deeper sorrow in it, tempering the judgment and anger he'd bandied about so far. "I still need your help."

The tight aching in her chest intensified, turning to a twisting pain.

Naago walked to the table and picked up his drink. He downed the contents in one swallow and stood there with his back to Deynas.

"I can't help you. Find someone else."

Deynas closed his eyes and ground his teeth. He stood that way for a moment, the muscles in his jaw working as he fought some inner battle, then he turned and stormed from the room, slamming the door behind him.

The Keeper rose and walked across the room, letting herself be seen. She placed a hand on the door, feeling the fast fading traces of the energy he'd used to slam it shut. It felt as if someone had torn a hole inside her. Why?

Naago moved up beside her. "You know him?"

"No."

"But she does?"

She looked at him, taking in the furrow in his brow and the tension in the set of his jaw. "What makes you say that?"

"It could be instinct." He reached up, brushed a finger over her cheek, and held it up to show her the dampness on it. "Or it could be your tears."

She brought her left hand up and touched her other cheek. There were tears there too. What madness was this?

She looked at the door again, every detail of the man she had seen there still crisp in her mind as if she'd seen him a thousand times before. "You should help him."

Naago exhaled. "Which part of you is saying that?"

She knew the answer to that, but she couldn't bring herself to admit it aloud.

He went to the credenza and dug the bottle out to pour himself another drink. "Will you come with me?"

"I can't. I don't think it wise for me to be around him… or you. I will go back to the Halls of the Blooded. The Keeper needs a new host."

He froze, his hand holding the bottle poised above the glass, the alcohol stopping a fraction from the lip. "What?"

"The mind and spirit in this body are too strong and too active. It is no longer a suitable host."

He poured the drink and slammed it then set the glass down and poured another. "You would kill her?"

"For a man who makes his living dealing in the lives of other creatures, you are very quick to question my ending one life." She regarded him, gaining insight

through the distress in his face, the weight in his movements. "But it's different, isn't it? It isn't just any life.
It's the life of an Endless woman, one you find attractive
no less."

"Of course it's different. It would be different for
you if I were to…"

"To kill another Keeper?" She shook her head.
"There has only ever been one of me. I will never
understand the difference of which you speak."

He set the bottle down then carried the glass to
the bathroom and dumped the contents down the sink.
Leaving the glass on the counter, he walked out to her
forcing a smile that didn't reflect in his eyes. "Come
with me. Let yourself live a little more before you move
to a new host."

"I have lived longer than you can remember, Endless."

He denied her words with a shake of his head, moving
close enough to brush his fingers into her hair. He placed
a light kiss on her lips. "You have only existed."

She couldn't argue with that. It felt true.

"Perhaps this is your chance to experience something more. Besides, I won't agree to help him unless
you agree to travel with me."

When she didn't answer, he kissed her again, a deeper
kiss this time, and she opened her mouth to him. The
mind within the body compelled her to press into him,
seeking solace from uncertainty in his arms.

Drawing back from the kiss, he murmured, "I'll
take that as a yes."

Then he slid his hands inside the cloak and around
her waist. Pulling her tight against him, he began to kiss
her again, igniting a fire in the body that was no longer
entirely hers and chasing her disconcerting response to
Deynas to the back of her mind for a time.

Deynas stormed through the lobby, aching to punch something. Anything. The whole journey had been a waste of time. Kochan was right to turn Naago away. The man was worthless. He could only hope the master wouldn't do the same to him after this.

He burst through the front doors and the two valets on duty started. The crossbreed youth took one look at his face and yanked open a drawer, scrambling through it to pull out the proper key tube. Deynas thrust out his arm for scanning. When the tube opened, the crossbreed took the key and tossed the empty tube to his companion who snatched it from the air without looking up.

"I'll bring your flyer right up, Sir."

Deynas gave a sharp nod as the crossbreed darted through a door behind the valet desk.

He'd been standing there only a few seconds when Kaira walked up beside him. He hadn't even noticed her on his way out. She slid her hand over his far shoulder and rested her chin on the other.

He tensed. "I already told Kato I was leaving."

She chuckled in his ear, the warmth of her breath on his skin bringing back the nights they spent together, the smell of her sweat, the taste of her, the way she touched him. The memories still aroused him, forcing him to adjust his stance in spite of his anger with Naago and with himself for being fool enough to go after the man.

"I know." She brushed her fingernails down his neck. "I almost feel like I should have paid you for your services."

He felt warmth rising up into his cheeks, uncomfortably aware of the other valet watching them, or watching her at least. "What do you want?"

"Don't be upset with Naago. He's broken…inside." She placed a hand on her ample chest, perhaps meaning to indicate that the Endless man's heart was broken, but the gesture didn't have the desired effect.

Deynas forced his eyes away from her breasts and stared out into the crowded nighttime street in front of The Firelight. Whores worked through the crowd, looking to snag customers, while two voluptuous waitresses from the casino offered up free shots on trays to any passers willing to come inside.

"He's a coward."

"Maybe he is." She seemed willing to let it go at that. Her lips brushed his neck in a soft kiss. "Don't be a stranger."

He held his silence, though he couldn't resist turning to steal a last glimpse of her shapely ass as she walked back into the hotel. She'd succeeded in muting his anger a bit, turning it to more of an intense frustration that opened the door to the slow rise of despair. At least Kato hadn't tried to keep him there. Deynas wasn't sure he could have fought the demon's glamour if he had. It would be good to put this place behind him and forget the whole mess, assuming he still had a home to return to.

The crossbreed came up on the red flyer and Deynas tossed him a few stones from the money he'd barely had to touch thanks to working for Kato. Then he strapped in and sped away from the building.

Night in the Undercity wasn't much different from any other time. There was a small increase in the population due to those residents of the upper levels who dared to come down and patronize the gambling dens and taverns at the end of their work day. He darted through the crowds, going faster than he should, though he doubted any of the few Undercity enforcers were going to bother challenging him. Lawlessness was the law in the Undercity now. Criminal order maintained by the warlords with the most power.

He was about to angle up out of the Undercity when he spotted a couple of men crowding a young woman a little beyond the ramp. At a glance, the youth looked disturbingly familiar. Deynas veered off toward them and gunned the throttle. He swung the craft around to an abrupt stop alongside the three and jumped off next to the girl. After giving her a quick a reproving scowl he faced the two men.

"This girl is with me. Go find your entertainment elsewhere."

The men, burly and blockheaded both in build and, he suspected, intellect, gave him boorish sneers and Deynas dropped a hand to his sword hilt. One man's lip, swollen and bruised from some recent altercation, lifted in a quiet snarl, but the other held up his hands.

He smiled a greasy smile that Deynas didn't trust for a second. "We don't want trouble, Mister. We'll just move on if ye don't mind."

Deynas nodded and kept his hand on the sword hilt until the two disappeared into a nearby building. Then he sheathed the weapon and spun around, rapping Misa firmly on the forehead with his knuckles.

"Ouch!" She ducked away from him and rubbed at her head, glowering. "What was that for?"

"For being a fool! What in the name of The Undying are you doing here?"

"I came to look for you."

"Why?"

"I…" She lowered her eyes, her face flushing. "You'd been gone a long time. I was worried about you. What if something bad had happened to you?"

His chest ached with a twist of sympathy and grudging appreciation for her concern, but it had been a foolish thing to do, no matter the reason. "What if something had happened? What exactly were you going to do about it?"

Her shoulders drooped and she stared at his feet, her sullen silence filling the space between them.

Deynas exhaled and ground his teeth. Kochan was going to skin him alive. Maybe not literally, but it would certainly feel like it when the master was done. At least he'd come upon her before she got into real trouble.

"Where is your flyer?"

She chewed her lip, moisture welling in her eyes. "A demon took it."

Bastards. He wiped away a tear that raced down her cheek. "This place isn't safe, Misa. You knew that before you came."

Her lower lip trembled as she nodded. Then something in her stance changed, a straightening of her posture, and she lifted her chin to meet his eyes. "So did you."

The stubborn defiance brought out her beauty and he found himself almost wishing she were a little older. Before he could say anything, her eyes focused on something behind him and widened. Deynas turned, placing his hand on the thick staff grip at his belt this time.

The two men who'd left them moments ago were coming back with another two large chaps flanking them now. He'd been right not to trust them. The man who'd said they didn't want trouble was smirking.

"Changed your mind?" Deynas asked, keeping his voice steady.

The man in front spit to one side and stopped a few feet back from him, out of reach of a sword. The others moved out to either side of him.

"I did. Pretty thing like that'll sell real well. Lots of folks pay a tidy sum for them young ones. Can't expect me to pass her up." His gaze moved to Misa.

"You'd best keep your eyes on me if you mean to make trouble," Deynas warned, pulling the staff grip away from his belt.

One of the big men drew a wicked looking axe from the sheath on his back and the other pulled a club from a loop on his belt.

Deynas switched the safety off on the staff handle with his thumb and flicked his wrist. The staff telescoped out both ends, the last foot of each end narrowing down into a sharp blade. He gestured Misa back and shifted his weight into a better stance for fighting.

The men did the same, but they didn't get a chance to attack. A band of seven crossbreeds raced over on their flyers and pulled up around them. The men backed off a several strides, lowering their weapons. A red-skinned part-demon youth with gold eyes and hair like flame grinned down at them. The expression was distinctly predatory, made more menacing by a mouthful of pointed teeth.

"You wouldn't be harassing these two, would you, Barl," the crossbreed purred, his tone made sinister by those bared teeth and narrowed eyes.

The lead man held up his hands in the same gesture he'd given Deynas, though this time he looked genuinely concerned.

"We was just having a chat, Settek." He nodded to the other men who put their weapons away.

Deynas wasn't comfortable yet doing the same.

Settek smirked. "Chat's over. Slink back to your holes."

The four men backed up several steps, then turned and made a hasty retreat into the building they had come from.

Deynas eased his stance and offered a wary nod of gratitude to the youth. "Thank you."

Settek gestured to the red flyer with one claw-tipped finger. "Did you kill the man who had this flyer?"

Was that the reason for the timely rescue? "No, he traded it to me."

That answer washed all trace of good humor from those gold eyes. "Did he tell you he stole it from me?"

Deynas tightened his grip on the staff. There was a pattern of escalating trouble going on and he wasn't sure whether to hope that it would come to a head with them or that some greater threat might come chase Settek and his band away.

"The man I got the craft from said he won it in a wager. I had no reason not to believe him."

Settek hopped down from his flyer and his six companions followed his example, gathering behind him. The red-skinned youth was the tallest of them by several inches, his reach long, his bare chest ripped with lean muscle.

"Then I will make you a wager."

Misa stepped closer and Deynas put a hand out, motioning her back again. "I'm not interested in wagers."

"I am and, if you want to leave here alive, I suggest you develop an interest."

Deynas felt vaguely sick. He couldn't make a run for it, not with Misa to think of, but he couldn't afford to get in a fight with her there either, not with all of them. The men he would have most certainly outmatched, but crossbreeds were different. There was no way to know for certain what advantages their mixed blood might give them. They had him in a corner. All he could do was hope for a better option to come up in conversation.

"I'm listening."

Settek grinned, his better humor returning. "If you defeat me in single combat, then you keep the flyer and your life. If you lose, I take the flyer..." his gold eyes flashed brilliantly, as if a fire had ignited within him, "and maybe, I take your life too."

"No. If I lose, you take the flyer and leave me alive to get her out of here."

The gold eyes moved to Misa and his expression turned thoughtful. After a few seconds, he nodded. "It is agreed. I would not bring the girl to harm."

That surprised Deynas a little. Maybe the situation wasn't hopeless.

Settek eyed his weapon. "You prefer the staff?"

Deynas nodded.

While Deynas set his sword belt aside and turned off the flyer, tucking the red key into a pocket, one of the other crossbreeds handed Settek a staff handle. He armed it with a flick of his wrist and they moved out away from the flyers. The other six crossbreeds formed a circle around them. Misa hung back, cowering next to the red flyer, her eyes moist and wide with fear.

Settek spun his staff with a flourish and dropped into fighting stance. Deynas touched the small bulge of the god's blood pendant as he moved into position, hesitating only a second before he lunged at his adversary. The crossbreed deflected his attack and came back with a swift counterstrike. He was strong and dangerously fast, but Deynas knew the staff as well as he knew his own flesh. He preferred to discourage the crossbreed without drawing blood if he could.

Settek wore no shirt, flaunting his exquisite musculature to the world, but also exposing a set of four symmetrical healing slashes on his side. They made a good target, a weak point where a strike would have more impact and perhaps cause enough pain to give him second thoughts.

They exchanged a series of attacks, each getting a feel for the other's style and skill. Then Deynas blocked a high strike and spun the other end of the staff around low, bringing it up in time to catch Settek a hard blow to the healing side with the rounded part of the weapon.

Settek grunted, staggering. He caught himself on one knee and sprang back up. A tiny glimmer of blood emerged from the healing wound that took the brunt of the strike and his eyes flared with rage, his flame-colored mane darkening a shade.

Settek looked past Deynas and gave an almost imperceptible nod. Deynas spun, catching the blade of another crossbreed's sword as it swept down behind him. The rest had pulled their weapons and were moving in on him now. There was no mercy in their eyes. He started to back away and remembered Settek behind him. Apparently, the young crossbreed wasn't going to chance losing the flyer a second time.

Three of them charged him at once.

"Deynas!"

He turned toward Misa's voice. She'd come around behind and jumped at one the crossbreeds, a dagger in hand. It sunk deep into his side. The crossbreed roared in pain, drawing the attention of his companions away from Deynas for a second. The crossbreed spun, wrenching the dagger still buried in his side from her grip, and swung his sword around in a low, upward arc. Misa's shirt and the flesh beneath opened, her blood spraying out bright red in the path of the blade. Her eyes locked on Deynas as she flew back. Time froze there for several seconds the way it had when she fell from the flyer, then she hit the ground and was still.

Rage and shock raced through Deynas, red closing in around the edges of his vision. He lunged at the one who had struck Misa, bringing his staff around in a powerful swing that separated the crossbreed's head from his shoulders. The body stayed standing for a moment, as if confused as to its fate, then fell. Deynas was already turning. He jabbed the bladed end into the chest of another who stood staring dumbstruck at his decapitated companion.

When he turned to go for the next one, they were already fleeing, rushing for their flyers. He caught one with a deep slash across his back, cutting through his spine. The crossbreed fell onto the wing of his flyer, howling in agony as he slid to the ground. The remaining four were speeding away, Settek in the lead.

Deynas stared after them for a second, blood dripping from both ends of the staff. Then he remembered what had started the bloodshed and rushed to Misa. He dropped the staff and knelt beside her. Her chest had been laid open by the crossbreed's blade. Her clothes were drenched with blood. Her eyes stared empty at the grime-coated lights of Undercity hanging high above them.

What have I done? He shook his head. "No."

The word seemed to come from miles away. So quiet. He pulled her up, holding her against him. Her blood soaked through his shirt, wet and warm, the thick metallic scent filling his nose.

This couldn't happen. "No!"

The anguish was too great for words, too great for tears. He cried out a third time only it came out as a hoarse unintelligible wail. He curled over her, squeezing his eyes shut against agony that tore through him in excruciating waves, and rocked her body. The child Argus had died to save was now dead because of him. He had failed Misa. He had failed Argus.

There was no answer to this, no solution. Neither weapons nor words could change this. Tears came then, pouring forth in a flood. He knelt in the street, rocking her against him until the tears finally ran dry, leaving him raw and empty. Somewhere in there, the crossbreed whose spine he'd severed had fallen silent.

Someone placed a hand on his shoulder.

"Deynas."

Kaira?

"Deynas. You can't stay here." Her voice cracked.

He didn't move.

Someone's feet came into view at the edge of his vision. "Try again."

Naago?

The man who had turned him away. The deserter who traded him the red flyer that brought this despair. He laid Misa on the ground. Her blood weighed down his shirt. His hand closed on the staff and he surged up toward the voice, bringing the blade around with murderous intent. The blade stopped inches away from Naago's shoulder, caught in the hand of a cloaked figure who materialized out of nothing next to them.

For a second, Deynas could only stare, then he let go of the staff and sank to one knee. Kaira and the many strangers who had gathered near the scene also knelt. Some of them began to murmur the Keeper's chant.

His mind raced. Why was the Keeper there? He couldn't bear it if she meant to keep the *umahk-ra* of the crossbreeds he had slain. They deserved to be forgotten. Why would she keep them? What could be so rare or special about any of them?

She knelt in front of him and rested her right hand on Misa's pale cheek. There were strange black vines or roots twined over the hand, tapering down past her fingernails.

"I'm sorry." She kept her voice low enough he didn't think anyone else would be able to hear her. Were her words meant for him then or for the girl she touched? "Her *umahk-ra* is gone. I cannot keep her. I am sorry, Deynas-ra."

He felt as if someone had a fist around his heart and was squeezing. That voice was so familiar. Was this some cruel trick of his mind? Didn't he hurt enough already?

The Keeper stood then and took a step back. He tried to look up into her dark hood, casting aside the fear that it would bring death to do so. What did he care if death came for him now? But the black depths revealed nothing. Then she vanished, denying his searching gaze.

Naago picked up the staff and stood, retracting the ends. He flicked the safety and held it out to Deynas.

Deynas ignored the offered weapon, staring down at Misa. Why would the Keeper even consider keeping the spirit of an Endless girl? Why had she known his name? Why had she sounded so much like Argus?

His gut twisted and the world spun around him, bringing a wave of nausea.

Kaira spoke, her shaking voice grounding him. "You have to get him out of here, Naago. The enforcers are slow to respond in the Undercity, but they will come. Those three are from wealthy families in New City. Their deaths will not be taken lightly."

"Go back to the hotel. I'll take care of this." Naago continued to hold the staff handle out to him. "Come. I can get you out of the city. Help me strap her onto your flyer."

Deynas took the staff handle, secured it at his belt and lifted Misa, following the deserter's directions.

CHAPTER THIRTEEN

Naago took them out through one of the illegal portals and they sped away from the city as fast as the lesser of the two flyers would go. The Keeper remained unseen, leaning back against him while he drove. She didn't want Deynas to see her, though she couldn't stop watching him. The dead girl had been someone important to the Endless woman whose body she wore and so was he. The woman's mind and spirit were more restless than ever since they found him and the girl in the street, to the point that her distress was becoming indistinguishable from the Keeper's own emotions.

She should have gone back to the Halls of the Blooded instead of leaving the city. The *umahk-ra* of the Endless woman was far too strong. It was straining against the barriers that kept the woman and the Keeper apart. Although she tried to tell herself it was simple curiosity that made her go along, she knew it was the Endless woman's growing fondness for Naago and her deeper attachment to Deynas and the dead girl that drove her to stay with them.

In the light of the rising sun, she watched Deynas as he stared ahead, his face devoid of expression, his eyes behind the clear goggles brimming with guilt and hatred. Her chest ached when she closed her eyes and saw the tortured black and grey storm that was his *umahk-ra*. He was in so much pain. Pain she couldn't fix. Pain she shouldn't want to fix. She did though, or the Endless woman did, it was becoming hard to tell the difference.

"Why did he try to kill you?"

Naago slowed the flyer, dropping back a little, perhaps so Deynas wouldn't notice him talking to himself. "He needs someone to blame I imagine. And I did give him the flyer that led to that confrontation. Damn fool should never have taken it into the city."

"Did you warn him of that?"

She could feel his muscles tense against her back.

"Are you defending him now?"

"No. I was only asking a question."

"He was a fool to come looking for me. I told him I couldn't help him."

"Wouldn't, you mean." The flyer jerked. Was she making him angry? Odd how people got so irritated when the truth was placed in front of them. In that, the blood of The Undying didn't make the Endless any different from the rest of humanity. "What would you have done if you were him? He believes you can help him and he is right. The only one who disagrees is you because you have come to think so little of yourself."

The flyer jerked more violently this time and one wing dug into the sand, almost ripping the controls out of Naago's hands. He braked them hard enough that she slammed forward into the harness, its straps bruising her skin. Deynas noticed their absence after a few seconds. He slowed and turned in a wide arc to come back to them. In the short time it took him to reach them, Naago had already detached her harness and his own and was stalking away from the flyer.

She followed him, although she got the sense he didn't necessarily want her to. He turned on her suddenly and she stopped, stepping back from the fury in his eyes.

"What the hell do you know about me? You're not even fucking human! You're just some stinking parasite!"

Deynas pulled up and stared at Naago as if the man had gone mad. For the elder Endless man's sake, she showed herself and Deynas started. His gaze locked on her then and his stare grew intense, as if far more interested in trying to see through the cloak than in their argument.

"Perhaps it takes something other than a human to understand one," she replied, choosing to ignore his insult.

"Don't give me that shit. You don't know what you are. You're in no position to tell me who I am."

She stared at him. A menacing blackness rose within her, familiar because it was the Keeper's wrath, but unfamiliar in that she could not recall any other time when it had come up so strong. It rippled through the black roots like a bolt of lightning ready to be unleashed. Beneath that, she could feel the Endless woman's ire. She embraced the latter because she wasn't sure what that blackness might be capable of.

"You wanted me here and I came. I should be back in the Halls of the Blooded now. Not skimming across the desert with two Endless warriors and a dead girl." A vicious twisting in her chest reminded her that the dead girl mattered and wasn't to be spoken of so lightly.

Naago sneered. "Yes. I forgot. You have someone to kill."

She almost pulled her hood down so he could see the fury in her face, but not with Deynas there. Instead, she turned from him and started walking back toward the city. She could disappear and truly end the confrontation, but she still wasn't so eager to leave them even now.

Naago stood his ground, refusing to come after her though she could feel the driving desire to do so in tendrils of his spirit that reached after her. Deynas did follow her after a moment, moving the red flyer up a few feet in front of her and releasing his harness with quick, practiced hands. He hopped down, leaving the quiet craft hovering, and knelt before her, forcing her to stop or go around. She stopped, knowing that she should have gone around.

You needn't kneel before me. I am no god. She held back the words. It had apparently been a mistake to say that to Naago. Deynas might be no different.

"Keeper. Your presence honors us. I don't know why you're here and I know it isn't right to make requests of you, but I would ask you to continue with us." He bowed his head lower and his voice dropped to little more than a whisper. "Help me see Misa to her rest. Please."

So much fear in him. He was afraid to return to his tribe. Afraid to endure the sorrow of bringing the girl to them and afraid of what punishment he might face. More than anything, he was afraid to do it alone. The Keeper could feel his fear, could see it in his spirit if she closed her eyes, but it was the Endless woman who understood it.

"Deynas-ra."

He drew in a sharp breath when she spoke his name. The Endless woman's voice. He must recognize it. She started to reach out to him and caught herself, pulling her hand back to her side.

No. I cannot go with him. This would all end the moment she returned to the Halls of the Blooded. The uncertainty would be gone and all of the discovery would come to an end, dying with this incarnation. "I will accompany you for as long as I am able, but for now I think I would prefer to ride in the passenger stand on your craft."

He nodded and stood, going to the red flyer to bring up the second stand. Once he had it locked into place, he paused there and rested a hand on the blanket he'd taken out of his hatch to wrap the dead girl. Sorrow tore at his spirit, grief strong enough that she could feel it as a physical ache passing into her through the black roots upon her skin. Naago's anger and now something else, jealousy perhaps, loomed dark behind her. His focus on her thrust his emotions at her with such force that she was beginning to feel crushed between the two of them.

She placed her normal hand on Deynas's shoulder. The woman's spirit flared within her like a struck match and she jerked her hand back. "Let us move on."

Deynas nodded and returned to his place at the front of the flyer. She buckled in to the stand behind him. Naago, already up and buckled in on the other craft, throttled away. Deynas followed him.

They flew through the day and into the night, neither man willing to admit the need for rest. Eventually, the need for fuel forced them into a traveler's haven and they secured a group cabin with a locked shed for the red flyer so that Misa's body couldn't be disturbed. They were within a few hours of the village, but exhaustion and hunger demanded attention now.

They ate a small meal in brooding silence and both men sank into sleep, emotional trauma and fatigue chasing them to the solace of dreams. The Keeper couldn't join them. The restless presence of the Endless woman kept her awake. After pacing around the cabin for a time, she found herself sitting on the edge of Deynas's bed, watching him sleep. She drew back her hood and sat studying his face, trying to understand the feelings the Endless woman had for him. Even in sleep, worry lines etched his brow and his handsome features remained drawn with grief.

A glint of metal drew her eye to the chain that hung around his neck, mostly hidden by the collar of his shirt. Ever so gently, she took it between two fingers and drew it out. A teardrop shaped stone hung upon it, gleaming black and heavy in her palm. Great power resided in that small stone, she could feel it resonating with the black roots on her skin as if its nature were somehow similar. She closed her eyes, gazing upon the gleam of that black stone, like a silver beacon hovering protectively over the tormented *umahk-ra* of the man who wore it.

"Argus."

The Endless woman's spirit flared within her, brighter than it had when she touched him before, and the Keeper opened her eyes, looking down into his startled blue ones. So much hurt, hope, and longing in his voice, in his eyes. She stood, dropping the stone, and stepped back. He started to sit up, reaching out for her. She retreated into the unseen sanctuary of the cloak's power, becoming invisible to both of them.

•

Deynas sat and stared at the empty place where she had been. His heart was racing and his thoughts were in so much disarray that he couldn't grasp one long enough to make sense of it. Naago was also awake now, sitting cross-legged on the bed, watching him. How long had the other man been awake? Had he seen her disappear? Had he seen her sitting beside him while he slept?

"Where did she go?"

"Either she was called to keep a spirit, you frightened her into leaving, or she is still here, but wishes not to be seen by us."

Deynas closed his eyes, grimacing. His head hurt trying to understand what had just happened. The Keeper, a being who had walked the world longer than legend could recall, had been sitting there beside him. Only she wore the face of the woman he loved just as she had spoken with her voice earlier. The hair and eyes had been a strange color, deep black with an odd silver sheen, but it had been her face.

He shook his head, trying to clear the confusion. "Frightened her?" What could he have said to frighten such a being?

"The name you called her, that was someone you knew?"

"Argus-ra," Deynas murmured. His entire being ached now with the longing to see her. "She died helping others flee the city after the takeover, but I saw her face just now. The Keeper…" It had to have been a trick of the light or an image of her pulled from some dream he'd been having. Perhaps the fragment of her *umahk-ra* inside him made it seem so real. Or was he going crazy?

"How did she die?"

"When the demons took the city five years ago, we were doing a final search to try to find some people who were still unaccounted for among the living or dead. We found two of the children…" *Misa.*

His throat tightened. Naago dug a flask out of his pack, took a swig and held it out to Deynas. There was sympathy in his ageless eyes. Because of that, Deynas accepted the flask and took a long swallow of the burning liquid. He coughed. It was strong, not the diluted alcohol he was accustomed to in the village tavern. How could the man stand to drink it like that?

For a few seconds, he just stared at the flask then he took another almost painful gulp and wiped his mouth before handing it back. He moved himself against the wall, sitting cross-legged on the bed in a mirror image of the other man's position. He let his head fall back against the wall and closed his eyes, remembering.

"Argus was my mentor. She had almost five years on me and had been Endless since she turned eighteen. We almost had the children out of the city when we encountered the Blooded Women. They did something to Argus, or rather, to her *umahk-ra* when she was spirit walking. It left her mostly paralyzed. She ordered me to leave her. It was my responsibility to get the children out of there." He ground his teeth, fighting the heavy press of misery. "I'd lost my mother in an accident three years earlier. My father and brother were both killed when the demons first attacked the city. Argus was all I had and I left her there to die."

"You loved her?"

He opened his eyes and nodded.

Naago took a long drink from the flask, swallowing it as easily as if it were water. "And it's a fragment of her *umahk-ra* that plagues you now?"

"Yes. I know there are fragments of many others I saw die in the attacks in me, but those were fragments taken from departing spirits. They're different somehow. Argus was *umahk-ra-en-mahde*. I captured a fragment of her spirit while she was alive. I think maybe that's why she haunts me and why I keep thinking I see and hear her in the Keeper."

Naago snorted wryly and held the flask out to him again.

Deynas waved it away, but the other man didn't retract the offer.

"Take another drink. You're going to need it."

There was a convincing ominous edge to his tone. Deynas accepted it and took a swig. He held onto the flask while Naago started to speak. The alcohol was working through Deynas now, relaxing his body and mind, though it made the pain of Misa's death feel like a raw, bleeding wound inside him. This was what he'd come to learn though, so he was determined to focus on Naago's words and hold that sorrow at bay.

"When an *umahk-ra-uden* captures a fragment of someone's spirit at death, that fragment still retains the original image, but it becomes a part of the spirit thief's *umahk-ra* and makes their spirit stronger. In the uncommon case of a spirit thief encountering a spirit walker, the person the spirit fragment came from is still alive, as you said, so it retains a connection to them and therefore can't fully integrate into the *umahk-ra* of the spirit thief."

"But Argus is dead now. If what you're saying is true, why hasn't her spirit integrated like the others?"

The elder Endless gestured for the flask and Deynas passed it back to him. "That is where things get more interesting. I've been travelling with the Keeper some of late."

"How did that…" he trailed off when Naago shook his head.

"How we came to be traveling together isn't important. I still don't know what the Keeper is exactly, but she seems to be a roaming entity. I don't believe that she has a functional form that is her own so she uses that of another. As I understand from talking with her, the Blooded Women choose a body for the Keeper to inhabit, usually the body of an Endless woman."

A sick feeling started to spread through Deynas along with a desperate itch in the back his mind urging him to run away. He wasn't ready to hear this. When he started to stand, Naago also started to rise, holding a hand out to him to stay him. He hesitated, one foot down on the floor and his hands on the edge of the bed ready to push him up. His heart was racing again, an uncomfortable thrumming sensation in his chest.

"Wait. I know this isn't easy, but you should know the truth. This woman, Argus-ra, she didn't die after you left her in the city. She is the Keeper now, or rather, her body is hosting the Keeper. The woman you loved still lives within that body, but in a dormant state."

Deynas shook his head. The quiet of the night had become suffocating, as if someone wrapped thick blankets around him and was pulling them tight, making it hard to breathe. "No. Don't tell me I condemned her to be a prisoner in her own body. I can't have left her to that."

He stood suddenly and Naago jumped up, grabbing his arm. Deynas refused to look at the other man.

"You didn't condemn her. You did what you had to. You saved the children."

It felt like some beast had broken free inside him and was trying to tear its way out through his flesh. "One of whom is lying dead out there!"

Naago let go of him and stepped back, lowering his gaze.

Deynas threw open the cabin door and stormed out into the night.

•

The Keeper followed Deynas a few steps past the doorway, then stopped outside of the cabin and watched him go. She pulled her hood down and let Naago see her. Perhaps she deserved to be alone, alone as Deynas was, but it hurt too much to be alone with the misery of the Endless woman crashing through her. She didn't know how to process this kind of pain.

Naago stepped up beside her. "I thought you might still be here."

"You shouldn't have told him."

Naago took another drink from his flask. She could smell the biting stench of the alcohol.

"He deserved to know."

How strange it was not to know what to do. "Should I speak to him?"

"Not right now. Right now, he's too upset. He could quite easily turn that into wrath toward you."

The longing to help him that made her ache inside wasn't really hers. At least she didn't think it was. It hurt just the same. "He thinks I have taken her from him."

"Haven't you?"

She stared into the night. Deynas was no longer visible, not until she closed her eyes and saw his anguished spirit glowing through the darkness. Then she saw Naago's spirit as he moved around in front of her.

"You're crying again, Keeper."

He kissed the trail of her tears, first on one side and then the other. Then he kissed her lips. More tears slipped free when she kissed him back. He tasted of the alcohol, and of distraction and comfort.

The summons came a little after dawn, an insistent itch in the back of her mind. The Blooded Women were calling her. Their call wasn't something she had to respond to like the call to keep, but she knew the time had come to return to the Halls of the Blooded. There wasn't much point in delaying it.

Naago stood looking down at Deynas where he lay unconscious to the world. He had returned to the cabin just before dawn and collapsed upon one of the beds.

She touched Naago's arm. "Don't wake him yet."

The Endless man nodded after a moment and tried to meet her eyes. She looked away.

"There's apprehension in your voice."

"I am summoned back to the city." She hoped he would assume it was the call to keep. The truth would only bring another argument. "I have to go."

He touched her face, his fingers light upon her skin. "I don't want you to." It was clear in his voice, he already knew why she was going.

"It isn't about what either of us wants." She stepped back from him when he tried to kiss her. With Deynas lying there beside them, she simply couldn't kiss him.

There was a small flash of irritation in his eyes, but he didn't let it come through in his words. "How will I find you again? What do I have to kill this time?"

A whisper of that ominous dark wrath moved through the black roots and she narrowed her eyes at him. "If you do that again merely to bring me to you I will give you the death pain of every spirit I have ever kept."

He drew back from her, perhaps as startled by her vehemence as she was. "What would that do?"

"It would kill you."

"You would kill me for that?"

She hesitated, trying to make sense of the confusion of thoughts and emotions that came in response to his question. "The Keeper would," she answered finally.

He lowered his gaze, his expression very much that of a sulking boy.

Did he actually dare to think there was something between them that would supersede centuries dedicated to a single purpose? If so, he was a fool. Still, there was something between them, she would be the fool if she tried to deny that. Whether that something had anything to do with the Keeper herself or was simply a result of the Endless woman awakening within her body remained unclear.

"There is another way to call upon me."

He looked up, hopeful. "How?"

"You carry a fragment of her spirit in you. Want me as I am now, in this flesh, with your heart and with your spirit. If I am able to," *if she still lives when you call upon me,* "I will hear you and I will come to you."

"If you're able?"

She put a finger over his lips. He already knew what she meant, or at least suspected, but was unwilling to accept it. She stepped back and disappeared.

•

"Why was the Keeper travelling with you?"

Naago turned to look at Deynas. There was a forlorn look on his face, as of a man who had said goodbye to someone dear, someone he didn't expect to see and was even less prepared to lose again.

"Because she is as broken as you and I are?"

"In what way?"

Naago turned his back on him and started putting his pack together.

Deynas got up from the bed and grabbed his things. He felt like hell. The alcohol had left him with a fierce headache to go along with the rest of his misery. He had hoped, rather foolishly, that the Keeper would accompany them back to the village and that her presence might somehow lessen or maybe even deflect Master Kochan's rage. With what he knew now, he didn't think he could bear to be around her. He was glad she had gone, even though he dreaded the return to the village more than ever knowing that Argus still lived, in a sense, but beyond his reach.

Should he tell the others, or would it be better if they never knew? Would it just be another burden on top of Misa's death?

While he secured his pack in the hatch and folded away the second stand, he considered telling Naago to leave as well. Kochan made it clear that the former tribe master wasn't welcome. To bring him back there might add to the general upheaval Misa's death would cause and worsen the punishment. Still, even Naago's questionable company was better than entering the village with nothing but a dead body and a substantial weight of guilt and misery.

They struck out a few minutes later. The high cliffs of the village were visible on the horizon, diminished by distance to a hazy lump of red and brown. It didn't take long for the lump to grow and take shape, rising up before them like a great hammer of judgment. Deynas kept them low to the sand, hoping to avoid notice for as long as possible, but a patrol flyer started tailing them when they got within twenty minutes of the village. That the pilot stayed just above them and offered no greeting didn't bode well for their reception.

I will be exiled.

A pod of sand dolphins approached them, but when none of the flyers joined their play, they moved on. The patrol herded them through the village and along the road that would take them up the side of the cliff. People stopped to watch them pass, their eyes lingering long on the bundle tied to the back of the red flyer. One woman turned away and covered her face with her hands. A few people even changed direction when they saw the trio coming and started walking up the road themselves. They would have known who was missing from the village. It didn't take much of a mental reach to figure out what was in the bundle and word would spread fast.

Ren came out of one hut and Deynas slowed down to a crawl despite the sour look the patrol gave him. No matter how the patrol pilot felt about it, Ren had the right to know that his sister was gone. The youth gave the bundle a long, heartbroken look then he trotted over and jumped up on the wing. Deynas tipped the craft away to counter the sudden change in weight balance and held a hand out to him. Ren took it and he pulled the boy over to stand in front of him as he accelerated up the road again. The lanky body pressed against him began to tremble.

Deynas took one hand and turned the boy around. Ren buried his head against his chest and his body shook with heart wrenching sobs. Deynas held him tight with one arm and struggled to keep the flyer on course with the other.

About two thirds of the way up, the patrol flyer sped ahead, going to warn Kochan of their approach. Three flyers passed them a few seconds later, heading down to bring the rest of Misa's family up along with some of the temporal tribe leaders.

They pulled up at the edge of the landing pad and Ren helped Deynas undo the ties holding Misa's body. The boy cried quietly now, big tears streaming down his cheeks. He showed greater maturity than Deynas would have expected given his age.

Naago stood to one side, a silent party to their mourning.

Deynas lifted the wrapped bundle and walked it into the temple, trying to get inside before the other flyers came back up. Kochan knelt facing them before the feet of The Undying. His head was bowed and a long, low table was already laid out in front of him. Incense burned around the feet of the statue, the smoke weaving up along the great stone legs. The soothing aroma was lost on Deynas as he walked up and knelt to lay her body upon the table. He stayed there then, keeping his eyes on the edge of the table. Ren walked up to stand at his shoulder.

A woman burst into the temple behind them. "No!" Her wail broke the silence, but someone caught her before she reached the table and pulled her back. Her hysterical weeping filled the big chamber.

"Your selfish actions have cost this girl her life, Deynas-ra," Kochan said in a low voice, tight with accusation and sorrow. "You are banished from this tribe for now and forever."

The words were like a knife blade through his gut. His breathing grew ragged with the effort of not begging for forgiveness or crying out against his fate.

"At least let us stay to see her off."

"That doesn't seem too much to ask, Master Kochan." Ren's small voice sounded strong and certain.

"No" Kochan shook his head. "He is banished. He shall leave this place now."

Ren took a step closer and moved the blanket to uncover his sister's face. He touched her cheek and another tear fell, landing on her pallid skin. "Misa chose to go after Deynas-ra even after he told her not to. I believe it would be her wish to have him here."

Kochan looked up at the boy. There were tears in the Endless master's eyes and the tightness of anger in his face eased a little. "You are wise and gracious beyond your years, Ren. I will grant Deynas-ra leave to use his old hut for the night at your behest. We will find a place for his companion as well. They are to speak with no one and no one is to speak with them. At dawn, we will send Misa to her place beside The Undying then they will leave."

Deynas forced himself to nod and stand, backing away so her family could take his place by the table. He would not belittle himself by begging forgiveness. If he knew Kochan, it would do him no good anyway. Naago shadowed him from the temple.

•

The Keeper didn't go directly back to the Halls of the Blooded. Instead, she appeared in the center of their complex, in the temple that still housed a towering statue of The Undying. The temple was unharmed out of respect for the greater god, but its doors stayed always barred and locked. For her, that presented little obstacle and, this once, gave her someplace quiet to steel her nerves before she faced the Blooded Women, not that she had ever needed such a place in the past.

The three faces of The Undying looked down on her, neither benevolent nor judgmental. A part of her found comfort in that serene stone gaze, a part that needed purging. There was only one way to fix things. The Endless woman had to die and the Keeper had to move to a new host. The host's death would end all of this confusion and Deynas's suffering. Something within her didn't want to let go yet. It might just be the Endless woman's indomitable spirit, but it might be something else, something the Keeper had found recently that made her want to do more than simply exist for her one purpose.

As soon as she noticed that she had started pacing, she stopped in front of the towering statue. Without taking the time to wonder why, she turned toward it and knelt, bowing her head.

This woman does not wish to leave and I do not wish to let her go. Not yet. Is there no way to keep things as they are for just a little longer?

What was she really? Was she only a vessel for those spirits she kept or had she once had an identity that was hers outside of her purpose? Was there a spirit among those within her that was actually her own?

How can I not know these things?

The Keeper stayed there, knelt and waiting for many hours. When the gleam of sunlight peeking in from windows high above The Undying turned to darkness, she finally stirred. Her muscles were stiff and sore from wasting the daylight in that position and she was no wiser for it. She stood to the popping of joints and started when a door groaned open. She spun around.

The center doors into the temple opened and the Blooded Women entered in their gliding little steps. There were eighteen of them, set apart in groups of six as they always were. They moved to form a semicircle around her in front of the statue, maintaining distinct separation between the three groups.

The Keeper clasped her hands before her to hide their sudden shaking.

Eighteen voices spoke the words in her head. *The Keeper has become compromised. The host is corrupt. We shall destroy it and find another.*

She bowed her head to them, fighting to ignore the panic rising in the Endless woman. *I do not believe this host is corrupted. The host's spirit is strong, but the Keeper still controls it.*

That you argue this proves the host's influence upon you. The time has come for a new flesh to become.

The Keeper searched her mind for a way to dissuade them, but she knew shockingly little of the Blooded Women and the terror coming from the Endless woman made it hard to think clearly.

The Blooded started to hum and opened their eyes, bathing her in ghastly pink light. Her body arched back, going into spasms of agony, every muscle rent with searing pain. It swept through her in waves and the flesh fast began to weaken. She sank to one knee. The Endless woman was screaming in her head and she longed to help her.

This was different from the many deaths she had endured while keeping. This was her death in a sense and the suffering of it belonged completely to the body she wore.

Was it always this painful? Why didn't she remember this?

Waves of agony continued to burn through her, tearing not only at the flesh, but also at the *umahk-ra* within. The wails of the Endless woman were fading, losing strength. The end of this host was very close and she could feel the black roots upon the skin and woven through the muscles and organs quaking in anticipation of the parting that would come with the death of the flesh.

Then the call came, charged with need and longing. That was all the assistance she required. The Keeper struggled to her feet and the Endless woman smiled bitterly at the Blooded Women, then they disappeared.

Deynas stood at the edge of the cliff and stared out into the night. He'd spent the rest of the day alone in his room. Naago had done the same, keeping to the room they had provided him a few huts further down the row. Deynas appreciated the chance to be alone almost as much as he regretted having so much time to himself to think. When long hours of self-berating offered no solace, he found his mind starting to drift to other things. He thought back on better times. On long days spent training with Argus, learning to fly or fight or simply be quiet and listen to the world around him.

At dusk, the banished Endless master had emerged and taken a seat outside the hut with a violin in hand. He'd played until full dark, a series of lonely laments, a few of which made silent tears run down Deynas's cheeks as he lay on his bed for what would be the last time, staring at the ceiling of the hut that would become someone else's home after tomorrow.

When Naago stopped playing and retreated into his hut, Deynas slipped out into the dark, walking to the edge of the cliff behind the temple where he was less likely to be noticed. Argus came with him, her memory clinging tenaciously to his thoughts.

The sky was a deep blue black, stars blazing through the darkness. There was no moon tonight and it was warm, the heat of the day lingering in the air and rest-ing over him like a soft blanket. The temperature hadn't dropped the way it usually did. It felt just like the night Argus had tailed him on his first nocturnal chase.

He'd been so intent on impressing her with his skill. She was very sparing with her praise and that night he'd gone out with the specific goal of earning some from her. It had been a perfect chase. After the wind spirit departed with its delivery, she had moved her flyer up beside him and given him a proud smile that made him feel like the richest man alive.

"Tenderfoot, it you're not careful you'll be the best pi-lot in the tribe soon."

"Helps to have the best teacher," he countered with a playful wink.

Her smile faded and her eyes locked with his. She gazed at him as if seeing him for the first time, a look that made time seem to stop for several heartbeats. He wanted to kiss her, to taste her lips and tell her how much he adored her, how much he needed her, but the separation of the flyers made that impossible. She held his gaze for a long moment, then her smile came back, if a little more tentative this time.

"Come on. I believe I owe you a drink." She spun her flyer and dove down toward the village.

He watched her for a few seconds. Tonight he would tell her how he felt about her. The decision spurred him to action and he spun his craft, accelerating after her.

He hadn't told her though. That had been the night the first refugees arrived and they'd gone immediately into action to help rescue those still trapped in the demon-infested city.

He stared at the sky. Her face filled his vision, an im-age burned in his mind. Then the image changed, the eyes and hair darkened to a gleaming silver black. He ground his teeth, fighting to get back the image of her as she had been. His chest ached.

"I still need you, Argus, more now than ever."

He started when someone appeared a few feet to his left. A cloaked figure. The Keeper. She took a step toward him. He stepped back away from her. Then she sank to her knees. He stared, bewildered. She wavered there for a few seconds then fell toward the cliff. Deynas lunged for her, catching her in his arms no more than a foot shy of the edge. He pulled her away from the drop and would have let go of her then, but she hung limp in his arms. It wouldn't be right to leave her there unconscious.

Supporting her with one arm under her shoulders, he brought his other hand up and brushed back her hood.

Argus.

That beautiful face that brought him such pain was perfectly still, her eyes closed. A small track of blood ran from one corner of her mouth and more trickled slowly from under her eyelids like red tears.

What to do? He couldn't take her to Kochan or one of the village doctors. They would recognize the woman she had been. He lifted her and hurried back to his hut. There he laid her on the bed and checked her pulse. It was weak, but steady. Should he get Naago?

He stared at her for a long moment, gazing into the face of the woman he loved while hating the creature that had taken her from him. After several minutes, he went and got a damp cloth. Sitting on the edge of the stone bed, he wiped away the drying blood around her eyes then started to clean it away from her mouth.

Her eyes opened and he froze.

"You?" Her eyes widened. Her voice was feeble and unsteady. "It was you who called me?"

He dropped the cloth next to her and stood. "I didn't call you."

"No. You wouldn't have, but you would have called her and remembered her as you last saw her, as me."

She wasn't making sense. He backed up a step and lowered his eyes, unable to look into her face without pain and resentment boiling up inside. She started to sit up and got almost halfway before her trembling muscles gave and she sank back down. He offered no help. Her eyes closed, her breath whispering through her lips in a soft exhale.

"What happened to you?"

She lay there for a while, her breathing soft, and he wondered if she'd fallen asleep. Then she spoke, her eyes still closed. She sounded as if the effort to speak were almost too much for her. "Why didn't you ever tell her?"

"Tell who what?"

"Tell the woman, Argus, that you loved her."

"Because I…" He hesitated, fingers of apprehension racing along his spine as he played back her words in his mind. "How do you know I didn't?"

He waited for at least a minute, listening to the soft sound of her breathing.

She didn't answer.

He looked at her, finding it easier to do so when her silver-black eyes weren't open watching him. "Please tell me."

She coughed and grimaced. The hand without the strange black roots over it tightened to a fist around a clump of new bedding. A small glimmer of fresh blood showed at the corner of her mouth.

"Can I do something to help you?"

"No. I need rest." She was silent again for a time, until the hand and her face relaxed again. Then she gave him the answer he'd been waiting for. "I know you never told her because she was surprised when Naago asked if you loved her and you nodded."

The implications made his mouth go dry. "I thought Argus was gone. Naago said she was dormant."

"She should be."

Did that mean that his Argus was alive in there, trapped and aware of her fate? Did she hate him now? A glimmer of agonizing hope rose in his chest. Could he set her free?

His gaze moved to the staff grip lying on a table by the door.

"Would you do it?"

He started guiltily and glanced back at her.

She was watching him now, her strange colored eyes gleaming in the starlight coming through an open skylight. "If it meant you could have her back, would you kill me and destroy the many spirits I have kept in all my years?"

His palm itched, his fingers closing part way as if he already held the staff in his hand. "Would it bring her back?"

She rolled onto her side, watching him intently now. A smear of blood remained by her mouth. "Answer my question and I will answer yours."

No matter how much he might want to bring Argus back, he knew the right answer. The Keeper had lived as long as time itself. She had kept spirits beyond count. He couldn't kill such a being without understanding what he was destroying, without knowing what purpose those spirits still had to serve. Besides, even if he could make an informed decision on the matter, he didn't think he could raise a weapon against her so long as she looked like Argus.

His shoulders sank and his hand opened. The truth defeated him. "No. I wouldn't kill you."

She closed her eyes and the barest trace of a sad smile curved her lips. "The Keeper cannot die and cannot be parted from this host unless it dies. I am sorry."

He sank to the floor and leaned back against the hard stone wall. It only took a few seconds for her breathing to even out in slumber. He couldn't bring himself to disturb her again. Whatever had happened to her that day, she needed to rest now and he needed to think.

•

A hand on his shoulder woke him. Deynas started to turn his head to see who it was and his neck seized in a sharp spasm. He'd fallen asleep leaning against the wall and his body intended to make him pay for it.

"How'd she get here?" Naago murmured, trying not to disturb the figure still sleeping soundly on the bed, the serenity of her expression broken by that last trace of blood by her mouth.

Deynas rubbed at the tight muscles in his neck. "She appeared last night. She said I called her."

"Ah. I'm not surprised."

"I'm glad it makes sense to one of us."

"You have a fragment of Argus's *umahk-ra* in you. If you were thinking about her, as she had been and as she appears now, wanting her and missing her as deeply as I imagine you were, it would have created a connection between you and the Keeper." Naago took a step toward the sleeping figure and Deynas grabbed his arm.

"Don't wake her. She collapsed when she appeared. She was hurt somehow."

Naago eased back away from her. "Will she be all right?"

"I think so. She said she just needed rest. We talked for a short time."

Naago looked down at him now, the shadows of the room hiding his expression. "Are you all right?" His tone made it clear that he didn't mean physically.

Deynas laid his head back against the wall and rubbed his temples. "No, I don't believe I am, but there isn't much I can do about it."

"Come on then. We'll let her rest and see the girl's body off."

Deynas glared daggers at the hand Naago offered him. "Misa. Her name was Misa."

"I meant no insult."

Of course he didn't. Deynas was just being sensitive. Could the man expect anything else? He'd spent the night with a creature wearing the body of the woman he loved in a room that he would never sleep in again and now he had to bear witness to the death rite for a girl he'd mentored and, if he were honest, loved as one loved a little sister. He was anything but all right.

He took Naago's hand and let the other man help him up. There was little point in changing and no privacy in which to do so. He would worry about clean clothes later, when he had time to dig through his things and decide what to take with him. The flyer would only hold so much. He also had to figure out where he would go now. After killing the three crossbreeds, the only way he would dare return to the city would be under the protection of a warlord like Kato, and that kind of protection would have a high price.

They stepped out into the pale light of dawn. Many people gathered in front the temple to accompany the accepted bearers to the Table of Returning. Deynas and Naago joined them, waiting for the tribe's master to emerge from the temple. No one spoke in the stillness of morning, the silence so complete that every shifting of a foot on the gritty earth was like a shout. By the time the sun was a third of the way up, the crowd had grown half again as large as when they first came out.

When the sun finally broke free of the horizon, Kochan emerged in the long sand-colored robes appropriate to the master in the rite of sending. The gathered people, ascended Endless and temporal alike, sank to their knees as one and bowed their heads.

"We come together for the passing of Misa of the Endless of Valbra." Kochan's voice was strong and serene. "Today we must bear her body to the Table of Returning so that her *umahk-ra* may be freed to return to the service of The Undying. Who among you will bear this burden?"

Deynas stood. "I offer myself as a bearer as one who loved her in life and as one who bears responsibility for her death."

Kochan pursed his lips and nodded one by one to others who had stood, family and friends of the family mostly, giving them each a chance to speak for their right to bear. Before he was through, Naago also stood. Kochan's expression darkened even more, but he nodded to give the man his say.

Naago spoke with the same strength and serenity as Kochan, his past as a tribe master showing through. "I offer myself as a bearer as one who also bears responsibility for her death."

Kochan scanned those who had offered, his composure fracturing with the hint of a frown when his eyes rested on Deynas and Naago. He opened his mouth to speak when the sound of approaching flyers interrupted the ritual of choosing.

One flyer was coming in fast toward the adjacent landing pad. The two patrol flyers in pursuit couldn't keep up with the sleek silver and black craft. It dove down and swung to a sharp halt at the edge of the landing area. Settek leapt off, tossing his long fiery mane and casting a defiant glare at the patrol flyers closing in. Then he strode up to the rear of the gathering.

Deynas put a hand on the staff grip at his belt and Naago's hand closed around his sword hilt.

Settek caught their movement, giving each a cool glance, then looked past them, meeting Kochan's eyes. "I am Settek. I offer myself as a bearer as one whose actions contributed to the girl's death."

"I do not know how you come to be involved in this, crossbreed," Kochan answered, a whisper of venom in his tone, "but only Endless can be bearers. You are not welcome in this rite."

Whatever Settek meant to say in response died on his lips when the Keeper appeared beside him in her cloak. Everyone standing sank to their knees again, including Kochan. Deynas and Naago were the last to go down. Deynas almost didn't, but that reaction would only inspire unwanted questions.

She placed the hand woven over with black roots on the crossbreed's bare shoulder. "This one has the blood of The Undying in his veins. His mother was ascended Endless. Perhaps it is right that all who played a part in this girl's death share the burden of bearing her body to the Table of Returning."

For several seconds, uncertain silence held them all. Finally, Kochan rose, keeping his head bowed. "There must be four bearers, Keeper. Those responsible for her death leave us with only three."

"I sense that you do not believe your own words," the Keeper returned. "Your spirit is heavy with its share of this burden."

"You wield truth like a blade, Keeper." Kochan's voice was tight as of a man on the verge of weeping. From where he knelt, Deynas could see Kochan's face and the tear that ran down his cheek. "Naago-ra, Deynas-ra, the crossbreed Settek and I will bear this burden."

A slight intake of breath passed through the gathering at his words and the Keeper disappeared again. Deynas glanced around for her as he, Naago, and Settek rose to follow Kochan into the temple. None of them spoke. It wasn't appropriate yet. Kochan directed them with gestures to different corners of the litter Misa now lay upon. Her body rested inside a clear casing on a bed of a white synthetic fabric that burned hot enough to cremate the body within. The casing was a fireproof material designed to allow visibility while protecting the observers from the intensity of the heat. Once they had burned the dead upon pyres of wood, but wood was too hard to come by in this part of the desert.

Misa's pale face was slack. Her hands lay crossed over her chest and Deynas couldn't help remembering the gaping wound hidden beneath the fabric. As they carried her out through the waiting crowd, he heard a few people comment on how peaceful she looked. He thought she looked empty.

They carried the litter up along a narrow path that led to a higher plateau upon which the stone Table of Returning waited. The rest of the gathering followed them, filing into rows and kneeling again while the bearers set her on the table. They stood in a row behind the table until all the attendees had settled. There were no words spoken aloud, but time was given in silence for those who had thoughts they wished to send Misa off with. The rite wasn't about comforting the living, but about freeing her *umahk-ra* from any connection to her flesh so that it might be free return to the service of The Undying. The living could remember her in their own ways when the rite was complete.

Kochan stepped forward after several minutes and lit the fabric through a small opening at the foot of the case. Bright flame began to consume the fabric and the body within. The four bearers knelt and bowed their heads.

At times Deynas could hear weeping from some of those gathered, or a soft cough, but they all respected the rite. No one spoke. For his part, tears ran down his cheeks at first, drying fast in the heat of the day. Then he simply waited, trying hard to only remember Misa in that time and not wonder about Argus or the Keeper, though both forced their way into his thoughts.

He wanted to hate the Keeper, but he couldn't hate Argus and, from what she said, Argus still existed within that body and was at least partly aware. Aware enough that she now knew he loved her. In a million years, he couldn't have dreamed up a more convoluted way for her to find that out. He itched to know more even while he dreaded what that knowledge might teach him. Did Argus have any control or was she simply a passenger in her body? Should he think of her as alive or was it better to try to go on as if she were dead?

The thoughts made his head hurt and his chest tighten. The only thing that made sense was to stay away from her. How could he though, when there were so many questions and so few answers?

Eventually, Kochan rose and everyone else rose with him, joints cracking with stiffness from kneeling so long on the hard ground. The case held mostly ashes now. The public portion of the rite was complete. The four of them took the sides of the litter and carried it back down to the temple. Those gathered stopped outside the temple doors and went their own ways while the bearers took Misa's remains back to a chamber deep within the temple where Kochan and other elders would tend to them.

Kochan turned to them once their shared burden had been set down upon a stone table in the candlelit room. "I have other rites to complete, but, after the events of this day, I think it important that I speak with all three of you before you leave. I ask that you remain here tonight as my guests. Settek, a room will be found for you within the temple if you will take it, but I must request that you remain apart from the tribe here in the temple."

Settek's gold eyes flashed with temper, but he nodded after a moment.

"Good." Kochan beckoned one of the elders over and asked him to show Settek to a room. As soon as they were gone, he continued. "Naago-ra and Deynas-ra, you will also remain apart from the tribe for now, though you may wander the grounds between the temple and your huts. A proper dinner will be served to you in one of the private rooms within the temple. We will speak upon the morrow. Go now."

Naago bowed and left. Deynas hesitated a moment, struggling not to show his surprise. Kochan ushered him out with no further guidance and shut the door behind him. They didn't speak, but rather left the temple and retreated to their appointed huts.

Deynas sorted through his belongings for a while, creating a pile of needed and not needed things, which eventually sprouted a third pile of things he could live without if he had to. Then he tried to sleep for a while, but he couldn't stop thinking about the Keeper lying on his bed. He would have given much to have Argus there, but she wasn't Argus, she just looked like her. Or was she?

Eventually, he left the hut and turned toward Naago's temporary residence, running into the man in the street halfway there.

Naago leaned close, keeping his voice low. "I take it she's not in your hut?"

Deynas shook his head.

"We should try to find her?"

Deynas glanced around to see if anyone was in earshot before speaking. "Do you think she's still here?"

"She could have gone back, but I doubt it. If she wanted to let Argus die, she wouldn't have answered your call."

Deynas stiffened. "Let Argus die?"

Naago rubbed his forehead as if it hurt and nodded. "She told me that the Keeper needed a new host because the *umahk-ra* and thoughts of the Endless woman were too active. The last time she left, I didn't expect to see her in that body again, but she apparently had second thoughts, and not a moment too soon judging from her condition when she appeared to you."

Deynas stared after a patrol flyer that had just swept overhead. Perhaps he could hate the Keeper. Then again, she hadn't gone through with it, not this time. Next time might be different.

"How can we look for someone who doesn't have to be seen if she doesn't want to?"

"Indulge me. Where would Argus be right now?"

Deynas didn't have to think about that for long. "Follow me."

The Keeper stood at the edge of the cliff within sight of the Table of Returning. The sun was already creeping down on the far horizon and, as weak as she still was, the gusts in the early evening wind were nearly enough to topple her. The fall would kill this flesh, though neither she nor the Endless woman cared much right then. Walking from the hut to the temple and then up here had sapped all of her energy. The rest of the mourners had gone back down some time ago. She stood and waited while the wind played through her hair. What she waited for she couldn't say. The call to keep perhaps, or for someone to come for her, someone who could help her rationalize her behavior.

An incessant summons from the Blooded nagged in the back of her mind. She didn't have to answer it, but they would find a way to get to her eventually. That she didn't doubt. Maybe it would be easier just to get it over with. And yet...

Individually, you and I are both remarkable beings, Endless. Together we make one complete fool.

There was an unsettling glimmer of amusement from the mind within the flesh. The separation between them had grown weaker still. Sharing of thought and personal memory remained diluted and unclear, like trying to communicate with someone underwater, but emotions were beginning to separate out and gain power much like the physical memories of flying and intimacy had. It was because of this place and the people, the one called Deynas especially.

The strongest emotion was the desire to continue living within this body. That had to be mostly the Endless woman, though it felt like the desire belonged to the Keeper and it stopped her from answering the persistent summons from the Blooded Women the same way it had compelled her to answer Deynas and flee her fate.

The Keeper stepped closer to the cliff, lining her toes up at the edge of the rock like a reckless child.

Why was there no childhood in her memory? Everything had a beginning.

Everything has an end too.

She looked down hundreds of feet to the desert below. One quick step and this would end. She would be born into another host by the Blooded Women and all of the emotions that tormented her in this flesh would disappear.

The one whose purpose it is to remember has forgotten herself.

Deynas and Naago came up the path then. She stepped back from the edge and watched them approach. They both glanced around, looking for her perhaps. They stopped at the stone table and Deynas stared down at it, his brows pinching together and a glisten of moisture showing in his eyes.

"She's not here," Naago muttered. He sounded disappointed. Then he took note of the other man's intense focus and lowered his gaze, waiting silently.

The Keeper walked up to the opposite side of the table. Her chest ached with the desire to comfort Deynas, a desire best ignored. When the two men started to turn away, her breath caught. She didn't want to be alone again, left here with no one but the Endless woman. Or was it the Endless woman who didn't want to be left alone?

She let them see her.

Naago exhaled, his shoulders sinking as he smiled in relief. Deynas glanced at her and away again. He looked, if anything, more distraught than before. Naago walked around the table and she turned slightly toward him, keeping her eyes on Deynas. When he got within a friendly distance, she shifted one foot away and he stopped there.

"I didn't expect to see you again, not like...this." Naago gestured at her body.

She forced her gaze away from Deynas. "The Endless woman wants to live."

"Argus."

The Keeper started at the forcefulness in Deynas's tone. He was glaring at her now.

"She has a name. Taking her body from her doesn't change that."

"I am aware of that, Deynas-ra." She saw him flinch at her sharp tone, but he didn't back down.

"Can't you show her enough respect to use it?"

"No." He didn't understand that to acknowledge the woman by name would give her that much more power. Somehow, it didn't seem wise to explain that to him. She met his blue eyes, holding his gaze until he finally turned away. It hurt him to look at her, she knew, and she didn't like hurting him, but he needed to remember that she would never be the woman he loved.

Someone else was coming up the path. The Keeper went unseen to all of them and watched as the newcomer summoned them down to dine in the temple. Naago glanced at where she'd been and scowled, then followed Deynas and the other man back down. The Keeper followed as well. Deynas excused himself to get something from his room and she waited in silence with Naago at the temple entrance. Deynas returned a few minutes later with a bottle of something that he carried into the temple.

Before they entered the private dining room, Naago asked for an extra plate. Anticipating or possibly just hoping that she would join them. They pushed through a warm wave of rich aromas into a small room with a low table surrounded by cushions. Settek was there and she felt a sudden rise in tension from the two Endless as they entered.

The crossbreed gave a slight nod of greeting, getting the equivalent in return from Naago. Deynas only narrowed his eyes and situated himself in the corner farthest from the crossbreed. Naago sat toward the center of the table. The man who'd led them there handed him the extra plate and bowed out, closing the door. Naago set the plate down next to him. Settek gave it a curious look, then the Keeper became seen and he started, his gold eyes widening.

She slid the plate down the table to put more space between herself and Naago before sitting. Then she looked up at the crossbreed. "Did you think the Keeper wouldn't need to eat?"

Settek shook himself and lowered his gaze. "I apologize for staring, Keeper, but I didn't expect you to be Endless."

"I am not Endless. I am the Keeper. Only this body is Endless."

Deynas made an offensive sound in his throat and she pursed her lips, trying not to let it bother her.

Settek dared another glance at her face, eyes burning with curiosity. "Why are you—?"

"It's a long story," Naago interrupted.

She gave Naago a chastising look. "Although rude, Naago-ra is right. That is not a tale for this evening."

Naago shrugged off her comment and began to serve her, which she knew wasn't going to improve Deynas's mood, but she didn't see a graceful way out of it. Deynas and Settek began to fill their plates as well, then Deynas filled their cups from the bottle he'd brought. Naago drew a flask out of one pocket and poured a sparing bit of the contents into his cup. When he started to put the lid back on, Deynas gave him a look and nodded towards his own cup. Naago complied, sharing some of the strong smelling alcohol, then capped the flask and set it on the table.

After washing his first bite down with a swig of the alcohol, Deynas glanced shrewdly at Settek. "How did you know we were Endless and where to find us?"

Settek took a long drink from his cup and smirked at it. Then he gave Naago a meaningful look and the elder Endless grudgingly opened his flask again and poured some into the crossbreed's cup. Settek took another drink and nodded approval before answering. "My sister, Kaira, came to me after you left the city."

Both Naago and Deynas stopped eating.

"She's your sister?" Deynas asked.

Settek nodded. "She told me that you were working for our father and convinced me to go speak with him about what happened."

The two men paled and Naago set his utensils down. "Your father being?"

"Warlord Kato," he stated as if it should have been obvious. "He told me that I should follow you and offer myself as a bearer for the girl."

"Misa," Deynas snapped.

"Yes." Settek continued, unruffled. For one who had been so hot-tempered before, he was remarkably composed now. "He said it would be the right thing to do and that it would honor my mother's memory."

"I assume your mother was banished from her tribe

for having relations with a demon." Naago remarked with more than a little bitterness.

Settek's composure faltered for a second, his lip lifting in a disgusted sneer that he quickly schooled away, though the darkening of his mane betrayed his ongoing displeasure. "Yes, but she was always Endless in her heart, even if her people refused to understand her."

"How the hell did Kato know where to find us," Deynas demanded, giving Naago a sharp look.

Naago glared back. "I didn't tell him."

Settek's mane flickered, shading from a dark maroon to a bright orange-red as he chuckled at them. "Father doesn't need to be told. He knows everything."

"That must make your life interesting," the Keeper remarked.

"You have no idea. I can't get away with anything." Settek grinned at her then as if she had, in that moment, become just another companion.

It was nice. She made herself smile back, ignoring the sour looks from Naago and Deynas who appeared to disapprove of her chatting with the crossbreed.

Settek's expression turned serious then and he inclined his head to her. "Thank you, Keeper, for defending my right to bear this morning."

More meddling she shouldn't have done. "Your intentions were good and your claim legitimate. I simply validated that for those who would not see it."

"Had she not defended you," Deynas remarked, "you might have been killed."

"And would I have deserved any less?" Settek's composure faltered, a pained look twisting his features for a moment and the Keeper felt a twinge of sympathy for him. Whatever his father's intentions, the youth truly regretted the outcome of his actions. "My father tried to warn me many times that my arrogance and hot temper would have a terrible price, but I was too arrogant to hear him."

Naago snorted. "You tried to stab me in the back. Pardon me if I'm underwhelmed by your show of regret."

Settek's features closed up, the candid emotion retreating. "I lost my temper, though I'm still not convinced it was a bad idea."

Deynas muffled a chuckle with a mouthful of food, though he didn't quite manage to hold back a grin.

The only sign that Naago noticed was a slight narrowing of his eyes. "How many did your temper kill before me?"

"None. I never lost before you and I never went into a duel with any intention of killing my opponent."

"Empty threats," Naago muttered before taking a long drink from his cup.

The Keeper followed his lead and took a drink, finding that the light alcohol Deynas brought wasn't so unpleasant after all.

Settek's gaze moved between the two men. "I don't feel so bad about being bested now, knowing I faced Endless."

"You should learn to accept defeat more graciously," Deynas snapped.

Those brilliant gold eyes dimmed and Settek looked stared at his plate. "Father said the same."

The Keeper searched her mind for another way to lift the mood, but Naago was there ahead of her.

"You have considerable combat skill, crossbreed. With some discipline and real training, you would do well."

The comment triggered a long discussion about sword technique between Naago and Settek. Deynas ate in morose silence and refilled his glass several times, refusing to contribute to the discussion. The Keeper watched them and listened. When Deynas stood and excused himself, she followed. The other two fell silent, watching them leave, but neither said a word to stop them or tried to follow.

There were many people out still and the sound of music rose up from the lower part of the village. Misa's death was a tragedy, but the release of her spirit was something to celebrate and they did a fine job of it. The Keeper followed Deynas up the path to the Table of Returning, remaining unseen to all except him. A few of those out nodded to him, but none gave him any more attention than that. When he reached the top, he walked to the edge, standing in almost exactly the same spot she'd been standing earlier. She walked up beside him. The few others up on the plateau moved to the opposite edge or started down the path after she gave their spirits a nudge of encouragement to do so.

"I don't want you here," he stated.

"But you do want her."

The muscles in his jaw jumped as he clenched his teeth. He swallowed hard. "I can't have her."

She stared out into the night. The stars seemed impossibly far away and cold. "I'm sorry."

He turned toward her and she faced him in turn, moving in perfect synchronicity as if she'd predicted him.

A light breeze played through his long black hair. His blue eyes narrowed. "Are you? Are you truly sorry?"

Her throat tightened when she looked into his eyes and saw the pain within him. It wasn't only the Endless woman's feelings for him that made her eyes sting and her chest ache and she didn't know how to react to that. Was the Keeper supposed to feel like this?

"Yes. I am sorry. I don't want to hurt you, Deynas."

He searched her face for a several seconds, the distress behind his eyes magnifying the pain in her chest. "Is that the Keeper saying that or is it Argus's influence?"

"Both."

Unthinking, she brought her hand up to his face. He jerked back and her hand hung awkward in the air between them. Then the summons from the Blooded went silent and a chill swept through her. She put up her hood and turned.

"Something's wrong." She closed her eyes.

There was a bright flash as the spirit of the demon appeared and she snapped her eyes open. The demon materialized on the plateau, a massive black beast with legs twice the size of a man. It sent two men and woman standing together near the far edge over the cliff with a sweep of one great paw. Their screams faded quickly. Then it turned to her and Deynas. It spread its leathery wings and opened the four-pronged outer mandibles of its jaws, shrieking an earsplitting challenge.

Behind the demon, two Endless were already charging up the path with weapons drawn. The beast twitched back its pointed ears and lashed out with two of its many barbed tails. The barbs found their marks and the two men dropped like stones.

The Keeper almost stepped back, but Deynas caught her arm, reminding her that back wasn't an option. He shoved her forward, over toward the stone table and drew his staff. The demon tracked her movement with its blazing eyes. It wanted her. The Blooded Women had sent it to kill the host and force the Keeper back to them.

"Run!"

She heard Deynas shout and saw more Endless trying to come up the path, Naago among them, but the lashing tails kept them back. She stood her ground. The beast snarled and lunged at her, but before it reached her, something else slammed into her from the side, throwing her to the ground. The beast hit the stone table with enough force to break it in two and send one of the halves flying over the cliff.

Deynas jumped up off her and stood over her, facing the demon as it spun back around.

"Get away," she warned. "It wants me. Let it have me and it will leave."

"I can't do that." Deynas lowered his stance, readying his weapon.

The demon lunged. The staff blade sank into its chest, but didn't slow it. It slammed into Deynas, throwing him to the ground and landing on top of him beside her. The beast drew its head back, opening dripping mandibles wide in preparation for a strike that would finish its opponent.

Death is not mine to deal.

The Keeper looked at Deynas lying trapped beneath the beast. Could she watch him die?

Reaching out, she grabbed the demons leg with her right hand and passed the pain of hundreds of deaths into the beast all at once. It threw its head up, emitting an earsplitting howl that filled the air with crushing sound pressure, then it shuddered and collapsed, blood running from its nose and ears.

The Keeper got unsteadily to her feet while Naago and two other warriors pulled Deynas out from under the beast. His left shoulder was dislocated. Between the three of them, they managed to hold him down and shift it back into place. He made a dreadful choking sound, but didn't cry out. She winced in sympathy and pulled up her hood that had fallen back when he knocked her out of the demon's path.

Several Endless had gathered around the two dead men on the path and someone barked out an order for flyers to go down and find the remains of those thrown off the cliff.

The call to keep came then and she let herself be seen by all of them. Most of them knelt and began speaking the Keeper's chant.

Naago came to stand beside her, staring at the dead demon.

"How did you do that?"

"I gave it the pain of too many deaths all at once." She started to reach her right hand out to the fallen demon and he grabbed her other arm, pulling her back.

"What are you doing?"

"This creature was the last of its kind. It must be kept."

Deynas, up on one knee and holding his arm, his face twisted in a pained grimace, was watching them now.

Naago shook his head, keeping his voice low. "You can't. If you receive the spirit, you take in the pain of its death, correct?"

She nodded.

"So you get back all the death pain you used to kill it?"

"Yes."

He held fast to her arm. "Wouldn't that kill you?"

"It might kill this host."

"Then you couldn't punish those responsible," he answered, apparently hoping to talk her out of doing what she had to do.

"This creature chose to ally itself to the Blooded Women. I killed it in self-defense, for it would have killed this flesh had I not. There is no one to punish. Still, it must be kept."

"No."

She looked at the hand still holding her arm then met his eyes. "I cannot deny the call to keep. If you won't let go willingly, I have the power to make you."

He held on. The call was insistent. She passed a flash of intense pain into Naago and he jerked his hand away as if burned. Argus trembled within her, afraid of what it would mean to take back all that pain, but the Endless woman didn't try to stop her, perhaps understanding that there was no choice. She stepped close to the demon and set her right hand upon the soft fur that covered its thick hide. Its spirit rose up instantly, blazing with crimson light, fierce even in death.

She closed her eyes and bowed her head. *Come to me and you shall be remembered.*

The demon's spirit consented and a storm of pain and emotion poured into her. So much pain from so many deaths burning through her mind, spirit, and flesh until she couldn't see or feel or hear anything else. She cried out, the Endless woman's voice screaming into the night while their shared body convulsed with agony. The pain and everything else ended in blackness.

CHAPTER SEVENTEEN

Deynas struggled to his feet, a deep pain flaring in his injured shoulder and along several bruised ribs. Kochan had arrived on the plateau and took immediate charge, directing a group to take the dead to the temple and ordering the few others to return to their huts for now. Naago, meanwhile, knelt alongside the Keeper and pressed his fingers into her neck, searching for a pulse.

Kochan walked up behind him and glanced down at the still figure, then sucked in a sharp breath. "Argus-ra."

Deynas stepped up next to the startled master. "Is she alive?"

"I don't think so."

Naago's voice was tight, choked with emotion and Deynas wondered, not for the first time, how intimate the man's relationship with the Keeper was. The way they'd argued the day they all fled the city he might have suspected they were lovers if she were only an Endless woman, but one didn't fornicate with such a being as the Keeper, did they?

Naago adjusted his fingers against her neck and checked again.

Deynas held his breath, as if breathing would chase away any delicate hold she might still have on life. It would be so much better if she were dead. This madness would end for all of them and Argus would be free of her prison in the only way she could be free now. If it was better though, why did it hurt so much to face that possibility?

"Wait. It's faint, but she's still alive."

Deynas let his breath out in a soft exhale, trying to reconcile a sting of disappointment with his substantial relief.

Kochan gave him a stern look and extended one finger to point at the Keeper. "I get the feeling you already knew about this."

Deynas nodded. There was no point denying it now.

"You will explain this, but bring her to the temple first and, in the name of The Undying, make sure you cover her face. We don't need more commotion."

Naago lifted her and Deynas pulled the hood of her cloak back up, positioning it so that her face once again vanished in shadow.

Settek trotted up to the plateau then and Kochan gave him a harsh scowl. "I believe I told you to stay in the temple."

A wave of bronze rippled through the crossbreed's expressive mane. Now that Deynas thought about it, it wasn't so hard to believe that he was Kato's son. They were both magnificent, although Settek's changing color in his mane appeared to be something he had little control over.

Settek ignored the master and turned to Deynas. "You look in pain. Do you need help walking?"

The offer surprised Deynas and irritated him a little. He wanted to keep hating Settek the way he couldn't manage to hate the Keeper. Why did everyone keep trying to undermine his rage? He took a few steps and shook his head. "No, but I wouldn't mind if you got my staff."

Settek walked over to the demon and pulled on the staff. It took him three tries to wrench it free of the beast's chest. He gave Deynas an appreciative look. "Impressive strike."

"Not impressive enough," Deynas muttered.

Kochan finally left off scowling at the crossbreed and turned toward the temple. "Bring her."

They took the Keeper to the private quarters in the lower part of the temple and laid her on a bed in the room next to the one the elders had assigned to Settek. Most of the rooms served as housing for the injured or sick and their caretakers when their condition was too dire for their families to manage their care at home. A few rooms were kept ready for the use of elders during long nights of ritual like this one when there were dead to tend to. With the Table of Returning destroyed, they would have more work than usual preparing for the sending of those who had died that night.

Deynas found himself standing between Naago and Settek watching through a blur of physical and emotional exhaustion and pain while Kochan checked the Keeper's vital signs. Throughout the process, the master paused many times, often becoming lost for a few seconds in the familiarity of her face.

"What happened to her up there?" He asked after shaking himself out of one of those moments.

Naago spoke before Deynas could gather his thoughts, explaining that the Keeper absorbed the pain of every kept creature's death when she absorbed their spirit. She had passed the pain of many of those deaths into the demon, enough pain to kill it. Unfortunately, because she had to keep the demon, she had no choice but to take back all of that pain the same way she had dealt it.

Deynas stared into the face of the woman he had loved, trying hard to remember that she was no longer that woman. She was something else. And yet...

Enough pain to kill a greater demon plus the pain of that demon's death. That she lived at all was impressive and she had done it to stop the demon from killing him. He had tried to protect her, something he probably shouldn't have done in the first place, and ended up the one who needed saving. Why had she bothered? Why not let the demon kill him?

She had no injuries he could treat so Kochan ushered them out into an adjacent room where they could keep an eye on her while they sat and talked. The master positioned himself in the chair with the best view of the unconscious Keeper.

"The only thing we can do for her is let her rest. While she is doing that, perhaps one of you would care to explain why the Keeper looks like our Argus-ra."

Deynas sipped at a brew one of the elders had brought down for him to ease his pain then nodded to Naago. "You know better than I." Besides, he was too tired, sore and unsettled to try to explain what little he did know and he was likely to learn more about their relationship by listening to Naago talk about her.

"I still don't know exactly what the Keeper is," Naago began, leaning forward in his seat to rest his elbows on his knees. The position allowed him to see the still figure in the next room, which Deynas suspected was no accident. "From talking to her, I know the Keeper, whatever she or it is, requires a host. She told me that the Blooded Women choose that host and somehow move the Keeper into it. She said they tend to take Endless because of their longevity and resistance to spirit corruption. In this case, they used your Endless warrior, Argus-ra, when she was captured in the city during the takeover."

"But why did she come here? Does it have something to do with that demon?"

Naago glanced from Kochan to Deynas then his gaze shifted to Settek and stalled there.

The half-demon moved to the edge of his seat. "Do you wish me to leave?"

Naago nodded. "Perhaps that would be best."

The crossbreeds jaw tightened and his mane darkened again, but he stood. "I'll be upstairs."

"Thank you." Deynas uttered the words without thinking and cringed inwardly at the icy look Kochan gave him. The master may have allowed Settek to be a bearer at the Keeper's behest, but he hadn't forgotten that he was half-demon.

Settek glanced down at Deynas, the fire in his gold eyes cooling. He bobbed his head once in a slight nod and left them. Deynas turned back to Naago, pretending not to notice Kochan's displeasure.

"I have a theory," Naago said when Settek was gone and he had their attention again. "From what I understand, usually the host is dormant and the Keeper is in full control. In this case, Argus hasn't been overly cooperative. I suspect that, at least initially, this might have been because the fragment of her *umahk-ra* that exists in Deynas kept her connected to the world outside of her body. The Keeper allowed Argus's *umahk-ra* to move outside her flesh when I was with her many nights ago, so now a fragment exists in me as well. Perhaps being around the two of us and the fragments that anchor her to the world outside her body has allowed Argus to gain strength. The Keeper is aware of what's happening. She said she should let the Blooded Women find her a new host, but I think Argus is making it difficult for her."

Deynas took a deep breath and winced at the pain in his ribs. They both watched him with varying degrees of concern. He took another drink of the bitter painkilling brew before speaking, giving the flare of pain time to abate.

"Up on the plateau she told me the demon was after her. That it would leave if we let it have her. Do you think the Blooded Women could have sent it?"

Naago chewed his lip for a minute and Deynas drank more while he watched the man think things through.

Finally, the pale eyes lit. "You said she was hurt when she arrived here last night?"

Deynas nodded.

Kochan's expression soured as they revealed more of what they'd kept from him. Having been banished once already, Deynas found it hard generate much concern over the master's irritation. What was he going to do, double banish him?

Naago's focus was entirely on Deynas now. "When she left us in the desert, she intended to go back to the Blooded Women and let them move her to a new host. Maybe they tried to, but she, or Argus, changed her mind so she fled from them when you provided her an escape route."

A flicker of alarm danced through his nerves. "If that's true, then the Blooded Women may be trying to get her back. We've already lost five people. We need to move her away from the village before they come up with something worse than that last demon."

Kochan held up a hand to catch their attention. "You can't move her yet. As weak as she is, it would probably kill her. You need to let her rest until morning if she lives that long. If not, and if I understand the two of you correctly, then it won't matter anymore. Argus will be truly dead and the Keeper will be gone."

Silence hung heavily on them for a moment and they avoided each other's eyes. Deynas suspected they all had the same thought. Kill her and the threat would go away. In her current state, it wouldn't take much.

No one said it aloud.

Naago leaned back in his chair after a minute, his gaze narrowing in on Kochan. "You studied many of the tomes in the Endless archives. Do you remember coming across the title *Umahk-ra-sehndo?*"

"No. It doesn't sound familiar."

"The Keeper was with me when the wind spirit you sent delivered its message. It called her by that title."

Deynas also sat back, the brew relaxing his muscles while his thoughts danced around wildly in his head. They had been traveling together before Naago came to the village the first time. The thought sent a spear of jealousy through him. He shoved it aside. *She isn't Argus.* "It named her in the Voice of The Undying."

Naago nodded significantly.

"That is very curious." Kochan rubbed his chin, heavy layers of braids waving with the motion of his head. "If we had access to the archives, there are several tomes I can think of that might provide more insight, but we can't get to them."

Naago drew the ever-present flask out of his pocket and took a long draw then handed it to Kochan who accepted it readily enough.

Deynas raised his brows inquisitively. "Don't you ever run out of that stuff?"

"Not if I can help it." Naago took the flask back from Kochan and passed it to him.

"I don't know that you should mix something that strong with the painkillers," Kochan warned.

Deynas shrugged and took a swig then passed it back.

Naago accepted it and took another drink before resting it on his thigh. "Why can't we get to the tomes?"

"Perhaps you've forgotten that the archives are in what they now call the Halls of the Blooded," Deynas remarked sourly.

"There has to be a way to get in there." Naago took another long drink then began to chew thoughtfully at his lip again.

"My father might know a way."

They all glanced up as Settek strode into the room.

He shrugged off their scowls. "Sorry to intrude. I needed something from my pack and happened to overhear."

Naago capped the flask and held it up, raising an eyebrow to Settek. The crossbreed nodded and held up a clawed hand, catching it easily when Naago tossed it over. He took a deep draw before tossing it back.

Deynas started to shake his head at the crossbreed, stopping quickly when the room began to spin. Perhaps adding the alcohol on top of the painkillers and the drinks he'd had with dinner hadn't been the best idea. He managed to focus on Settek with some difficulty. "You know your father is a demon, right?"

Settek grinned and sat down, apparently not *needing* anything from his pack as badly as he thought. "If you'd set your species prejudice aside and think about what else he is, you might understand why I say that. First, he's an Undercity warlord. He liked the status quo before the Endless were ousted. Second, he loved an Endless woman who died in the takeover. He might be more willing to help than you think."

"Not for free," Naago remarked caustically.

Settek lifted his broad shoulders in another shrug. "Nothing's free in the Undercity, but you two already knew that."

Naago glowered a warning at the crossbreed.

Deynas picked up the brew to finish it off. His coordination failed him and the contents spilled down the front of his shirt.

"Shit!" He snapped to his feet only to have his legs give out.

Kochan managed to catch him and help him upright, fighting a losing battle with a superior smirk as he did so. "I warned you not to mix it."

The room tipped and swayed like a flyer with faulty balancer sensors. Deynas leaned on the elder Endless.

"Naago, help me get this shirt off him. We'll put him on the other bed in there."

They pulled the wet shirt off him and supported him into the room where the Keeper lay. When they finally got him onto the other bed, he closed his eyes and lay there wishing the damned flyer would balance out so he could sleep.

•

It didn't feel like morning when he woke. The time candle on the table by the door still had a few hours of burn left. His battered body screamed in protest as he sat up and leaned back against the wall. The room no longer moved on its own, but his head ached and his stomach felt like someone had poured corrosive acid down his throat. His shirt was gone and he had a vague recollection of spilling something on it. He closed his eyes and rested his head back on the cool stone while he rolled the god's blood pendant between his thumb and forefinger.

"It protects you."

The soft voice caught him by surprise. He dropped the pendant and glanced at the other bed. The Keeper lay there on her side, watching him. Her eyes were glassy and bloodshot.

"Did you say something?"

"The pendant," she murmured. "It protects your *umahk-ra.*"

He lifted the stone. It looked so simple, but he had no reason to doubt her words. Had his mother known that? "I didn't know."

An amused smile flickered across her lips. "That's why I told you." Her lips pressed together into a tight line then and she squeezed her eyes shut. Tears spilled from the corners of her eyes.

Deynas got stiffly to his feet and walked over to her. He knelt and sat back on his heels, bringing his face to her eye level. "Is it pain?"

"Yes. Everything hurts." She opened her eyes and looked at him, her gaze lingering on the bruises over his shoulder and ribs. "I hope I look better than you."

He managed a teasing smile. "Sorry to disappoint, but with those bloodshot eyes, you look rather frightful."

Her eyes drifted closed again and she smiled wearily. "Be nice, tenderfoot."

Argus.

His breath caught in his throat and he clenched his teeth against a wave of longing and misery that left him feeling crushed inside.

I can't take this. Argus, why couldn't you have just died?

As soon as he thought it, guilt swept in, adding to the turmoil. He brought one hand up, stopping with his fingers a few inches from her cheek. He wanted so badly to touch her. No. Not her. He wanted to touch Argus and she wasn't Argus, not really. He had to remember that.

He heard someone moving in the other room and pulled his hand back, getting to his feet and moving away before Settek stepped into the doorway.

The demon's gold eyes swept over him. "You look like shit."

"Thanks. I feel about as good."

Settek nodded as if he expected as much. "How is she?"

"Alive. I think she'd benefit from a little more rest though." Deynas gestured with his chin toward the door.

The crossbreed took the hint, stepping back out of the room. Deynas followed him. Naago had never made it back to the hut he was using. He lay stretched on one of the couches fast asleep. The flask was lying open on its side on the floor, apparently empty.

"He finished it?"

Settek grinned, showing off his pointed teeth. "I helped some."

Deynas rubbed his aching head and sank into a chair.

Settek put his clawed hands on the back of another chair and stared down at them. His shoulders hunched, making him look like an overgrown child and, for the first time, Deynas wondered how old the crossbreed actually was. It could be hard to tell with demons and Endless were, well, Endless.

"I've wanted to talk to you."

Deynas put his feet up on another chair. "I'm not going anywhere."

"I told father about what happened with my red flyer."

Deynas gave him a cautionary look.

"Your red flyer," Settek amended amiably enough, though a flicker of bronze swept down his mane. "Father bought that flyer for me. He said I deserved to lose it and maybe he's right, but I can't let it go at that."

Deynas sneered. "You'd challenge me in this state. That's about as sporting as having your mongrels gang up on me."

Settek looked at him, his gold eyes blazing bright. "Endless arrogance," he snarled. "Perhaps you would listen rather than cast insults upon the dead and assume you know my mind."

Fury swept through Deynas and his hands tightened on the arms of the chair. Pain flared in the injured shoulder, forcing him to relax his grip on that side. It made his temper flare hotter, but Settek didn't give him time to give voice to the rising outburst.

"I never meant for your Misa to come to harm. I lost my head at the thought of being defeated again. My own reckless arrogance, I suppose. I came here to make what amends I could for that, but nothing can undo what is already done. As for the flyer, I wish to offer you a suitable trade. The flyer I came here on was commissioned by my father for one of his favored guards, only that guard was killed. The one whose position you filled briefly, in fact."

That didn't help assuage his anger. "And your father gave it to you so you could get yours back?"

"No. He is making me pay for it. He said I would learn nothing if it came free. I'll be paying for it for a very long time and perhaps that is how it should be." A trace of frustration and something else, something that sounded suspiciously like regret, edged into the crossbreed's tone. "Mechanically, it's a superior craft to the one you have, but…"

Deynas held up a hand and Settek trailed off. The crossbreed's manner and the fact that Kato was making him take responsibility for his own mistakes had begun to cool his anger. "But the red flyer is more complimentary to your good looks," he remarked with only a hint of sarcasm.

"Well, yes." Settek flexed his hands on the chair back and one claw sank through the upholstery. He jerked his hands away. "Shit!"

Despite himself, Deynas laughed, then groaned and grabbed his side as pain shot through the bruised ribs. Naago rolled over, turning his back to them, and began snoring.

Settek just stared at Deynas, holding his hands in the air above the seat back as if unsure what to do with them now. "I apologize. I didn't mean to—"

Deynas waved him to silence. "Don't worry about it. I'll take a look at this flyer you brought later and see if I think it's a good trade. Right now, I'd like to know what else you three discussed last night."

Settek stepped around the chair and finally sat. "The Endless master went up to tend to the dead after you succumbed to your drug cocktail. Naago agreed to talk to my father about the archives. He said he had to start somewhere." Settek glanced over at the sleeping Endless man and lowered his voice. "I think he's jealous."

"Jealous?"

Settek nodded. "Of your relationship with the Endless woman."

Deynas gritted his teeth, his brief better mood guttering out like a windblown flame. "She's the Keeper, not an Endless woman. Not Argus."

"I think the two are not as separate as you're trying to make them."

Deynas stared through into the other room at the sleeping figure. She was still beautiful. He was already getting used to the odd color of her hair and eyes, though the strange root-like black tendril at her temple forced him to remember what she was. She wasn't Argus, but she had called him tenderfoot the way Argus always had to tease him in training. Regardless, if he couldn't keep the two separate in his mind, it would only bring more pain.

"Why are you really here, Settek?"

The crossbreed's fiery gaze turned cold. "I am part demon, so deceit must motivate my every action? You Endless are so wrapped up in yourselves you couldn't recognize a good intention if it hit you in the head."

"So I'm supposed to believe that your primary reason for coming here was to atone?"

"You will believe what you want to believe, as my father is fond of saying. Many things led to the girl's death, my arrogance and temper among them. For my part, I regret that she died and that some of my companions died in your rather potent backlash."

He kept forgetting that Settek had lost three friends in the confrontation. It was easy to overlook that with everything else, easy for him at least. Probably not so easy for the crossbreed. "Maybe your intentions are good. Maybe not. What about your father though? Kato sent you here. I'm willing to accept that he wanted his son to learn a valuable lesson, but I can't believe he doesn't have some other purpose beneath that."

Settek glanced at Naago who still appeared to be soundly asleep, snoring on occasion. "For what it is worth, he loved my mother a great deal and I believe that he wanted me to take responsibility for my part in what happened and also have a chance to connect with the Endless side of my lineage. However, I did get the feeling he is more than a little interested in the two of you, though I haven't a clue as to why. He doesn't share that kind of information, not even with his offspring. He did seem especially intrigued when Kaira mentioned the Keeper appearing at the scene of our fight."

Deynas tensed. Maybe speaking with the warlord was a bad idea. "Do you think he might mean her harm? He could be working with the Blooded Women."

Settek gazed into the other room where the Keeper lay. "No. I am sure his interest wasn't malicious in any way." The bright gold of his eyes softened as he continued to watch her.

Deynas cleared his throat and the crossbreed looked at him, the candid warmth in his face disappearing.

"You sound quite certain of that."

"I am."

Deynas followed the crossbreed's gaze as he turned toward the room again and they both watched her sleep. Anger and longing began to creep in on him again. Maybe if he put some distance between them he could get a little relief.

"Shall we look at this flyer you brought?"

Settek was on his feet in an instant, holding one clawed hand out in offering. Deynas stared at the hand for a few seconds, deep loathing rising defiant to the surface. He swallowed those black emotions. Whatever his motivation, the crossbreed was trying to make some amends. Could he do any less?

Deynas took the offered hand, letting the crossbreed help him up.

Deynas wouldn't meet the Keeper's eyes when he entered the room. "Kochan said you wanted to talk to me."

She nodded, hiding her frustration, and gave the open door a meaningful look.

He turned and shut it with a respectful gentleness then faced her, standing rigid and staring past her like a man facing trial. Perhaps she had been wrong to ask for him.

She stood. Despite sleeping through most of the day, exhaustion made rising hard and claws of pain raked through every muscle as she moved, but Deynas needed to believe she was capable of moving under her own power, so she kept her expression neutral and her motions as smooth as possible.

"Master Kochan has asked that we stay another night. He believes that you and I both need more time to heal."

His eyes flickered toward her and away again. "And you disagree."

Pacing might ease the anxiety his tension caused. It might also betray how fragile she still was, so she settled for clasping her hands tight before her.

"Honestly, no. He asked me to talk to you because he believed you would be resistant to the idea of staying here another night and that I could convince you to stay." An overestimation of her influence on him, she suspected. "However, the Blooded Women are calling me." *And I should answer.* She pushed the thought aside. That was something she could think about when she was away from here. "The demon failed to kill this host, but they made it clear in sending it that they will go to extremes to bring me back. I cannot continue to put the village in danger. I want to leave here as quickly as possible. Naago said that you were up packing the flyer earlier. If you're ready, I think we should go now. At speed, we could reach the nearest travel haven before nightfall."

Deynas moved his injured shoulder in a small, careful circle, his lips pressed together, pain apparent in the tightness around his eyes. When he'd completed a slow circle both forward and back, he frowned and stared at the space to the right of her face. "I share your concern, Keeper, only I'm not sure how good this arm is going to be for piloting."

She'd expected as much. He wasn't going to like her next suggestion. It had to be made, however, and she would simply have to convince him it was a good idea. "Let me pilot your flyer."

He immediately shook his head, as she'd known he would. "No. I can't do that."

"Why not?"

"I just..." He shook his head again, staring at the floor now so that his dark hair fell forward, partially obscuring his face. "No."

"You would let her do it."

She could feel the surge of aggravation in his *umahk-ra*, a cyclone of frustration and defiance. *So stubborn.*

"You're not her."

The vehemence in his words stung. It shouldn't, but it did. She was almost getting used to things not being as they should. How would the Blooded Women feel about that? "I'm not, but I fly with her memory and her ability. Trust her."

He closed his eyes and exhaled, still trying to resist. There was a growing weakness in the wall he'd put up between them, however. She could sense it, and for all that she hated to leverage his pain, perhaps it was necessary.

"Trust her or let her go."

His eyes snapped open, finally meeting hers. "What?"

"If you won't accept that she and I both exist in this body then stop wanting her to live. It isn't fair to either of us. Forget her. Let me go back to the Blooded Women so they can move me from this host and be done with it."

"Go then. I don't care." He snarled the words and turned his back on her, reaching for the door handle.

"It does no good to say the words if you don't mean them."

He kept his back to her, but didn't open the door. "What am I supposed to do?"

The torment in his voice pulled at her. How badly she wanted to comfort him. She kept her hands clasped and stayed back. "There is nothing wrong with loving her, Deynas-ra. Just know that it puts me in a difficult position."

He turned around. His blue eyes blazed with fierce passion and torment. "Why? Why does it even matter how I feel?"

This time she was the one who looked away. "A fragment of her spirit lives in you. I... Maybe that..." *What am I?* Her throat tightened. An unfamiliar swelling of emotion made her eyes sting. "I don't know. I only know this isn't how it should be." Why was she trying to explain this to him? It was pointless. She couldn't even explain it to herself.

He watched her, waiting for some explanation that

would help him reconcile the situation.

She sank down on the edge of the bed. "It's like wearing a leash."

He started to walk toward her and she looked up at him, startled by the change in his presence and the intent in his spirit. Her chest felt as if a weight pressed upon it, heavier and heavier, a weight she had to escape if she wanted to stay in control.

"I can't silence her so long as the two men who carry fragments of her spirit continue to want her."

He stopped and clenched his teeth, the brief compassion in his eyes going cold.

She shouldn't have brought Naago up. The two Endless men nurtured a rivalry because of their interest in her that festered below the surface, threatening to break through in some ugly fashion if they remained in one another's company too long. There was something else between them though, the potential for a comradery born of their shared caring for one or both of those who shared her body. If only she could nudge them that way.

"Why did you even consider keeping Misa?"

The question came as a surprise and she flinched away from the unexpected stab of regret. "Because she mattered to this host and to you."

"I didn't think you kept Endless."

She lowered her eyes. It was hard to think with him staring at her like that, his expression demanding and his eyes full of restrained affection that wasn't truly meant for her. The conversation was escaping her control. "I have done so before. I remember their spirits and the pain of death, but not the reasons they were kept."

Someone knocked once then opened the door without awaiting an answer.

Deynas stepped back from her and over to one side as Kochan entered the room.

"Ah, Deynas-ra. I had hoped to find you here. I'm sure the Keeper already said something, but I believe it would be best if you both took one more night to rest and recover before deciding your next move. Your other guests may stay the night as well if you wish it."

Deynas looked stricken. He turned to face Kochan. "My guests?"

"Yes. I spoke with Naago-ra for some time while you were out with Settek. I've decided to revoke your banishment. If I hadn't been selfish, putting my disgust for him above your needs, perhaps Misa would still be with us. I cannot make you suffer for a mistake I helped you make."

Deynas bowed his head, his spirit reverberating with an overwhelming mixture of happiness and sorrow. "I am grateful, Master."

The Keeper's hands clenched tighter, the black roots pressing into her other palm. Now Deynas had no need to leave the village. It would be foolish of him to risk returning to the city with Naago and Settek. In a sense, it was a relief to know that he could stay here where he would be safe, and yet...

"Deynas-ra?" She murmured his name in query.

He glanced sideways at her then away. His jaw tightened.

"Is there something you wish to say, Deynas-ra?" Kochan encouraged.

"I am grateful, Master, but we must leave today, before more harm comes to the village. It comforts me to know I have someplace to return to after we figure out what we can about the Keeper, but the time has come for us to leave."

"There is no need for you to leave," Kochan stated, his tone more that of a loving father than a superior. "Naago-ra can take the Keeper and go to speak with Settek's father. He has promised to return with whatever information he finds."

The Keeper didn't dare start pacing, though the need to release some of her anxious energy was starting to make her skin itch. The Endless woman took care of it for her, storming back and forth in her head, torn between asking him to come and urging him to stay behind, away from danger. It wasn't only the Endless woman who wanted him close either. Whatever the catalyst, curiosity or something else, the Keeper wasn't ready to part ways with him yet and the realization made her head hurt.

I want you with me, Deynas.

Deynas stiffened and started to turn toward her, then caught himself. His *umahk-ra* flared with a black distress. "I request your permission to go with them, Master. I believe that understanding the Keeper and helping her could prove important to the future of the Endless tribes. We shouldn't continue to risk the safety of this village by lingering here."

Kochan's brows pinched together. "If this is really what you wish, Deynas-ra, I will not deny you. Your shoulder, however, should have another day of rest at the least before you attempt piloting. Consider the damage you could do."

"I've considered it. The Keeper will pilot my craft today."

A stifling tightness in her chest released. For his sake, she held back a relieved smile.

Kochan turned a questioning look on her and she nodded.

"Very well, then. At least allow me to provide a faster flyer for Naago-ra in exchange for your old one. It will slow you down."

"Thank you, Master. I'll go check that my flyer is ready." With that, Deynas all but sprinted from the room.

Kochan turned a shrewd look on her. "You didn't try to discourage him, did you, Keeper?"

She pressed her lips together and shook her head. "He is right, we must leave here."

"All four of you?"

She drew up the hood of her cloak. It was the easiest way to hide her doubt from him. "He made his own choice."

"Did he? Or did the influence of the woman he once loved serve to persuade him?"

Still loves. "Perhaps that is a question you should ask him."

Kochan stepped to one side, clearing the doorway for her to precede him out, and inclined his head with grudging respect. He didn't like the decision, but he would not fight with her on it. No matter what she looked like or what questions he now had about her, she was still a revered being. She would rather rest more, but the decision was made. It was time to go and show that she had the strength to pilot. The Endless woman had no doubt, so neither would she.

It didn't take long to move Naago's things to the newer flyer Kochan gave him. Deynas and Settek had already swapped their belongings between their two crafts. A powerful tension filled the air, growing more potent whenever Naago and Deynas came within speaking range. The most the two Endless men exchanged was a frosty look. Naago avoided her questioning gaze. For once, both men appeared more at ease in the crossbreed's presence than in each other's. Whatever brought about this fresh animosity would have to be resolved soon if they were going to work together.

The Keeper buckled herself into the pilot stand on the silver and black flyer Settek had traded to Deynas, aware that Naago was scowling at her all the while. Settek hooked himself up on the red flyer with a broad grin made menacing by his pointed teeth. If she closed her eyes, however, she could see no malice in the pleased glow of his spirit. He was more at peace with himself now and delighted to have his flyer back. Perhaps he would be less eager to throw it out as a bargaining chip in the future. It was good that Deynas had traded him.

Thinking of Deynas, she glanced over one shoulder to where he stood staring at the passenger stand. He seemed loathe to take his place there. When he caught her watching, he shook himself and climbed up. She twisted around as far as her harness would allow.

"I am honored that you would trust me to pilot for you, Deynas-ra."

"It's out of necessity. Don't read too much into it." He set his jaw and finished buckling in.

Even knowing that his words were just a shield, an effort to keep her away and protect himself, it felt like he'd jabbed her through the heart. Still, the truth in his *umahk-ra* told her far more than his words. In it she saw pain and longing, anger and pleasure all blended into a convoluted mess of emotion. No wonder he was defensive. He was a cyclone in human form. There had to be some way to relieve that.

Convincing him not to come might have been a good start.

She faced forward, her jaw now set as tight as his. When everyone was ready, she started the flyer, bringing it up to a low hover and shifting her weight to test the balance of the unfamiliar craft. Kochan wished them a safe journey and she accelerated, diving over the cliff and letting it fall. The exhilaration of the drop cleared her head and she breathed deep of the warm afternoon air then pulled the craft out of the drop and sped across the crisp blue sky, riding just above the dunes. Despite her pain and weariness, it felt good to fly again. The Endless woman was calm and content, guiding her movements as easily as if they were truly one being.

The pleasure was short-lived. They weren't more than an hour from the village, the sun already dipping low on the horizon, when the nagging call of the Blooded Women stopped again. The strength of the arriving demon's spirit served as a warning and she pounded the throttle to full, jumping the flyer ahead of the other two to catch their attention.

The beast appeared ahead of and slightly above them, a great hawk-like creature, covered in feathers of gold set to flame by the light of the setting sun. The magnificent demon angled into a dive, its wingspan great enough to reach across all three flyers. Naago and Settek veered their crafts out in opposite directions, sweeping clear of the line of attack. The Keeper dove down, skimming below the creature's belly.

The demon twisted in the air, its tail striking the top off a dune into a cloud of sand as it came around to give chase. Naago and Settek were both coming back around to the center behind it, but the beast had no interest in them and there was little they could do to stop it. The flyers weren't equipped with anything powerful enough to take on such a creature. Despite that, Naago fired a wind chasing net from his flyer, wrapping one of the beast's taloned feet with it. The demon twisted and swept its wing out, striking the side of Naago's flyer and sending it careening out of control.

Naago!

"Drop us down lower," Deynas shouted.

She complied, diving the craft down close to the sand. The demon couldn't fly as low without striking its wings, but it didn't let up, keeping close above and a little behind them. She couldn't see what had become of Naago, but Settek was still with them. He swung low over the right wing, trying to interfere with its flight without getting hit. The demon veered toward him, forcing him to back off, then turned back to harry them.

Deynas grabbed hold of her support stand and clipped himself onto it, holding on tight. He leaned close. "I need you to swing out and up fast. Get me above its right shoulder," he shouted.

Whatever he was planning, it couldn't help being dangerous. Her chest tightened with dread. "No."

"Do it! You know it won't give up until it kills you."

And with him on the same flyer, it would kill them both. She clenched her jaw and jerked the craft out to one side and up, easing the throttle at the last possible second, positioning them above the startled demon's shoulder. Deynas unclipped and she leaned hard to the opposite side to counterbalance when he sprinted across the wing and jumped. Her heart felt like it stopped, watching him drop through the air, telescoping out his staff with a flick of his wrist on the way down. Settek cried out something that sounded like encouragement.

The blade of the staff sank in before his feet made contact and he drove it down hard through the demon's spine with the momentum of his fall. The creature shrieked and twisted over. The Keeper lost sight of Deynas then and had to accelerate up to get out of range of a flailing wing. Then the beast plowed into the dunes, sending a wall of sand spraying up high into the air as it slid to a stop.

The Keeper landed beside the dead demon and peered around, looking for some sight of the Endless man while she unclipped her harness.

Deynas.

Settek landed beside her and hopped off his flyer. A ways back, she spotted Naago heading their direction, still on his craft. The sight of him brought only a tiny glimmer of relief. Now she had to find Deynas. The call to keep drew her then, an irresistible demand, and she got down from the flyer.

"Settek, look for Deynas-ra, please." Her voice was shaking.

The crossbreed's grave nod wasn't at all encouraging.

She turned to the dead demon, placed a hasty hand upon it and invited it to her. At least its death had been quick. Even so, in her weakened state, the pain drove her to her knees and brought tears to her eyes.

"I see him."

Settek's words gave her the will to get her back to her feet. She stumbled across the sand after the crossbreed to a still figure lying several yards back before the point of impact. He must have fallen when the demon first twisted over. Fear drove her hard enough that she reached his side at the same time Settek did and sank to her knees, throwing back the hood of her cloak to see him better.

He lay on his side, breathing shallowly, eyes closed. Not dead. She closed her eyes. His *umahk-ra* flickered, weakened by pain, but not even close to death. Opening her eyes, she breathed a soft sigh and brushed his hair away from his eyes with a careful touch.

Naago landed a few feet away and jumped off the flyer.

Deynas murmured something. She leaned down, putting her ear near his lips. After a few shallow breaths, he spoke again.

"Don't ever let me do that again."

She couldn't stop a soft, relieved laugh. She swiped away a rogue tear, brushing it off before Naago could see. Then she sat back on her heals, leaving a hand resting on Deynas's shoulder.

"What hurts?"

He chuckled. It turned into a cough followed by an agonized groan. "Maybe I should tell you what doesn't. It'd be faster."

Settek lowered himself down on one knee. "Can you stand?"

Deynas rolled over on his back and looked up at the crossbreed, squinting against the bright orange glow of the sunset. Blood streamed from a wound above his eyebrow and sand mixed with blood covered the side of his face.

"Help me get this shoulder back in place and I can manage."

Naago stepped in then. "Dislocated it again, huh? Probably should have stayed behind and let it heal."

Deynas gave the other man an icy look.

"Perhaps you missed him saving our asses just a moment ago," Settek remarked, his tone almost flippant though his gold eyes flashed a challenge at Naago.

"Ah yes. I suppose so." Naago gave a hard swallow. Pride was always painful going down. "Let me in here and we'll get this shoulder straightened out again."

The Keeper rose and her knees buckled.

Naago caught her and guided her to one side, then lowered her gently down, his eyes full of concern.

"Are you all right?"

She looked past him at Deynas. "Help him. I'll be fine."

Naago did as directed, though he didn't look happy about it. The shoulder moved back in easier this time. Deynas ground his teeth and squeezed his eyes shut, which made the bleeding worse from the cut above his brow. He stayed that way, battling the pain while Naago went and dug a cloth out of his flyer. He gave the cloth to Deynas who pressed it to the wound to stop the bleeding.

"Anything else need immediate care?"

"No," Deynas answered through gritted teeth.

The Keeper got unsteadily to her feet and brushed past Naago to kneel by Deynas again. "Get me some water and another rag if you have one."

Naago complied, wearing his silence like armor.

"Settek, could you see if his staff is salvageable."

"Anything you ask, Keeper."

The crossbreed strode away. A few minutes later, Naago returned with the requested items. Then he went to sit in sullen silence beside his flyer while she cleaned the blood and sand from Deynas's face, being slow about it so they could both rest before trying to travel again.

His brilliant blue eyes opened, glazed with pain. "You fell a moment ago. Are you fit to fly?"

"More so than you. I can manage the last few miles to the traveler's haven."

"What happened? Is it weakness from last night still?"

The worry in his strained voice caused a ridiculous flutter in her stomach. She deliberately avoided his eyes, turning her focus to removing every trace of blood from his face. "It is partly that. The Blooded are deliberately selecting demons that I must keep. That way if the demon fails to kill me, it will still weaken me. They know the physical and emotional toll the deaths will have on me, though they can't know how badly the last one went. Perhaps they hope to wear me down enough that I'll give up from exhaustion if they can't kill me outright."

"Kill you? Don't you mean kill her?"

She gave him a hard look. "Don't complicate things." She touched the hand still holding a cloth over the wound. "Move your hand so I can see."

He took the cloth away. The bleeding had slowed. A little more pressure and it would stop. She took the cloth from him and pressed it on the wound while cleaning closer around the edges.

He closed his eyes again. "You do fly like her."

She pressed her lips together, keeping quiet as she lifted the cloth again then gestured Naago over to help her bandage the wound. Settek returned with the staff handle, apparently undamaged, though he was breathing hard from the effort of wrenching the weapon free. Then the crossbreed and Naago got Deynas to his feet and helped him to his place on the black and silver flyer.

The Keeper followed, allowing Naago to help her up into the pilot's place. She glanced at Deynas before attaching her harness. This was the second time he'd almost died because of her. Perhaps she *should* have encouraged him to stay behind. Then again, where would the three of them be now if he hadn't been there?

Once she was in place, she leaned back into the stand and rested her head against it for a moment.

Behind her, Deynas gave a ragged chuckle. "We're a fine pair."

"That we are." For some reason, her cheeks flushed when she said it.

She took the control handles with shaking hands and they resumed their flight, leaving the second sacrificial demon behind.

CHAPTER NINETEEN

Deynas stood on a dune within sight of the group cabin they'd rented. The night was brisk and the cold made his shoulder ache as if something gnawed at the joint from within, something with very sharp teeth. His ribs were stiff and achy along with much of the rest of his body after his unplanned airborne tussle with the demon. As much as he needed the rest, the painkillers they had with them weren't strong enough to help him sleep for long. To avoid waking the others with his restlessness he came out here.

"Is it the pain keeping you awake?"

Apparently, he hadn't been quiet enough leaving.

The chill breeze brought the smell of her to him. She smelled like Argus. Like the desert. Salt and sweat with a certain heady undertone he couldn't quite name. He glanced over at her. The silver in her eyes and hair shone in the starlight, framing her fine features in dark radiance. Breathtakingly beautiful. It took him a moment to remember what she'd asked and gather his wits enough to respond.

"Yes, mostly."

She turned to face him.

He tried to look away, but the worry in her eyes caught him and held him fast. "Is something wrong?"

She wrung her hands, the gesture disarmingly

human. "I sense the call to keep coming."

His stomach twisted. He still cared far too deeply for Argus and it was becoming harder to remember that this woman wasn't her. If he'd never known Argus still lived in her, it might be easier to let go, but now the lines were blurring, not just for him, but also, he suspected, for the Keeper. Or was he just seeing what he wanted to see in her behavior?

He took a deep breath, drawing crisp air into his lungs to ease the emotional aching. "How soon?"

Her shoulders lifted in a helpless little shrug. "Very soon."

"You think it's a trap?"

"It seems likely."

Deynas reached up, wincing at the flare of pain in his shoulder. Without her, he would have to pilot the flyer, but that was a minor concern. He unclasped the chain around his neck and took a step closer to her.

She shifted back from him. "What are you doing?"

"You said this pendant protects my spirit. Maybe it will help protect you from them."

"But I'm not..."

He silenced her with a fierce look then walked behind her and drew the chain around her neck. "Lift your hair."

She obliged and he hesitated a moment, his attention captured by the black roots that twined down along the right side of her neck, disappearing into her cloak. Physical proof that she wasn't the woman he loved anymore. Where else did those roots weave upon her skin?

The desire to touch her caught him unaware. He took another deep breath, searching for his ever more elusive will. His fingers brushed her skin when he clasped the chain and let the pendant down gently to hang around her neck.

Soft. Warm. Real.

She dropped her hair.

When he moved around in front of her again, she was holding up the god's blood pendant in her fingers, her striking eyes riveted upon it.

"This was your mother's. I can't take this."

"How do you know... Nevermind." He shook his head, ignoring the poignant ache in his chest. Argus was part of her, more so all the time it seemed. He shouldn't wonder at her knowing such things. "I want you to wear it and promise to bring it back to me."

She let it slip from her fingers and fall down to slide beneath the clasp of her cloak. Her eyes moved up to meet his. "Deynas, I can't..."

He held up a finger to silence her. "I know what you're going to say. Think me crazy if you wish, but I don't want to hear about it. Just accept that."

She smiled wistfully and he saw his Argus in her features more distinctly than ever. "You were always a little crazy."

He stared into her eyes then, a question weighing heavy on the tip of his tongue, one he knew he shouldn't ask.

Her smile faded. "What is it?"

"Do you know if..." He fell silent. It was a foolish thing to ask.

"If what?"

Foolish. He shook his head and looked away. "Nothing."

"If she ever loved you?"

His gaze snapped back to her face. *Damn her perception.*

"Yes. She does." She smiled once more, an expression full of sorrow, and disappeared.

"No! Not yet," he snarled, glaring up at the stars.

He felt as helpless as he had the night he left Argus in the city. It was a terrible feeling and not one he cared to experience again. He also felt naked without the pendant against his skin. It really had been foolish to give it to her, but it was the only thing he could think of that might protect her. If they killed her, then Argus was truly gone. Maybe that was the way it should be, but if Argus wanted to live, even this way, then he had to try to help her. He'd come along to do just that because he'd heard her spirit speaking to him in the room in the temple. Her voice inside him saying she wanted him with her. How could he refuse that?

The pain in his shoulder flared and he gritted his teeth against it. Tears stung his eyes and he blinked them back. Footsteps approached from behind, making a soft squeaking noise in the sand. He glanced back, spotting Settek as the part-demon strode purposefully toward him. He didn't have the energy for hating the crossbreed anymore and he was too confused to know if he even should, so he nodded acknowledgement then turned to gaze at the sky once more as he had been when the Keeper joined him.

"I expected the Keeper to be with you."

His hands tightened into fists. Even that increased the pain in his shoulder. "She was called to keep."

"Ah." Settek's grim look said he understood the possible danger of that. He also caught on to the other implications of her departure. "If you're piloting tomorrow, you'll need sleep. I have something that will knock you out for a few hours."

Deynas gave him a questioning look.

"I didn't offer before because of the Keeper. With her gone, it seems less likely that we'll need you to save us from any enraged demons." Settek gave him a sly, teasing grin.

The crossbreed was turning out to be reasonable and disturbingly likeable. "Why are you awake?"

"I'm a light sleeper." He looked up at the stars, his gold eyes gleaming with an inner fire Deynas almost envied. "I woke when you left and again when the Keeper went out. We can't all sleep as well as Naago-ra."

Deynas chuckled, unable to keep bitterness from the sound. He needed to have a few words with Naago. That would go easier if he had some rest as well. Just a day or so ago, he'd have turned Settek's offer of drugs down with no little hostility. Strange how fast some things could change. "I'll take you up on that offer."

•

The Keeper appeared deep in the ruins below the Undercity in an unlit temple. The place had an eerie familiarity that prickled up her spine. Her eyes pierced the darkness, making out the rubble of a destroyed statue of The Undying that littered the interior. The typically towering central chamber came to an abrupt stop, the cut down walls butting up into the metal substructure of the Undercity above. The temple in the Undercity was the oldest such temple in existence. It wasn't the passage of time that destroyed it or drove the ancient Endless from the place. Legend said the Endless angered a greater god and that god had sent demons to destroy this temple and much of the original city in retribution. A thousand years later, the Endless returned to the site and built the current city on top of it, a city that they would be driven from again almost four hundred years after their return.

The call to keep came from behind the remains of the statue, in the long room to the rear where the Endless elders once prepared the dead and performed the ritual of ascension along with many other important ceremonies. She wound through the maze of debris around the side of the statue, her nerves fired up with the Endless woman's dread. Or was it her own? What did the Keeper have to fear?

One of the tall double doors behind the statue stood cracked a few inches. Dim light flickered through the narrow opening. She touched the door with her right hand, feeling a thick layer of dust under her fingertips. There were cleaner marks above her hand on the door where others had touched it quite recently. The black roots constricted and a tingling sensation swept through her everywhere they pressed against the skin. A warning?

The call to keep drew her inexorably on. She pushed the door open.

Thirty-six Blooded Women lined both sides of the long room, set apart in six groups of six with tall candelabra between each of the groups. The flickering flames of the candles, six on each candelabrum, provided the only light. The women faced the center, standing still as statues and silent. At the far end of the room, a creature lay upon a stone table. It looked like a furry white moth, though several times the size of a normal man. Its wings hung over the sides of the table, fine circular patterns in icy pale gray softening the bright white of the delicate appendages.

I'm sorry, Argus. Our time may be at an end.

The Endless woman's sorrow was powerful, but an even stronger sense of pride rose to the surface and the woman rode along with the Keeper while she walked down between the Blooded Women. It was strangely reassuring, as if someone walked beside her, offering support in whatever happened next. Even with that comfort, the room grew colder with each step. The Blooded Women didn't move. They were so still it was almost hard to tell they lived at all. Then the chant started, singing out in her mind in thirty-six identical voices.

That which is lost, she will find.
That which is forsaken, she will cherish.
That which is forgotten, she will remember.

That which is, she will keep.

She stopped before the table and placed her right hand upon the dead creature. A lesser god. Its spirit rose up from the dead flesh, glowing with a gentle violet light, its aura so beautiful and serene that brought forth tears.

Come to me and you shall be remembered.

As expected, the spirit complied, moving gracefully into her. The pain of its death was familiar, the all-consuming pain that came from the eyes of the Blooded Women. This one had not come to its fate of its own free will as the other two had. They had killed the creature themselves this time.

She had to grip the side of the table to keep from sinking to the floor, but she didn't cry out. They would not see the true extent of her pain or how weak she still was from the demon she had killed to save Deynas. When the pain ceased, she took first one hand then the other deliberately from the table and rotated around to face her audience. There were punishments to deal out.

The Blooded were moving out from the sides of the room now. The nearest group of six slid toward her, their slippered feet hissing along the gritty floor. They were the ones responsible for this death. All of them together. The Keeper walked toward the first group. A few feet away, the Blooded Women stopped. They began to hum and their eyes started to creep open.

Did they think to kill this flesh before she could punish them for killing the lesser god?

She reached out a hand as the ghastly pink light washed over her. Extraordinary pain pounded through the flesh and spirit of the Endless woman, arresting her motion. Then she felt a spot of heat against her chest and bright silver light blazed out from the god's blood pendant. The pain receded, leaving in its place only a sensation akin to a sharp itch throughout her borrowed flesh. Unpleasant, but not debilitating. The Keeper closed the remaining distance and placed her right hand against the cheek of one Blooded Woman.

"You have committed an unforgivable crime. Your life continues at the whim of greater powers, for death is not mine to deal, but you must pay in suffering."

You cannot punish us.

"I think I can."

With those words, she passed all the pain of the lesser god's death into them. All six of the Blooded Women started shrieking in her head and the Endless woman within her reveled in the sound, urging her on. The Keeper smiled and passed more pain through, the agony of a hundred deaths, a thousand. The tubes that ran from the Blooded Women's jaws burst, spraying blood, and all six collapsed, twitching on the floor. Their voices fell silent. The ghastly light in their eyes faded to dull, lifeless black.

To kill only one had destroyed all six within that group. Could they really be so fragile?

The Keeper looked around the room. The other five groups of Blooded stood back now, neither coming closer nor backing away. They hadn't expected this. She took a few steps toward the nearest group and they shuffled back, their eyes staying closed.

You know a new host must be found. Give yourself to us. Let us care for you as we always have.

The Keeper hesitated. *Death is not mine to deal.*

She had just killed some of them. They were the ones who moved her between hosts. They weren't her enemies. What would happen when this flesh died if she didn't have them to help her?

You belong with us. Where else can you go?

She could feel Deynas and Naago calling her. The call from their spirits was almost as strong and constant as that from the Blooded Women. If she returned to them, however, she would be putting them in danger again. Maybe the Blooded Women were right. Maybe it was time to stop fighting the inevitable. What point did it serve to cling to this flesh?

The pendant was still warm against her skin, though the silver light no longer blazed in her defense. Deynas had entrusted it to her because he loved her.

No. He loves Argus.

Making the differentiation weighed her down as if the city itself rested upon her shoulders. Did she care for him? Was the Keeper even capable of such emotions on her own? Whatever the reason, she couldn't let the Blooded Women destroy this host without first returning his mother's pendant to him. She owed him a great deal. The least she could do was see that he got his remarkable keepsake back and there was only one way she could think of to do that without going to him directly.

She glanced around at the Blooded Women again. "I am leaving and you will not try to stop me. I must finish something before you move me from this host."

Animosity thickened the air in the room, but the remaining Blooded Women shuffled back to the sides, leaving her an open path. Her neck and back prickled with expectation of an attack as she left the room. The sensation didn't go away until she made her way up into the crowds of the Undercity. Hidden by the cloak, she moved unchallenged through the streets and into the hotel adjacent to The Firelight.

She sensed the Warlord Kato in his suite that took up the entire top floor of the hotel. She didn't need to request an audience with him. No one could stop her.

The magnificent demon was standing with his back to the door when she arrived, gazing out a window down at the main street. His tail swung back and forth, color moving down from base to tip in a slow, mesmerizing cascade.

The Keeper watched him for a moment, staying hidden. As soon as she entered his presence, the black roots warmed against their skin and she experienced an odd feeling of nostalgia. Had she dealt with him in some manner before? It didn't seem likely that she would feel this way if all she had done was punish him at some point. This was something different, like encountering an old friend, only a disturbing unease was rising quickly up beneath that sense of familiarity.

"You needn't hide from me, Keeper, I have known you and cared for you in many of your iterations." He turned as he spoke, his scaled hide rippling with warm color, his voice rich and soothing. His gold eyes, when he stopped moving, trained upon the spot where she stood.

"Cared for me?" She let herself be seen and pushed her hood back. "Why don't I remember you?"

"They don't want you to remember. I am a threat to their careful balance because I know what you are supposed to be. I know what they have done to you."

"They?" She put her left hand to her brow, hoping to stop the sudden spiraling sensation in her head.

Kato gestured to a chair. "Please sit."

"We can't linger here."

His expression darkened to something more like that of a disapproving father, a look she suspected Settek was exceedingly familiar with.

"Sit," he repeated in a firmer tone.

The dizziness forced her to oblige him and she sank down into a leather chair that could have comfortably sat another two people alongside her. The seat was too long for her to rest into the back so she leaned against one tall arm. She felt like a child sitting in her father's chair, though the memory that accompanied the thought was something from the Endless woman's childhood.

Kato gave a curt nod. "Better. You said *we* can't linger here. I assume you were referring to yourself and this host."

She thought back through the strange fog now filling her head. He was right, she had said we. Her stomach began to tie itself into knots. She could barely open her mouth to speak for the sudden fear of being sick. "Why do I feel like throwing up?"

"They've conditioned you to react this way so that you will not linger in my company should you and I cross paths."

In addition to spinning, her head was starting to hurt now. "By they, you mean the Blooded Women?"

"And the one who controls them."

"Who controls them?" she blurted, craving as much information as he could give her before she gave in to this rapidly escalating misery.

He smiled faintly though she couldn't find anything amusing in the question. "Another. That is not important right now. What is important is that this host is very strong. She can help you, but you must stop fighting her. You fight her only because they have made you believe that she should be dormant."

Her eyes were starting to tear up with the increasing pain in her head. She started to curl forward around her rebellious stomach. "What..." She swallowed a rush of bile. "What do you mean?"

"The relationship between the Keeper and her host is meant to be a partnership, not a hostile domination. The Blooded have desecrated that sacred joining. Embrace this Endless woman and her memories. Make her your ally."

A partnership?

Were the Blooded really in the wrong? Were they controlling her?

That silent black rage Naago had found in her began to well up again.

Kato's smile broadened, showing his bright, pointed teeth. "I sense fury in you. Good. Be outraged by what they have done to you. The anger will serve you well."

"If they control me as you say, how can I stop them?"

He moved closer. The churning in her gut grew more turbulent and a thousand hammers pounded at the inside of her skull.

"Almost a thousand years ago they tore away the spirit of the Keeper. They have used it to control you and to leech away your memories when they move you between hosts. That spirit waits, imprisoned in the Halls of the Blooded now. Not the Halls in the New City, but those deep down below, in the caverns beneath the ruins where the blood spirits dwell. You must find your spirit and take it back."

She wanted to scream. The nausea and pain were becoming too much to bear. "Where? How do I find it?"

He leaned over her, his gold eyes gleaming like stars. "Listen for the call of your spirit. It will guide you."

She stood and scrambled away from him, nearly falling over another chair in her haste. Leaning against a wall for support, she reached around behind her neck and unclasped the chain. She let the god's blood pendant fall to the floor.

"That belongs to Deynas-ra. He is coming to see you. Please make sure he gets it back." With those words, she jerked up her hood and went unseen as she sprinted from the room.

When morning came, Deynas at least didn't feel completely exhausted, though a few more hours of sleep would have been welcome. Every muscle in his body ached and the pain in his shoulder and ribs wasn't much improved, but he could reduce it all to a tolerable level with the painkillers they did have and not impair his flying ability too significantly. The absence of his mother's pendant left him feeling naked and he felt hollow without Argus there. No matter how often he tried to tell himself she wasn't really his Argus, some part of him insisted that she was and loved her as much as ever.

Naago and Settek were both out by the flyers in the fast rising heat of a bright day. A strong, inconstant breeze picked up occasional funnels of sand, dancing them across the landscape before dumping them in a small pile somewhere new. Even if the wind stuck around, the afternoon heat was going to be blistering. They would want to make good time heading for the city.

Naago was stuffing his things into his hatch as though each item had done him some wrong. He'd been quiet and brooding all morning, ever since they told him of the Keeper's departure during the night. Deynas got the feeling his sour mood was as much irritation that she hadn't told him she was leaving herself as it was worry about her wellbeing. That possessive attitude toward her made it even more important that they talk things out. He could hear Master Kochan in his head telling him countless times that calm and rational conversation was always more productive than an emotional confrontation. Despite those wise words, just thinking about the other man's quietly hostile conduct got his ire up.

Deynas stalked over to Naago and watched him shove things around the hatch for a few seconds. The other Endless did nothing to acknowledge him, which only served to make him more cross.

"You told Kochan to convince me to stay in the village, didn't you?"

Naago glanced sideways at him, his pale eyes narrowing a fraction. "You're injured."

"Don't give me that shit." *So much for calm and rational.* Ah well, he'd never been much of a diplomat anyway. "You didn't do it out of concern for me. You did it to get the Keeper away from me."

On the far side of Naago's craft, Settek sat on the wing of his flyer, watching them with a bemused smirk. At least someone was enjoying the morning.

Naago faced Deynas. "What if I did? It's obvious that having you around is making things more difficult for her."

"What things would those be? The decision to kill Argus perhaps? I can't say I feel too bad about making that harder for her."

Naago clenched his jaw. The muscles twitched. He turned back to the hatch.

Deynas reached out and slammed it shut, narrowly missing the other man's hand. "What gives you the right to make decisions on her behalf?"

Naago spun to face him again, one hand sinking

toward his sword hilt. Anger flushed his features. "She isn't Argus!"

A flare of pain in his shoulder prompted Deynas to take a step back, wary of the confrontation growing physical in his current condition. He struggled to achieve some level of calm. "I know that. Believe me, I do. But Argus is still there and I can't turn my back on her." *Not again.* "Why do you care so much, anyway? What is she to you but a fascinating puzzle?"

Naago deflated then, all the anger draining away, seeming to leech his energy out with it. "She's something… someone completely different," he muttered. "An Endless woman, and yet not. Someone who never knew my *ra'sen.* Someone I could touch who didn't make me think of her."

Touch? Deynas bit back a flare of jealous temper, trying hard not to become caught up on that one word. It was clear from the sorrow that gave sudden age to Naago's face that the *ra'sen* he spoke of was no longer alive. Deynas could think of nothing to say short of several cruel remarks fueled by senseless jealousy, so he said nothing.

Settek stood and tossed his head, the bright sunlight giving life to his flame-colored mane, then bared his pointed teeth in a grin. "If you're not going to entertain me with a duel, perhaps we could get moving. It would be a shame if the Keeper returned to find us loitering in the same place she left us, no closer to any answers."

Naago and Deynas locked eyes for a moment, sharing the same thought. Would the Keeper return this time? That uncertainty made their disagreement feel petty. Besides, they were bickering over a woman who was much more than just a woman and whom neither of them could truly have. It was an inane argument.

Deynas turned away and stalked to his flyer. It was past time to move on.

•

It was well after dark when they reached the city. Even at this hour, the lingering heat from the day was enough to keep them sweating, all except Settek whose demon blood gave him a higher tolerance to such temperatures. With both Naago and Settek there, it was a cinch to gain admission through one of the illegal Undercity portals. Deynas and Naago donned hooded jackets before venturing out in the streets. The city enforcers were still likely to be watching for Deynas and they had no way to know if Naago might have been spotted leaving the city with him. Until they reached Kato, they were better off staying hidden.

Settek took them to a secured garage he frequented to park the flyers. Traveling on foot would draw less attention, though it would take a little longer, especially on the route they took. The tall crossbreed knew the back alleys, rooftop walks and hidden corridors of the Undercity better, it seemed, than most knew the hallways in their own homes. Deynas questioned that intimate knowledge while following Settek down a damp hidden corridor infested with black rats and well-fed blood grubs.

The crossbreed paused and grinned at him. "Father always knows when I'm up to something. Occasionally, if I'm planning something that's going to draw too much attention, he sends his guards to intervene. The only way I can get away with anything worthwhile is by staying a step ahead of his guards. I've invested so much time finding hidden ways around the city that the simple act of driving his guards crazy trying to find me is sometimes more fun than whatever I else I might be trying to get away with."

"Perhaps you would get in less trouble if you spent less time in the city."

Settek nudged a plump rat that was sniffing at his toe out of the way and continued walking. "Where would I go? The desert is good for racing, but has little else to offer. The nearest city of any size is Ginakwa and the gods that run that place are too damned restrictive. You can't even carry a weapon within the inner city walls. Demons aren't allowed in the inner city at all and anyone with demon blood has to serve a two-week probationary period in the outer city before they can be admitted. They even detain most humans, unless they have the precious blood of The Undying in them." He rolled his eyes.

Deynas couldn't hold that against him. Becoming one of the unwelcome ones gave him a new insight into how damaging such restrictions could be. However, the last part wasn't so true in Ginakwa anymore. Endless could enter inner Ginakwa, but they were encouraged to wrap up business and move on quickly in an effort to maintain peaceful relations with the new owners of this metropolis. Deynas didn't bother to correct Settek on the subject. His stomach turned when the tail end of a bloated blood grub burst under his heel and he was busy trying not to be sick. The copper stench of warm blood that wafted up didn't help matters.

He swallowed hard and tried to focus on their conversation. "Perhaps you could go train in an Endless village. Refine your combat skills."

Naago snorted. "Without the Keeper there speaking in his defense, they would never allow a crossbreed to stay in one of the villages, much less train there."

"True, but he is part Endless. Perhaps it's time we opened our minds and our borders a little."

Settek gave Deynas a measuring look when he turned sideways to move through a narrower opening leading out to a dim alley. "Perhaps it is. There are more like me than your elders would care to admit, the offspring of Endless who found love in a demon's embrace. The blood of The Undying doesn't dilute, not through the many generations that separate you from the first Endless or through the introduction of demon blood in the mix. It always runs strong and true."

Deynas glanced over his shoulder at Naago. "Is that right?"

The other man nodded distractedly, watching his footsteps. With the lingering smell of burst blood grub still thick in his nose, Deynas turned his attention to the ground as well.

One of the rats scurrying past had a human finger gripped between his teeth, probably a leaving found in one of the fighting ring drainage channels. Several of its opportunistic brethren gave chase, squeaking excitedly. More rats gathered around a chunk of unidentifiable flesh that pulsated with blood grubs and reeked of decay. It was becoming debatable whether the risk of stepping on another ripe grub might be worth not having to look at the floor of the snug alleyway.

After almost an hour spent in grimy, rank smelling alleys and hidden passages, the back door of Kato's hotel was a welcome sight. They kept their faces hidden and let Settek take the lead. The door guard let them through, scowling at their dark hoods, and directed them to the office above The Firelight to find the warlord.

The gambling den was in full swing and there were no less than five of the large centipede-like hypnotists moving around the building. Now that Deynas thought about it, though it was almost too loud inside to think, they were probably more effective crowd control than any of the burly guards. If someone got out of line, they could hypnotize the troublemaker into behaving and continue to profit from their patronage. It wasn't the most honest way to operate, but an honest business wouldn't last long in the Undercity.

Kato stood behind his desk, watching the door as if he had expected them, which he probably had. Settek strode boldly into the room. Naago and Deynas stopped inside the door and inclined their heads to the magnificent warlord. Kato glanced over their heads and the door slid shut behind them, then he turned his gold eyes on Settek. Now that Deynas knew they were related, it was remarkable how obvious the similarities were.

"Did you present yourself as a bearer for the girl?"

Settek's brilliant mane dimmed a shade and he bowed his head. "I did, Father. I would not have been allowed, however, had the Keeper not intervened on my behalf."

Kato's eyes flashed. "The Keeper spoke for you? Perhaps she is beginning to connect with some of her own memories through the Endless woman. That's promising."

The demon's words caught Deynas by surprise. They implied that he might know quite a lot about the Keeper. Deynas opened his mouth to question that and Kato held a palm out to silence him. Glorious color rippled over his arm with the movement. Obedience was inevitable. Deynas closed his mouth and waited.

"Do you know why the Keeper was there?"

Settek started to turn toward them for assistance, but Kato's eyes narrowed and he shifted back to face his father. "As you suspected, she and her host seem to feel a connection with Naago-ra. However, the dead girl and Deynas-ra are from the same tribe as the host. From what I understand, they knew her well before the Blooded Women took her. I believe they're the primary reason she was there."

Kato turned to Deynas and Naago now, bronze and red rippling over his scales as he moved. "And you two have come here to ask something of me."

Naago stepped forward. "We need to find a way into the Endless archives."

Kato's gaze held Deynas for a moment, resting so heavy upon him that he had to fight not to sink to his knees before the warlord. Then those gold eyes released him and moved to Naago. "What do you hope to find there?"

"When the Keeper was traveling with me, a wind spirit came with a message. He addressed her as *Umahk-ra-sehndo* in the Voice of The Undying. We want to find out more about this."

Kato nodded to the door behind them and it opened to admit Kaira. The voluptuous crossbreed brought potent sexual energy into the room, grinning unabashedly at Naago and Deynas each in turn. Naago let desire show through in his smile. Deynas offered a more formal nod, trying to ignore the effect her sumptuous curves had on him and she responded with a perfect teasing pout.

"Kaira, my dear, please get some drinks for our guests. Add something a little extra for Deynas-ra. I sense that he is injured..." Kato leaned closer to Deynas and inhaled, "...from fighting greater demons, it would seem."

"Yes, Father." She turned and swayed out. The door slid shut again behind her.

Kato's gaze lingered on the door for a moment, the gold warming a touch before he returned his attention to them. "You do not need your archives. *Umahk-ra-sehndo* means Spirit Keeper. It is what The Undying chose to call her when he made her."

The Undying made her? A shiver passed through Deynas.

Naago swayed ever so slightly, then shook himself and walked to a chair to sit down, crossing his legs in the wide seat.

It was Settek who put voice to what they were all thinking. "The Keeper was made?"

"Yes. Created by The Undying and others. Several greater demons and gods banded together to create the Keeper. She was our answer to the problem of death, a being that would preserve certain spirits with the ultimate goal of bringing them back later, after we perfected the art of creating new flesh for them. Of course, we made certain that her creators would be among those kept, should the need arise. The Undying gave her life with his blood. She is his child, in a sense, and kin to the Endless. He meant for her to live with the Endless tribe in the village that became the ruins beneath us."

Deynas shook his head and Kato's gold eyes regarded him with infectious serenity, encouraging him to speak his mind.

"If that's true, why don't the tribes know more about her?"

"The Endless tribe that built those ruins was killed off in their entirety by demons roughly fourteen hundred years ago. Much of their knowledge was lost with them."

Naago nodded, confirming the warlord's words. "We know they existed, but we know almost nothing more than that about them."

Settek took a seat as the door opened and Kaira returned with a tray of drinks. She passed them around then took the last and sat next to her brother, curling her legs up into the chair like a little girl. Deynas took a swallow of his drink. Soothing warmth moved swept through him, concentrating at the worst of his injuries and easing the pain. Something this potent certainly wasn't legal, but now didn't seem a sensible time for embracing moral conceits. He took another long swallow.

The door slid shut once more and Kato went on. "The Undying kept that tribe isolated from the others while we perfected the Keeper. Acting as the Keeper's host was intended to be a position of great honor. The host and Keeper were meant to coexist within one body, two spirits living in harmony, a joining that proved strongest when the Endless woman was *umahk-ra-en-mahde.*"

"Is the host always a woman?" Naago asked when Kato paused.

"Yes. The Keeper's nature is female. We needed a being that would be naturally inclined to nurture and protect the kept spirits. She has her own thoughts and memories, but her only physical form without a host is as a seed meant to house her spirit and those she has kept. She is not designed to exist alone. When placed in a host, that seed expands throughout the body and over part of the flesh as the black roots you have both seen."

Naago nodded as if the answer was everything he expected. Deynas found himself wondering again how much of her skin those roots covered and exactly how much of them the other Endless man had seen.

"When demons destroyed the original tribe, the Blooded Women stripped the Keeper's spirit from her and imprisoned it. I'm unsure of the motive behind their actions. They may simply be trying to prevent the rebirth of the spirits she keeps or those controlling the Blooded Women may be looking for a way to use those spirits to strengthen their own the same way a spirit fragment strengthens the spirit of the *umahk-ra-uden.*" Kato gave Naago and Deynas both significant looks. Somehow, he knew that about them as well.

"The Blooded Women take away her memories every time they move her to a new host and store them with her spirit so that they can manipulate her and make her believe this is how she is supposed to be. Sometimes those memories start to return to her and they have to move her again. This time, they made the rather significant mistake of placing her within an *umahk-ra-en-mahde.*"

Deynas felt a little like a child newborn and ignorant of the world. It was an irritating sensation. "How do you know so much? How do you know what we are and what Argus is?"

Kato didn't acknowledge him this time. The warlord would only give them the answers he wanted them to have.

"If The Undying created the Keeper, why would he allow demons to take control of her? Why hasn't he done anything to stop this?" Naago asked.

"Those are things we can discuss at another time. There are more important matters that require your attention now." The warlord turned toward Deynas and held his hand out. Something dangled from one claw, sparkling in the light of the room. It was the chain with the god's blood pendant. Deynas grabbed for it and Kato drew it back out of reach. "You gave her this?"

Deynas forced his hand back to his side, his pulse pounding in his ears. The healing heat in his shoulder was like a small fire now, making him feel feverish. "How did you get that?"

"Why did you give it to her?"

"To protect her."

Kato's expression was unreadable as stone, his body and the colors unchanging for the first time since Deynas met him. "To protect the Keeper or to protect the Endless woman who is hosting her?"

The gravity in the warlord's tone told Deynas that the answer was of considerable importance to him. Nevertheless, it wasn't a question he was keen to answer, nor could he see how it mattered. Still, he couldn't bring himself to defy Kato. The Keeper and Argus existed in the same body. To protect one was to protect the other, wasn't it?

His face grew warm when he thought of her, the Keeper as she was now, Argus as she was then. It made very little difference how he thought of her and that surprised him.

Kato shifted his folded wings. Color rippled through them, rich, comforting color.

"Both," Deynas answered.

Kato held the pendant out to him again and he took it, the reassuring weight of the stone sliding into his palm as Kato released the chain. "She came here to give this to me because she knew you would come. I think her plan was to give herself to the Blooded Women."

Naago jumped up from the chair. "Where is she now?"

"I sent her to find herself in the Halls of the Blooded beneath the ruins. She is *Umahk-ra-sehndo'en-mahde* now. She is as strong as she has ever been, but I don't think she is confident enough yet to free her spirit alone. She will need help."

Deynas closed his fist around the pendant. "Then we have to go after her."

"Don't fret. I didn't tell her precisely how to get to what she is searching for, though she will be drawn there eventually. With you, I will send a guide. You have time to finish your drinks. You especially, Deynas-ra. No matter how much you care for her, you will be of no use to her if your injuries get you killed along the way."

As if of one mind, Deynas and Naago both slammed the remainder of their drinks.

Settek chuckled and followed their example.

Kaira shook her head at them and did the same.

Naago put a hand on the arm of his chair and sank back into it. Deynas wavered on his feet as the room spun around him. He dropped into the nearest chair.

"What..." Naago hung his head, unable to finish the sentence.

All at once, the room stopped spinning and came into sharp focus, every color brighter than it had been a moment ago. The effect was strongest with Kato whose scaled hide gleamed, as if lit from within, the gold of his eyes flickering like candle flames. His claws looked longer and sharper now and his wings rippled with continuous subtle waves of color. He was truly the most magnificent creature Deynas had ever seen and he was looking them all over shrewdly now, his color darkening to a deep maroon.

"For as long as Endless can live, I would have expected you to be more patient," Kato grumbled. "So be it. As you've noticed by now, there was something extra in your drinks. The Keeper will be able to enter the Halls of the Blooded beneath the ruins because her spirit resides within and because she is... unique. In order for you to enter, you need to see the world with the vision of a spirit."

"But the Blooded Women aren't spirits," Naago stated, his gaze zeroed in on one of Kato's spectacular wings as he spoke.

"The Blooded *are* spirits. The Blooded Women, however, are flesh constructs. Each group of six women has one blood spirit bound to it." He held a hand up to silence the question forming on Deynas's tongue. "We can discuss your questions later, Deynas-ra, if there is a later for you." The gold eyes swept over them. "The Halls beneath the city belong to the blood spirits. The vision I have given you will get you inside, but it will not get you out again. The way out is unknown to me. You must enter the Halls knowing that you may not ever leave. You must be willing to risk your lives for her." Kato looked at Deynas now. "Are you willing to risk that, Deynas-ra?"

Deynas stood and inclined his head to the warlord. "I am."

Kato's gaze flickered to the next seat over. "And you, Naago-ra?"

Naago was a little slower to stand, but he also inclined his head once he was on his feet. "I am."

"As am I."

They all turned to Settek as the young crossbreed stood.

Kato shook his head, a red so dark it was almost black cascaded down his scaled hide. "You are not going, Settek. This is not your fight."

Settek took a step forward. In the new sight the drug gave Deynas, the crossbreed's mane rippled with shimmers of defiant gold. He was every bit his father's son.

"It is my fight, Father. I will stand beside the Endless and help the Keeper for my own reasons."

"It has taken a long time for you to find your worth, Settek. I would not choose to lose you now. Are you certain you want to do this?"

"I must, Father, if I wish to keep that worth."

Pride and a hint of sorrow shone in Kato's eyes when he inclined his head slowly to his son. "Then it shall be. Kaira will lead you to the entrance, but she will not go in with you." He turned a firm gaze on his daughter. "Will she?"

Kaira stood and held up her hands in a show of concession. "Of course not."

"Wait." Settek scowled at his sister. "Why does she know the way?"

Kato chuckled. "Because, until recently, I could not trust you with such knowledge. Go now. The drug will only last so long."

Settek set down his glass and stared at it for a moment. He smirked. "You knew I would go or you wouldn't have had her put the drug in my drink."

Kato only smiled, the expression still tinted with sorrow, and gestured toward the door with one clawed hand.

Deynas put the pendant around his neck then turned to follow Kaira out, but he felt a hand on his shoulder, holding him back. The other three continued out the door as he turned. There was no one close enough to have touched him.

Kato regarded him solemnly from where he stood before his desk. "Naago-ra and Settek do this for the Keeper. Would you still do this if you found her in a new host? Would you be willing to die for her if the Endless woman you love was gone?"

"Yes."

Kato shook his head. "I do not care what your answer is now. Think about it while you follow my daughter. If both you and Naago-ra are with the Keeper then the host's *umahk-ra* will be complete and they will both be stronger for it. However, when you stand before the entrance to the Halls of the Blooded, if you have any doubt, do not go in. You will only do more harm that way."

"If this matters so much to you, come with us."

"I cannot. If you survive, perhaps I will explain this to you." Kato turned his back to Deynas, putting his glorious wings on full display. "Now go."

Deynas inclined his head once before hurrying after the others.

They followed Kaira down to the ruin level and through a long corridor that took them around behind the arena. Thick as the walls were, they did little to muffle the sounds of fighting and the bloodthirsty roar of the crowd. At the end of the corridor, she turned them away from a door that led, from the sounds of it, out into the stadium and gestured to a square slab of stone inset into the floor in an alcove. The alcove saw little use judging from the layer of dust over the slab.

Naago and Settek knelt next to it, brushing away ages of dust to reveal finger holes.

Deynas let them handle the heavy lifting. Although his shoulder felt much better, he saw no reason to test it yet. Kato's words suggested there might be ample need for that soon enough. While they slid the heavy stone out of the way, Deynas fingered the staff grip at his belt. Despite the hit it had taken from the demon plowing into the ground with the weapon stuck in its spine, the staff was still fully functional. He wouldn't have expected to be using it again after that. Of course, he was a little surprised to be doing anything at all after that encounter.

Twice now he had fought to protect the Keeper and he had entrusted her with his mother's pendant. Was it all just because she wore the body of the woman he loved? Was it because the Keeper was a revered creature of legend? Was there something deeper to it? If she wore another flesh, would he have risked so much to keep her safe? He couldn't hate her, but how much of that was because he could see Argus bleeding through in candid moments? Was there any way to know the answer for certain?

He glanced up to find Kaira watching him. She immediately turned her gaze to the dark hole Naago and Settek had finished uncovering. The stench of blood and waste wafted up through the opening, more concentrated than anything he'd smelled in the Undercity.

"I'll go first," Settek announced, his nose wrinkling as he stared into the depths, his long hesitation betraying how he really felt about making the descent into the pungent region below the Undercity.

Kaira nodded. "Naago, you come last and slide the stone back in if you can."

Settek stepped down onto the ladder and descended out of sight. Kaira started to follow, but Deynas cut her off.

She batted her thick lashes at him. "Trying to be gallant?"

He found himself grinning back and wondering if she had some of her father's glamour ability or was simply that charming. Either way, she was a pleasure to be around. "Maybe a little."

She slid the shoulder pack she carried around behind her and tapped a dagger at her belt with one long fingernail. "I'm not completely helpless."

"Get a move on," Naago snapped.

Kaira turned a delighted smile on the other Endless man, perhaps pleased by the show of jealous temper, then she stepped back and gestured for Deynas to precede her down into the hole.

Deynas shrugged the moment off. It made little sense to take offense at Naago's jealousy, not when he would much rather see it directed at Kaira than at the Keeper. He stepped down on the ladder and began his descent. A hand caught his wrist as he passed below the level of the floor. He looked up at Kaira.

She held a small silver ball down to him. "It's a light. Right now, your spirit sight will help you see in the dark. When that goes away, you will be nearly blind down there. Keep this with you." She turned it to show him a little silver bump. "Press and rub the nodule here to turn it on." She winked then. "For future reference, that turns me on too."

Deynas chuckled and took the ball, tucking it in a pocket as he resumed his descent. The rungs were narrow and the ladder creaked with each step. Looking down, he could see a large corridor opening up below his feet, the ladder dropping down in the center of a four-way intersection. Settek was stepping out of view down one corridor. When Deynas dropped below the ceiling of the corridor, Settek cried out and came flying back out of the dark as if thrown, landing hard on the floor. Something that looked like a large dog, only covered in white scales instead of fur, landed on his chest, sinking its teeth into the arm the crossbreed threw up in front of his face. Settek grabbed the beast around the neck with his other hand, claws digging in, searching for access to the softer flesh beneath the scales.

Deynas shoved off from the ladder and landed hard next to the struggle. His staff grip was already in hand and armed by the time his feet hit the ground. With an overhead sweep, he brought the blade down through the beast's neck, severing his head. The jaws slackened and the body slumped to one side, leaving the head hanging in Settek's grip. The crossbreed stared wide-eyed for a moment at the blade of the staff where the swing stopped no more than a finger's width away from his chest. After a second, he took a breath and turned the head in his hand, eyeing the cut a hairsbreadth back from his fingers.

He tossed the head to the side and looked up at Deynas. "Very…precise. Thank you."

Deynas moved the weapon away and offered a hand. Settek accepted without any of the hesitation he had shown when their roles had been reversed in the village. Admirable. He was starting to like the bastard.

Deynas pulled him up. His shoulder felt strong. Whatever Kaira had put in his drink, it was potent stuff.

Kaira was hurrying down the ladder, hips swinging back and forth in a distracting way with each step down. The pants and shirt she had on hugged to her skin in such a way that he found it almost more arousing than the scanty bits of clothing she wore when working in the hotel.

She glanced down over her shoulder at them. "I heard someone shout. Is everyone all right?"

Blood flowed from the bite on Settek's arm. The crossbreed sniffed at the wound and snorted. "Venom," he growled. "I could use a dip in the medical kit."

Naago began his descent while Kaira gave Settek a vial of something to drink. She cleaned and wrapped the wound in the quick, efficient manner of someone familiar with minor injuries. With that done, she gave him a rag to wipe the beast's blood off his chest.

Deynas inspected the dead creature, its scaled hide leached of color by life underground. "What is it?"

Kaira glanced at the beast. "Darro. Cave-dwelling canines. I've never seen one before, but I've heard of them. I thought they would be bigger than that."

Once on the ground, Naago gave the bandage and the blood-soaked rag a cursory glance. He met Settek's eyes. "Place seems less then welcoming. Are you still fit to fight?"

Settek nodded. "I'd be even better if this place didn't smell like corpse rot."

Kaira started walking down one corridor. "It's better when you get away from the fighting rings."

Deynas hurried after her, matching his pace to her long purposeful strides once he caught up. "How big is this place?"

"These corridors are part of a natural cavern system hidden beneath the ancient Endless settlement. They were kept secret from the human races for a long time, protected by some of the spirits and demons that live here. There was no surface access from the city until Father had the arena in the ruins restored and an entrance cut down into them. A few other warlords have accessed this section since. They work well for moving illegal supplies if you can contend with the occasional beasts like the one Settek scared up. Father initiated a project to reinforce and improve the portion beneath the city. Farther out, the caverns are mostly untouched by such development. You could spend several weeks down here and not see as much as a third of the chambers and passages."

Deynas looked around the corridor. In places, new formations were growing on the walls, ceiling and floors. The natural cave working to reclaim developed corridors. Even the steel pillars set at regular intervals along both sides of the passage had developed a layer of new growth over their surfaces. In many places, the new growth bore stains of red and brown due to the blood and filth draining down from the Undercity.

He tried not to breathe the rancid odor of the Undercity waste in through his nose, but breathing through his mouth made it so he could taste the filth on his tongue. Better to smell it, he decided.

"Kaira is our guide and I understand why Deynas and I are here. Why are you here, Settek?"

Kaira gave Naago a cutting glance. "Don't pester him."

"It's fine. All our lives are in danger here. He has a right to ask."

Settek fell into step beside the other Endless and Deynas dropped back next to them, curious. The crossbreed met his eyes for a moment, the bright gold in his gaze dimming. The change sent sorrow through Deynas in a slow wave. Settek also shared some of his father's mood altering glamour it seemed.

"When the demons took the city five years ago, Kato told our mother to flee with the other Endless. She refused. She told him she would rather die than live her life without him."

Naago gave a derisive snort and Settek grabbed his arm, jerking the man around to face him. The crossbreed's claws pressed against Naago's skin, his arm trembling with the effort of restraint, and Deynas couldn't help remembering how easily one of those claws had sunk through the fabric of the chair in the temple.

"If you are unable to believe an Endless woman could love a demon that deeply than I would ask that you keep your bigoted hands off my sister. I will only ask nicely once."

Naago jerked his arm free, cutting himself on Settek's claws as he did so, and reached for his sword. Settek's gold eyes were on fire, his mane flaring bright, but he didn't make a move for his own weapon. Deynas dropped his hand to his staff grip, a little shocked to realize he meant to use it in the crossbreed's defense if necessary.

"Stop!" Kaira stomped one boot in a manner that might have been charming if the situation were less serious.

Settek's blazing eyes stayed locked on Naago, but the elder Endless man turned his pale gaze to Kaira. After a moment, he moved his hand away from his sword and faced Settek again.

"I apologize. It is because of your sister that I know such love could be possible. I just haven't quite reconciled the idea with so many years of trained prejudice. I have lived a very long time and yet it seems that I still have much to learn. Please go on."

After a few more tense seconds, Settek nodded and they continued walking, though Deynas found himself walking between the two now, his hand still poised near the staff grip. Damp ground squished under their feet and the steady dripping of water sounded in the dark.

"Mother asked Kato to end her life, knowing that end would be gentler than anything the invading demons would do to her. He granted her wish. I think that is the only time I've ever seen him cry. I remember him kneeling over her, his scales faded to a wretched charcoal. How I hated him at that moment." A flare of dark red swept down Settek's mane as he spoke those words. "Then the Keeper appeared. She looked confused and said that she'd heard him calling her. What he said to her then has always stayed with me because the words seemed so odd. He said, 'I beseech you, keep her spirit. Please. For all the times I tried to help you and all the years I have cared for you, I ask only this one thing.' She did as he asked and kept Mother's spirit."

"*Umahk-ra,*" Deynas corrected under his breath.

Settek nodded, his expression rife with remembered sorrow. "Yes. Father used that word when he spoke to the Keeper. When she was done, the Keeper fled. She seemed to become agitated and uncomfortable in his presence. He said that it was because the Blooded Women didn't want her near him. That was the last time I saw her in that host. Father never told me anything more about his relationship with the Keeper, but I knew from his voice and his color when he spoke to her that she was very important to him and he to her, even if the Blooded Women wouldn't allow her to remember why. Because of those things, though I do not fully understand them, she is also important to me and I would see her freed from her captors."

Ahead of them, Kaira sniffed and wiped at her eyes. Naago trotted up beside her and put an arm around her shoulders, whispering something in her ear. Deynas warded off a spark of jealousy when she leaned into him by calling the Keeper up in his mind, her smile and her odd, yet beautiful silver-black eyes.

"The Keeper told me she had kept Endless before, though she couldn't remember the circumstances. If Kato helped create her, it makes sense that she would be drawn to him when he called and be willing to keep the woman he loved." In Naago's defense, it did feel odd to speak of a demon loving an Endless woman. If one listened to the tribe elders, children like Settek and Kaira only ever came from rape and were born unredeemably corrupted by the loathsome circumstances leading to their conception. Settek's story contradicted that.

"I suppose that makes her almost family." Settek visibly pushed down his sorrow and bared his pointed teeth in a friendly grin.

Deynas almost smiled back, then the image of the crossbreed nodding to his companions while they were having their duel, a gesture that had led rather directly to Misa's death, flashed in his head. Because of that, they would never be friends. Deynas hoped Misa would understand the circumstances that brought them to be on the same side in this. If things hadn't gone so badly that day, he could easily learn to like Settek, but then they probably wouldn't be traveling together now. That was how life worked.

"You all right?"

The muscles in his shoulders tightened at the concern in the crossbreed's tone. He shrugged his shoulders, forcing the tension away. "Fine. How long did it take you to forgive Kato for killing your mother?"

Settek stared at the two walking ahead of them, his mane changing to a dark dull bronze. "I don't know that I have any more than I've forgiven her for asking him to do it. I'm not sure I know how to."

Deynas watched Kaira's feet. Her boots had two-inch heels. They were the shortest heels he'd seen her in yet. Impractical as hell in the underground passages, but they did keep an attractive sway in her hips. "I suppose that's one of those things that fades over time."

Settek's chuckle had a bitter edge. "Good thing both demons and Endless tend to live a long time."

"Indeed." Deynas smiled wryly. If things didn't go poorly down here beneath the ruins then maybe they could be friends someday. Fifty years or so would take away some of the sting of the lives lost between them.

The steel pillars and the brick lining the corridor ended abruptly and they moved onto bare stone. The floor curved down and the ceiling rose up. The walls spread away to either side. They had come to a massive natural chamber. Great limestone columns spotted the room, set out randomly as if arranged by a mad architect amidst hundreds of stalactites and stalagmites spearing up and down like the misaligned fangs of some deformed beast. To one side of the room, seven glowing silver forms swayed back and forth around a deep pool. They didn't acknowledge the intruders in any way.

Kaira disengaged from Naago and slowed enough for them to catch up. She indicated the forms with a quick glance and spoke in a hushed voice. "Water spirits. They're very private creatures. If not for the spirit sight, you wouldn't see them at all. You'll be doing them a kindness if you simply pretend they aren't there."

Deynas nodded, though it was harder not to look at them now that he wasn't supposed to than it would have been otherwise.

Settek leaned down closer to him and murmured. "You ever notice how being told not to do something makes you really want to do it?"

Deynas exhaled a soft laugh and kept his eyes on the path ahead.

They left the room through a smaller passage and moved on into another chamber much like the last, only the formations here had been largely destroyed, pieces of them strewn over the floor all around. A closer inspection showed that many were reattached where they lay by new rock formation growing slowly over the top. It had been a long while since the original destruction took place.

"What happened here?"

Kaira glanced back at him. "There are claw marks on many of the stones. Father says some demon probably threw a tantrum down here. A couple of the adjacent corridors are also significantly damaged."

The large corridor they turned down then smelled powerfully of wet dog. The new stench made Deynas realize that the smells of blood and waste from the city had faded. This odor was familiar somehow, though he couldn't quite place it.

Settek leaned close to him again and murmured, "The beast that attacked me earlier smelled like this."

Kaira glanced back at them and put a finger to her lips.

They navigated the uneven terrain around a high wall of stone draperies. The sound of growling reached them, coming from somewhere within an opening just past the drapery wall. They crept forward. As Deynas moved past the opening, he could see five of the scaled white canines tearing at a corpse. He caught a glimpse of toes sticking out under the belly of one beast and looked away, barely breathing for fear of alerting them. A lone darro was something they could deal with. A whole pack of them would test their collective combat ability.

They had cleared the opening and were moving on when a huge, oddly patterned boulder to one side of the corridor shifted. The beast had been lying curled away from them so that its scaled form appeared, at a glance, to be nothing more than another limestone coated rock. Now it swung its long snout around and started to rise, a deep growl vibrating through the air around them.

The growling in the adjacent chamber cut off abruptly. The pack's, or rather, the litter's mother had woken and was not happy about having company. She was at least three times the size of her offspring that were now emerging from the opening behind them, creeping out in a low hunting stance.

Settek caught Kaira's arm as she started to back away from the agitated mother. There was nowhere to back away to. They were caught between the mother and her offspring.

"What now?" Kaira's voice was steadier than Deynas would have expected under the circumstances.

Naago glanced at him and Settek. They all dropped their hands to their weapons. He nodded faintly. They stepped apart enough to give each other fighting space and drew.

Deynas armed the staff with a sharp flick of his wrist. "Now we survive. We're no good to the Keeper dead."

CHAPTER TWENTY TWO

The Keeper had never worn a sword before, not that she could recall, but Argus insisted they find one before going beneath the ruin level. The weapon they were drawn to in the fighter's quarters beneath The Firelight felt unexpectedly comfortable sheathed at her side. It was an Endless blade, light and strong and the Endless woman delighted in the weapon's presence the same way she delighted in piloting a flyer.

For her part, the Keeper didn't think they would have need of a physical weapon with the cloak hiding them, but she didn't see where it would hurt anything to carry it. What interested her most was that the decision to obtain the weapon had been a conscious compromise between her and the host. Whatever Kato might be to her, whatever his motives, taking his advice to work together with Argus instead of fighting her felt right. Even with the weight of the towering city bearing down from above, she felt lighter and stronger from the first moment she gave up the fight to keep the Endless woman's mind in submission.

Now, with her own memories lost to her, she took pleasure in wandering through Argus's memories, feeling what she felt and taking in the Endless woman's motivations and emotions as if they were her own. Argus welcomed her, accepting their union and facing the possibility of her death with strength of character the Keeper admired.

It was not hard to see now why Deynas loved this woman, and the memories of their time together made it easy to see why she loved him too. The only shame was that he might never truly know how Argus felt or how she felt, for she could no longer help feeling the Endless woman's love for him whenever he crossed their mind.

The caverns beneath the ruins fascinated Argus. The Keeper had been there before. She remembered keeping several spirits in those dark depths. Despite how dark it was, she had no trouble seeing there. The changes the Keeper's presence wrought upon her host gave her eyes a spirit's ability to see in the darkness. Maybe, if they succeeded, she would finally understand her nature and what place she held among the creatures that shared this world.

There was much life in the caverns, from the microscopic life forms she could sense, but not see, to the serpentine demon she spotted filling an entire side chamber with is almost translucent coils. Water spirits abounded, gathering around the many pools. When she approached them, they bowed respectfully, but any attempt to communicate sent them diving down to disappear in the water's depths. She would get no guidance from them. Without help, she followed her instincts and hoped they would be enough to lead her to what she sought. If not, then a call to keep would eventually drag her out of this place – that or hunger.

She knelt beside a large pool and brushed the tips of the roots on her right hand through the water, gazing down at the formations deep within that blurred with the ripples she created. There was no telling if all of her fascination with the uniqueness of this underground realm came from Argus or if some of it came from her, though she suspected the former. Either way, she took pleasure in seeing the dark underworld through the Endless woman's perspective.

The harmony they'd found in their relationship had its down side. Her anger gradually faded to the background and reluctance to risk losing this peace overpowered her sense of urgency. If they failed and Argus died, the Blooded Women would erase all of this and things would go back the way they had been. She wouldn't know it was wrong. Kato said this host was strong. Without such a host, would she ever get another chance to fix what he said was broken?

Two of the darro that roamed the caverns raced through the chamber. They were just pups, bounding about and snapping playfully at one another as they ran. Their mother would have a den somewhere close by, but the Keeper wasn't concerned. Such beasts could not see her unless she wished them to. She watched the pups for a while, brushing her fingers absently through the water and smiling at their antics.

A few water spirits lifted their heads from one of the other pools and the darro pups stopped their play to investigate, inching close then leaping away when one silvery form reached toward them. Water spirits shied away from the more sentient beings, but they appeared to enjoy tempting the pups. They splashed water at the two and one jumped up to snap his teeth on the spray. It soon became a game, with the water spirits kicking up sprays of water and the pups forgetting their caution to leap after the water in the air.

She enjoyed watching the game until a call tugged at her awareness. It came from both Naago and Deynas. The call wasn't direct. They weren't intentionally summoning her to them, but they were both thinking of her and there was an edge of distress in their thoughts. More importantly, the call came from somewhere very close.

The Keeper disappeared and reappeared in another corridor of the caverns. Deynas, Naago, Settek and Kaira were there, blocked in front by a full-grown female darro and behind by five juveniles, her litter. They had weapons drawn and the female was poised to attack. Deynas was stepping forward, bringing his staff around for a strike, when the Keeper appeared.

Argus drew the sword and tossed it into her left hand, bringing it up in a quick motion to block Deynas' strike when the Keeper stepped in front of him. She placed her right hand on the beast's nose. Metal clashed and Deynas froze. The beast also froze in place, calming at her touch the way simple creatures tended to. The juveniles shifted, restless and confused by the sudden change in their mother's temperament.

"You will not harm this creature," she stated. "Go around behind me and move on. When you are safe, I will follow."

Deynas hesitated, staring at her with a peculiar expression, then he lowered his staff and led the others around behind her and past the mother. The Keeper let the sword sink to her side and stroked the beast's muzzle. It settled, sinking down to curl on the ground beside her. The juveniles approached, inching near, and the mother began to groom the first one that ventured within reach. When Deynas and the others had gone around a bend in the corridor, the Keeper went unseen. The juveniles started at her disappearance, but their mother's lack of concern soothed them.

She found the others waiting for her in a small side chamber well away from the mother and her pups. They were all staring at her with an odd fascination when she entered and fingers of dread crept slowly up her spine. Naago took a step toward her then stopped when Deynas, who was closer to begin with, cut him off.

"You're okay." There was relief in his voice along with a breathy enthrallment.

The Keeper looked into his blue eyes and saw herself reflected there. She placed her right hand on his cheek and closed her eyes to see what he was seeing. Then she understood. Her hair and the tendril at her temple gleamed with silvery light that also speared out through the narrow slit between her closed eyelids. A dark violet aura flickered around her. He was seeing her the way a spirit would see her. They all were. That could only mean one thing.

She opened her eyes and jerked her hand away, taking a step back from him. Her glare encompassed all of them. "You've taken spirit essence," she hissed. "You realize that no less than two elemental spirits must die to create a single ounce of that." Understanding clicked within Argus at her words and the Endless woman suddenly shared her anger.

"Argus… I mean…" Deynas faltered, his words failing as he stared at her with tormented longing.

Naago spoke in the awkward silence. "Kato said it was the only way we could pass into the Halls of the Blooded with you."

The Keeper felt a stinging in her eyes as she looked around at them. Settek and Kaira nodded in support of Naago's words.

"We're here to help you get back your *umahk-ra*," Deynas stated, his tone daring her to try disputing the idea.

"You would help me? Even if it means putting your lives at risk?" Her gaze moved inexorably back to Deynas. "Even if it means putting Argus at risk?"

He nodded, holding her gaze, his resolve unshaking. "Yes. The Blooded Women can't be allowed to hold you prisoner any longer."

Pride welled in Argus, but it was the Keeper herself who yearned to embrace him. This was the part of him

Argus loved most, defiant, confident, and willing to face whatever life threw at him, but now wasn't the time or place for indulging their feelings. "I appreciate your intentions more than I can possibly express, but must insist that all of you go back. This is my battle."

Settek shook his head, his mane, shot through with defiant crimson, snapped back and forth with the vigorous dissent. "Not anymore."

Their set expressions told her all she needed to know. Fighting with them over this would be a waste of valuable time. "I don't suppose you know the way then?"

Kaira, who'd been hanging back behind the others, finally stepped forward. "I do."

The Keeper exhaled a mix of frustration and relief as the manipulations of Warlord Kato became apparent. He had known all along where to find the Halls. He never intended for her to face this alone. Whatever their history, it appeared that he was trying to protect her. "We will follow you then."

Kaira walked ahead of the group to lead them on. Both Naago and Deynas appeared inclined to watch her as she moved and it wasn't hard to see why. Argus might be a lovely woman, but Kaira's every curve spoke of intimate pleasures, her movement overflowing with sexual promise. It was almost as if she had been manufactured for seduction. Did she ever get weary of being an object of lust for any male that looked at her?

When Deynas finally moved to follow, the Keeper fell naturally into step beside him.

Naago deliberately moved around to her other side. "That was a skilled block you made back there. I didn't know you could even wield a blade."

"Argus is quite adept with a sword. I let her handle Deynas-ra while I took care of the mother."

"If we get through this, perhaps she'd be up for a friendly duel."

There was a suggestive tone in Naago's voice and Deynas tensed beside her. He gave Naago a cross look. "If you're so eager to duel, perhaps you'd be willing to try me first."

"We have a common goal for now. Let us focus on that, please." The Keeper maintained a soothing tone and she discreetly touched Deynas' arm.

Argus found their rivalry over her amusing and even a little flattering, but she agreed with the Keeper's inclination to keep them from each other's throats. Argus also savored the brief contact with Deynas and they were both pleased that he didn't pull away. They still cared for Naago, but the intimacy they shared with him didn't supplant the preexisting connection Argus had to Deynas. At some point, if they all lived, she would have to speak with both men about those things. For now, retrieving her spirit and surviving the process in this flesh were the priorities. If that failed, none of the rest mattered.

The path they followed, weaving through the complex maze of the cave, took them ever downward. Other life appeared deeper in. Centipede creatures, like the hypnotists only with translucent white flesh, crawled on the walls and ceiling. They paused now and then to reach out with their antennae, seeing the intruders through delicate sensors that picked up vibrations in the air. Rock spirits, disturbed by their passage, faded in and out of the walls, glowing a blue so dark and rich it was hard to look upon in the blackness of the caverns.

The passage they followed ended, the floor dropping away into darkness below, the walls and ceiling opening out so dramatically that they couldn't make out the dimensions of the chamber beyond that point. Water could be heard flowing, a distant rumble somewhere below them. To the right of the passage, before it dropped off, a stone door was set deep into the rock with symbols etched around its perimeter in the language of the spirits. Only spirits could see those symbols normally, spirits and the Keeper. With the aid of the essence they had consumed, the other four would also see those symbols, shining like starlight in the dark.

They stopped, facing the door with the solemn look of those attending death rites. Rock spirits moved in and out of the walls around the door, curious about them.

Kaira hugged her arms around herself. "This is it," she announced into the silence, perhaps seeking comfort through the familiar sound of her own voice. "I'll wait here for you."

Naago cleared his throat. The sound echoed around them. "Before we go in there, I'd like to ask a favor of you all."

They turned to him. He continued to stare at the door and the Keeper felt an itch of apprehension building.

"If I die, assuming the rest of you don't share my fate, someone must take the violin out of my flyer and return it to my daughter Maro in Valaya."

"You have a daughter?"

Naago offered Deynas a solemn nod. "Yes."

"I don't suppose it would do any good to tell you not to go on for her sake."

"No."

Deynas nodded and turned to the door. "It will be done."

"Thank you."

A civil exchange for the two men. Perhaps there was hope for this situation.

The Keeper stepped forward and closed her eyes. The symbols shone brighter still, painful to look upon. The space between them revealed an opening with a long corridor stretching beyond. The entrance was only passable by those who could see the symbols.

For now, they were all capable of entering, but what would happen when it came time to leave?

She moved through and turned around to see what it looked like from within. The stone appeared solid behind her, not even the outline of the door visible. There were no symbols on this side. Spirit sight would not get them back out. Her chest tightened.

Don't come through.

Even as she thought it, Deynas appeared and Naago almost stepped on his heels he followed so close. Settek followed only a few seconds behind. They all turned to look at the door and their sour expressions negated any need to explain. There was no going back.

They moved in unison, turning to face what lay ahead. The corridor that stretched away from them looked as if some large creature had tunneled it. The stone walls were devoid of formation as if they had only just been made, but the Keeper could feel great age in the air around them, age that preceded her existence at the very least. It was warmer here as well, warm and faintly clammy, creating a light layer of moisture on her skin.

Settek, Naago and Deynas all moved their hands nearer their weapons as they walked down the corridor. Argus started to move her hand toward the sword, but the Keeper resisted. Weapons would do no good in this place. Life could not exist long in here. Only the blood spirits lived here and no mere weapon was going to harm them.

At the first intersection they came to she turned right without hesitation, following a pull that grew stronger with every step she took. The others followed without question, trusting her, believing in her.

Settek spoke into the tense silence. "We won't be coming this way again."

They all paused to look behind them. The corridor they had come down was gone. Seamless rock covered the way as if the passage had never existed. They continued on.

I will see you all safely from this place. I promise.

Naago and Deynas moved closer to her. Had they heard the thought? They were *umahk-ra-uden* after all. They would be sensitive to such a desperate sentiment directed at them.

She hoped it wasn't as desperate as it felt, but this place felt like death. It had a scent to it reminiscent of the fighting rings. The smell of blood, both stale and fresh, whispered through the air around them, clinging to the bored-out stone walls and floor.

Fingers of fear crept insidiously up her spine and her nerves screamed at her to leave this place, but the pull ahead was still growing stronger and the corridors continued to close up behind them. It began to feel like an endless trek. Only the draw of her spirit, as intense now as the call to keep, kept her going. The others wouldn't falter, she knew, so long as she appeared certain of her path.

They turned a corner into a large circular chamber. At the far side, behind a rippling, translucent barrier, an ethereal violet form glided forward. Its shape was inconstant, but two translucent tendrils reached out toward her, the hint of fingers or claws almost taking form. Her breath caught in her throat. The spirit of the Keeper.

We know why you have come, Keeper. A voice whispered in her mind.

Five more ethereal forms moved into the room from side passages, gliding out to stop between them and the barrier. These forms were pale red, almost pink. They had no distinct shape beyond a sense of tallness as they hovered in the center.

Her three companions moved as if to draw weapons and she put her hands out to either side, using a small downward motion to discourage them. They stopped, but didn't relax. She gestured for them to stay back and walked forward. Argus cringed within her, recalling the night the Blooded Women took her and the Keeper shuddered with remembered fear that wasn't her own. She pushed it down and faced the spirits.

"Will you give me back what is mine?"

We did not take it from you nor are we beholden to those who placed it here. You are welcome to it.

Could it be that easy?

The barrier vanished and the violet form swept forward, diving into her like a spirit for keeping. The Keeper closed her eyes…

…and raced back through over a thousand years of memory, starting with the death of each host and running back through to her first thought in that flesh, then moving on to the death of the host that came before. She plunged through memory, revisiting host after host, the longest-lived surviving almost two hundred years before the Blooded Women destroyed her. Few had died natural deaths. Most shared the same end. At some point, the Keeper was drawn to the city, to Kato specifically, and that encounter marked the beginning of the end for each.

Kato had called her to him during the takeover of the city, called her to keep an Endless woman, and she had answered, dooming the host that preceded Argus. The moment was crisp in her memory. Kato, his color dark and dulled with misery, kneeling on the floor and pleading with her to keep his love. Then the Blooded Women destroyed that host. After that, they did everything wrong. They moved into the New City and put the Keeper in this host. A host with the ability to move her *umahk-ra* independent of her flesh. A host already anchored to the world outside her flesh by the fragment of her *umahk-ra* in Deynas. Once again, she'd gone to Kato. Why had he never come to her?

Memory drew her back even farther, back to the time the demons overtook the original settlement here, when the ruins were still the home of an ancient Endless tribe. They had come for her. An entire tribe demolished because the ones controlling the Blooded Women wanted control of the Keeper. Kato had stood protecting her outside of the arena, his wings outstretched and his color splendid with rage. Blooded Women faced him, no fewer than fifteen groups of six women each. Their white dresses and faces glowing in the light of a bright half-moon.

Give her to us, they demanded.

"Never. She will never be yours."

There had been no negotiation, no attempt to persuade him. All of the Blooded Women had simply opened their eyes, bathing Kato in that ghastly pink light. They tore half of his spirit out of him and imprisoned it somewhere deep in the caverns beneath the arena, using it to bind him to that place. Then they had ripped her spirit from her completely and made her theirs. That was why Kato never came to her. He was trapped by his sundered spirit.

Memory drew her back to the time before that night. The host that she resided in then had been her first. That first host trained for long hours and competed in rigorous physical, moral and intellectual trials to prove her suitability as the Keeper's host. The roots upon her skin were a source of great pride. The Undying, the father of the Endless, had entrusted her with his most treasured creation.

They had existed as The Undying intended, working together almost as one, with the memories, goals, and ambitions of the host dominant. The Keeper was only a controlling force when a spirit needed keeping. The rest of the time, she was a part of the Endless woman, like an extra facet of her personality, their thoughts and decisions shared. That was how the relationship was intended to work.

Argus had been wronged. All of the hosts since the first had been. And The Keeper had been wronged as well.

The Keeper opened her eyes, letting the memories sink to the back of her mind. Argus was present now, more present than she had ever been, almost more so than the Keeper herself. Anger burned in them, one shared sense of rage, but the spirits around them were not to blame.

"How do we leave this place?"

Deynas inhaled sharply behind her. She didn't have to ask why. She'd spoken not only with Argus's voice, but with her confidence. She emerged from her memories as part of Argus. They were one being and a wonderful sense of completion united them.

Naago stepped forward, taking his eyes off the blood spirits for a quick second to look at her. "Are you all right?"

"More so than I have been in some time."

"Are they speaking to you?"

She glanced over at him. "You can't hear them?"

He shook his head.

We do not speak to them, Keeper. You alone have any right at all to be in this place. But it is good that they have come. These are the true Halls of the Blooded, not some mockery made by the blood spirits bound to the Blooded Women. For you to leave here, someone must pay the blood price. It is the only way.

"What is the price?"

The others shifted around her, unease rippling through them. They knew a discussion was going on, but they were only getting one side of the conversation.

Blood must flow, strong and true. So long as the blood flows, the passage will open up before you. If the blood stops, the passage will close. The rest may pass through the door only when the one who pays passes from this life. We leave it to you to choose which of them will pay this price.

The Keeper became acutely aware of her companions, the smell of anxiety on them, the turbulent restlessness of their spirits. This time she spoke to the blood spirits through her reclaimed spirit.

One of us must die?

Yes. That is how you open the way out.

The Keeper fought an urge to look around the others. *You say you are not beholden to those who imprisoned my spirit here. Why not just let us leave?*

The rock around us is alive. It responds to our needs. If we hunger, it opens, allowing the scent of blood to lure in living creatures. When we are sated, it opens again to let survivors leave. The spirit forms shifted and pulsed now, illustrating an impatience to feed.

Can you not let us leave and lure in some other creature?

You misunderstand. We do not control the rock. It responds to our needs. Your intrusion woke us. Now we hunger and there is food within. It will not open until we are sated.

The increased flickering gave her the sense that they were losing patience with the conversation. Their hunger was growing. If she did not make a decision, they would soon make one for her. She and Argus made the decision together. It came easily.

Then I will pay the price.

The spirits stilled, surprise muting their hunger for a moment. *You would sacrifice your spirit and this host for these others. Does this host agree?*

We are of one mind.

Then it shall be so. There was a sharp pain on the inside of her left wrist, like a dagger slicing down it, and blood began to flow warm over her palm and down her fingers. The spirits pulsed brightly. *Go now.*

CHAPTER TWENTY THREE

The Keeper turned her back on the blood spirits. Something was wrong. Deynas could see it in the forced calm of her expression.

"Are you all right?"

She nodded. The motion was too abrupt. "We must leave this place now. We can talk later."

Why did it feel like she was lying to him? And why did it seem like he could read her again the way he used to be able to read Argus?

Naago and Settek turned, so Deynas reluctantly followed them. The corridor behind them was still blocked, but when the Keeper stepped toward it, the rock receded. None of them hesitated then. They all wanted out of those corridors that smelled of death.

The dripping of water was louder now, a constant patter that moved along the passages with them. It was getting harder to see as well, the spirit essence losing its potency. Soon he would not be able to see the flickering violet aura around the Keeper that had flared so blindingly upon the reclaiming of her spirit. He would have to take out the light Kaira had given him. For now, he only really needed enough sight to follow the Keeper. She led them out with the same confidence that she had led them in with, if perhaps more haste.

Kato had been wrong. She hadn't needed them at all.

So far, they had only caused her trouble by drawing her to their conflict with the scaled beast. Only Kaira had been useful in her ability to lead them to the entrance. Had the warlord expected trouble from the blood spirits? As far as Deynas could tell, they had been rather obliging. Still, there had been something bothering the Keeper when she turned back to them. Maybe not all was as right as it appeared.

After a time, their pace slowed, as if the Keeper were no longer so sure of her direction or perhaps weary of walking. The aura around her and the silvery gleam of her hair faded away. Darkness closed around his vision. He drew out the small orb Kaira had given him. Trying not to think about her rather evocative comment when she explained how it worked, he rubbed firmly at the small nub. The orb lit, casting a pale yellow light over them. Naago, who had another light orb in his hand, glanced at Deynas and tucked his back in his pocket. One was sufficient for now.

The Keeper stumbled and reached out, catching herself on the arm Naago threw in front of her. Her skin looked unusually pale in the warm light. When she let go of Naago's arm, his sleeve was stained red in the shape of her hand. Deynas met Naago's startled look then reached out to catch her as she took another step and stumbled again. She leaned into him and her head sank onto his shoulder as if too heavy for her to carry any further.

Naago grabbed her arm and jerked up the sleeve. In the yellow light, they could see a clean cut down her wrist, blood running in a continuous stream from the wound to drip from the tips of her fingers. The other Endless man drew a dagger and used it to slice into the sleeve of his shirt at the shoulder. While he ripped the sleeve off, Settek helped Deynas lower her down on the cold stone with him, holding her against his chest.

"No." Her voice was weak, shaking.

"How did this happen," Deynas demanded.

"We're almost out. We have to keep going."

Settek lifted the wounded wrist and Naago brought the sleeve forward to wrap it. The Keeper reached out to try to push his hands away, but Deynas grabbed her arm, pinning it down, wary all the while of the pain she could inflict on him if she chose to.

"The blood must flow," she protested.

Naago proceeded to wrap her wrist, holding pressure on the wound.

Deynas forced a gentle tone. "What is this about?"

"The blood spirits' hunger must be sated or the door will not open. Someone must pay the blood price." When she finished speaking, she sagged against him as if the explanation had sapped the last of her strength.

Deynas looked at the other two. They both looked grim. Her words were clear enough. Someone had to die in order for them to leave. It wouldn't be her. Not if any of them could help it. They had come all this way to get her spirit back. If she died now, their efforts would have been in vain.

"It should be me," Naago stated. He was staring into the Keeper's face as if trying to memorize her every feature. "I've had a long life already."

Settek jumped to his feet and stared back the way they had come, his eyes burning, his mane flaring with molten gold. "Take me then. I will pay your blood price," he shouted.

"No," the Keeper whimpered and Deynas hugged her close.

"Crossbreed fool!" Naago also surged to his feet. "We will decide together."

Settek's eyes flared like sunlight and his body stiffened, every muscle tightening. Deep vertical slits opened in both of his wrists and on either side of his throat, releasing a torrent of dark blood. The crossbreed made a wretched sound in his throat, his eyes glazing over while his body jerked in the air as if held up by some unseen force.

Naago backed away, watching in horror. It was already too late to help Settek. The Keeper curled against Deynas and trembled with silent grief.

In seconds, it was over and Settek's body collapsed. His blood sank into the floor as if it were sponge rather than hard cold rock. The Keeper started to push away from Deynas then, reaching toward Settek with her right hand. He caught on and helped her turn around. She reached out toward the crossbreed. Tears streamed down her pale cheeks. Her eyes slid closed and her arm fell limp, her fingertips landing just shy of Settek's leg.

A hollowness filled Deynas as he stared at their dead companion. He touched the Keeper's neck, making sure she was only unconscious and nodded to Naago. The pulse was week, but still there.

The rock opened, revealing the cavern beyond and Kaira sitting across the passage from them, waiting. She didn't seem to see them.

Deynas held the Keeper close and nodded to Settek's body over her head. "Can you drag him out? We can't leave his body here."

Naago pressed his lips together and nodded. He moved around to slide his hands under Settek's shoulders and began to pull, grunting with the effort. Deynas lifted the Keeper in his arms and got to his feet. He walked to the opening and stepped through.

Kaira leapt to her feet when he emerged. She looked wide-eyed at the Keeper in his arms then peered frantically around him. The rock behind them looked solid, but Naago came through a moment later, dragging Settek behind him. Kaira cried out. Naago laid Settek outside the rock and she sank to her knees, grabbing her brother's shoulders and shaking them.

"Settek! Wake up. Please wake up." Tears had already begun to stream down her face. She knew he was gone. "You can't die like this. I need you."

Naago knelt alongside her and placed a hand on her shoulder. She shoved it away and curled over her brother, sobbing.

There was nothing they could do for her. Deynas lowered the Keeper down and sat with her.

She had been willing to die to get them out alive. Had Argus been part of that decision? It was exactly the kind of misguided self-sacrifice she would make. It hadn't occurred to her what it would do to them to go all this way only to lose her now. Even Settek would rather die than let that happen. He hadn't expected that.

Her breathing changed then and her eyes blinked open. She glanced at Kaira then pressed her face against his chest. Tears streamed down her cheeks.

"I couldn't keep his spirit."

"You tried." Deynas kept his voice soft so as not to disturb Kaira in her grieving.

"Yes," she murmured. "I made the choice, Deynas. Why couldn't you let me go?"

He glanced down at her wrist. There was a hint of blood on the bandage, but the bleeding was slow. He took it in his hand, holding pressure on the wound and sat quiet for a time, listening to Kaira's heartbroken sobs. Eventually, Naago tried to comfort the crossbreed woman again and this time she turned into his arms and her sobs worsened for a while, then finally began to quiet as he held her.

The Keeper had been hiding the truth from them when they left the blood spirits. He had been able to read her the way he could read Argus before, but he hadn't trusted himself. He took a breath, bracing for disappointment. "Argus?"

She didn't move. Her voice was little more than a weak whisper. "Yes."

There was a painful clenching in his chest. He didn't trust himself to speak. Instead, he kissed her head and held her a little tighter.

When Kaira calmed, Naago brought her attention to Argus's injury. Rock spirits gathered to watch them while they removed the bandage. The cloth stuck and blood started to flow heavier again when they pulled it away from the wound. Argus made a whimpering sound in her throat. Her eyes were closed and she made no effort at all to pull away this time. There was no point.

Kaira dug into her pack. She pulled out a small container and twisted off the lid. The greenish jelly within smelled oddly of bread. She scooped some out on her fingers and nodded to the wound. "Wipe it clean quickly then get out of the way. It won't adhere properly if there is too much fresh blood on the skin."

Naago did as directed. It took two tries to get proper adhesion, but the second time the green jelly closed down on the wound, sealing to the skin and pulling the edges of the cut together. It was fascinating and more than a little disturbing to watch.

Kaira settled back on her heels and stared at Argus. "The jelly's hardened. It won't come off now until the wound has healed. She's very pale. I don't expect she'll be walking out of here."

Deynas moved the injured arm back into a position that looked more comfortable. Then he brushed her hair back away from her face. One finger touched the root at her temple. He didn't mind it so much. Argus was there, even if the Keeper was an inseparable part of her. He could love them both.

Naago stood and stared down at Settek's body, frowning thoughtfully. "I don't see how we can carry her and move him too."

Kaira stood and faced Naago, her eyes flashing with defiant anger. "We're not leaving him here."

"You don't have to." They both looked down at Argus, but she was gazing up at Deynas. A tear slid down her cheek. "I'm so sorry."

His gut twisted and he clutched her tighter still as if strength alone could keep her there. "No. Not now." Then he was holding only air. "No!"

He clenched his fists and his long cry echoed through the caverns. The rock spirits startled, vanishing back into the stone.

"Fuck!" Naago spun and slammed his fist into the nearest wall. It came away bloody. He didn't seem to notice.

Kaira sank into a crouch and buried her face in her hands. Her shoulders shook with renewed sobs.

Deynas let his head fall back onto the stone, not caring that it hurt. He closed his eyes and drew in a ragged breath.

They had done it all for nothing. Settek had died for nothing. If this was another trap of the Blooded Women, and he didn't doubt that it was, he wouldn't be surprised if keeping the spirit and absorbing its death were enough to kill Argus in her current condition. He hadn't given her back the pendant either, though he had meant to, just in case. Now it was too late.

He cried out again, so loud that it made his throat hurt. It was all for nothing.

•

Argus retreated when they disappeared, letting the Keeper take control. She appeared in the Halls of the Blooded in the New city and sagged against the door-jamb of the main doorway leading into of the Temple of The Undying. Blooded Women filled the main chamber.

How many were there? The room blurred. She couldn't focus well enough to count them. The call drew her toward something on the floor in front of the statue of The Undying. Whatever it was, it stank worse than the tunnels beneath the fighting rings.

The Keeper closed her eyes, finding it easier to focus with pure spirit sight. She staggered out into the room with slow, dragging steps. The Blooded Women began to chant softly, satisfaction brightening their voices in her mind. They knew she was beaten and she hated them for it. She hated them for everything. This time, they would kill Argus and strip the Keeper of her spirit along with all of the memories she had only just reclaimed.

It wasn't the thought of losing those memories that made her heart ache. She hadn't had them back long enough to mourn their loss. It was the memory of traveling with Naago after she first met him. It was Settek giving his life so that she would survive. It was Deynas, holding her close and kissing her head. They had tried so hard. Even if Naago and Deynas called her to them now, she was far too weak to hear them and respond.

The floor stretched out long before her, each faltering step barely bringing her closer to her subject. She could see the spirit of the creature, some form of rare demon, starting to rise out of its flesh. The call to keep surpassed the need for dignity. She sank down to her knees and crawled forward because crawling was easier and faster. The spirit was almost free of its flesh when she reached it, placing her hand upon the moist flesh and making her offer.

The spirit flowed down into her, bringing with it the familiar pain of death brought by the Blooded Women. She shuddered with that pain and sank down, resting her cheek on the cool stone floor. There were punishments to deal out, but she needed to rest first. She couldn't do it without rest.

Many pairs of slippered feet whispered over the floor, moving in to gather around her, their smug satisfaction stinging like a slap across the face.

We knew it would end this way. It is time for you to return to us.

Her eyes stung, but enough tears had fallen. She would not add to them. *I'm sorry, Argus.*

CHAPTER TWENTY FOUR

Progress was slow moving back through the caverns. It wasn't only the difficulty of moving Settek that slowed them. Sorrow and defeat weighed heavy upon them, bearing them down as they trekked along in silence. Even the few creatures they encountered on the return trip, one of the translucent white centipedes and a few darro, gave them a wide berth as if despair created a miasma around them that none dared to enter.

Numerous rock spirits followed them at a wary distance, weaving in and out of the rock like sand dolphins jumping in and out of the dunes. That thought, however, made Deynas think of Argus and he almost gave in to the selfish impulse to lie down on the hard stone and wait for something to come feast upon his flesh. He didn't do it because Kaira and Naago needed his help to move Settek and because he never had learned how to give up properly.

When they reached the improved corridors, the rock spirits abandoned them.

Kaira led them along a different route this time and, though they didn't question it, she explained, perhaps needing a break from the silence. "This way we don't have to use the ladder. There's a staircase up into Warlord Unag's shop. I can probably convince him to lend us a flyer for moving Settek."

Naago grunted. That was the only feedback they gave her.

She nodded and strode along, keeping her head up despite the shine of tears in her eyes and the twitching of muscles in her jaw that betrayed the urge to cry again. Deynas admired her strength. She was a remarkable woman, demon blood or no.

Many of the Endless could learn a lot from crossbreeds like Kaira and her brother, who had more than atoned for his crimes. It didn't matter now, but Deynas would be proud to call Settek a friend. He didn't think Misa would hold it against him.

When they finally made it up the stone staircase and gained access, under the callous watch of two crossbreed guards, to Warlord Unag's cellar overflowing with containers of powders, fluids, raw ingredients, and odors that made their eyes water and their noses itch, they were almost too worn out to carry Settek any further. Only the motivation of escaping the olfactory assault kept them moving up the next set of stairs.

At the top of those stairs, one guard opened the door into a dimly lit shop. The interior was done in worn dark wood and a few arrays of candles provided minimal illumination to shelves full of small glass bottles containing varied supplements and medicinal preparations. The overall effect was one of antiquity and exotic secrets found in hidden places. An intentional ambiance heightened by the wizened old man who sat in the dark behind the counter. He appeared mostly human, with the exception of two horns that spiraled up from his forehead, eyes that were completely emerald, devoid of distinct whites or pupils, and long brown nails that twisted out several inches from his gnarled old fingers.

The old creature took one look at their burden and his wrinkled features pinched together in distress. "You bring such a thing to Unag's shop," he shrilled. "Do you wish to see him executed?"

Deynas and Naago set down the body, taking a quick break while Kaira hurried over and knelt before old creature.

"Warlord Unag, we apologize for this intrusion. We would not have troubled you with this had there been another way, but you must look at it as an opportunity. Provide us a flyer to transport Settek's body home and Warlord Kato will hear of your generosity."

Unag leaned back and eyed her warily. "Unag sees that you are Kato's daughter. Your flesh carries the whisper of his glamour and you speak with his clever tongue. How can Unag trust you?"

Kaira's expression darkened. A chill fell over the room. Threat hung heavy in her tone. "We've suffered significant losses this day. If you do not wish to suffer the same, don't let it get out that you refused to aid the offspring of Warlord Kato. I cannot begin to imagine his wrath."

Unag paled and looked up at one of his guards. He said nothing at all, but the guard nodded after a moment and left the room. Unag turned his gaze back to Kaira. "Unag's guard will meet you in front with the flyer. Unag thanks you to leave now."

Kaira snapped to her feet and gave him a cutting glare. "Your generosity is humbling," she hissed before turning to give them a curt nod and heading for the door.

With arms that felt like jelly, Deynas lifted his share of their burden and they shuffled out front. When their burden was on the flyer, Deynas climbed up in the pilot position. Naago and Kaira crouched down on either side of the passenger stand, each with one hand on the stand for safety and the other holding Settek to be sure his body didn't slip free. Deynas took them on a slow, steady course through the Undercity that way, aware of the many eyes watching them pass, many with cautious indifference, a few with hostility, and even some with sympathy.

They were almost to the door of Kato's hotel when a howler surged out of a side street and into their path, raising its head in an ear-splitting howl. Deynas pulled the craft up as slowly as he could, trying not to disrupt their burden. The crowd in front of The Firelight turned to watch and more emerged from within, drawn by curiosity and the hunger for conflict.

A large mantis-like creature followed the howler from the side street, its long legs moving in a sharp, jerky cadence. Bulbous green eyes scanned them and it lowered its long neck to take a closer look.

The howler sat back now, its many amber eyes reflecting the scene before it while its black tongue lolled to one side of a self-satisfied grin.

"Your companions will be arrested. You are sentenced to death."

Deynas groaned. It fit with their luck that day to draw the attention of an elite enforcer. This wasn't the kind of creature they could bribe or negotiate with. Apparently, his crimes merited no trial under the city's new management.

One long, spiny arm rose up as if to strike him down and Deynas leapt away from the flyer, giving himself room to draw his staff. Naago dropped a hand to his sword and Deynas gave him a sharp look then glanced meaningfully at Kaira. Naago nodded and climbed in front of the pilot stand to move the craft over in front of Kato's hotel.

The enforcer adjusted its aim and struck, but Deynas was ready. He blocked, catching the creature's foreleg and deflecting it to one side. He didn't really want to harm the beast. Injuring it would only guarantee his death sentence. However, not injuring it was just as likely to get him killed. He dove under a swipe, hitting the ground on his shoulder and rolling to his feet. Pain flared in the shoulder, a reminder that he wasn't in the best condition for this battle.

Hypnotists emerged from The Firelight now and formed a weaving row between the crowd from the gambling den and the conflict. They made no move to interfere. It looked as if their only concern was keeping the patrons out of harm's way.

Deynas ducked, blocked, and danced away, his arms shaking with fatigue. The crowd that was gathering started to shout out taunts and advice to both sides like the audience at an arena fight. The enforcer was lightning fast and to match that speed would only draw attention to the fact that he was no mere human. Not matching that speed, however, would mean taking a hit soon and the power behind those strikes was such that it was breaking chunks out of the concrete.

Over by the hotel entrance, Naago stood watching from beside the flyer, his hand hovering close to his blade. Kaira was gone.

When the enforcer started to bring down another strike, Deynas leapt forward, under the attack and in close to the body of the beast. He swung with all his might, catching one leg with the rounded part of the staff and sweeping it out. With its weight already forward, the enforcer toppled and Deynas had to sprint clear to avoid being crushed. The ground shook as the massive beast hit. One flailing leg caught Deynas hard across the back and he flew forward, folding his arms in to protect his face from the concrete. The skin scraped away from his forearms as he skidded to a stop. Then he twisted around and sprang to his feet.

The enforcer was getting back up. Deynas turned to grab for his staff only to find it pinned under a large scaled foot. He looked up at Kato. The warlord was staring over him at Settek's body.

Deynas froze.

Did Kato mean to let the enforcer have him? Perhaps as punishment for Settek's death.

The enforcer rushed toward them. Kato spread his wings wide and let out a roar. Deynas covered his ears. The sound stunned the place to stillness and silence. The only sounds as the roar faded were those of the howler panting and Kaira's footsteps as she walked out of the hotel and went to stand next to Naago.

After several seconds, the enforcer's head began to weave back and forth on its long neck and it made an impatient clicking noise. "That one is dead," it hissed, gesturing to Deynas with one foreleg.

Kato stepped toward the beast and Deynas grabbed his staff, feeling much better with the weapon in hand, though the lull in the action was drawing his attention to the stinging in his arms.

Color swept along Kato's scales, moving over his wings in a mesmerizing and beautiful cascade. The enforcer settled, becoming still. Even it wasn't immune to his influence.

"That one is not dead. My son saw fit to give his life so that man and his companions might live," Kato boomed. "From this day forth, they are all under my protection." He took two more steps forward and the enforcer shrank back, looking suddenly small even though it towered over the warlord. "And if you ever try to arrest my daughter again, I will tear off your head and feed it to your howler."

Kato drew in his wings and turned his back on the enforcer then. He walked to the flyer, lifted Settek from it as if the crossbreed weighed nothing, and strode back into the inn. Deynas glared at the enforcer as he disarmed his staff then followed Naago and Kaira after Kato.

•

The violin sung a soft lament, its rich notes resonating through the halls around the ruin level arena. Kato had given Naago and Deynas a set of joined rooms in which to rest while he retreated into mourning. It was in the shared front room, a sparsely furnished sitting area, that she found Naago, his eyes closed and his music pouring forth like a river of sorrow.

Argus leaned against the doorjamb and closed her eyes, resting while she watched the colors of his sorrow dance languorously around the room. Then the tune changed, the color turning to warm bright hues of pleasure. She opened her eyes to find him watching her, his pale gaze full of delight and wonder.

Pushing away from the door, she walked in and went to sit in a chair beside him. He finished the song and set the violin down.

"How can you be here? You were barely alive when you were called."

She folded her hands in her lap. The hardened jelly on her wrist itched, but it would take some time for the wound to heal, so she did her best to ignore it. The body that she shared with the Keeper now was weak still and their spirits raw from being nearly torn out by the Blooded Women. Her salvation this time had come from an unexpected source.

"The Blooded Women nearly got what they wanted this time." Her voice shook, so she paused, taking a few slow breaths to steady it. "We fell unconscious before the Blooded Women and woke in one of Kato's rooms. He wouldn't speak much, but did explain a little."

She paused, thinking back. When she'd woken, she'd found Kato in the next room. Settek's body lay on a bed and he stood staring out the window. Kaira slept curled up in one of the big chairs, the salt of many tears drying on her cheeks.

"How am I here?"

He didn't move. "You should be resting. You are weak."

"I need to understand."

Kato ignored her.

She walked up to the bed and set her hand on Settek's shoulder. "I wasn't able to keep his spirit."

Kato turned then and stared at her for a long time, his eyes dim with grief. "Thank you for trying," he said finally. Then he turned back to the window. "When The Undying created you, he gave you his blood, but I gave you a piece of my spirit. Now that you have your spirit back, I can call you to me when I wish and you can refuse me no more than you can refuse the call to keep. That connection also made it possible for your spirit to call out to me for help when the Blooded Women tried to take you back. I took you from them." The hatred in his voice rippled black down his scales.

She was silent. Startled by this new revelation. Something that hadn't been in her memories. The warlord had given no reason for her to distrust him, but the thought of being at his mercy made her uneasy all the same. Still, he had saved her.

"Thank you."

His shoulders lifted and sank in a mournful shrug. "Soon, you will assist me in reclaiming the rest of my spirit. For now, I wish to be alone."

"Keeper?"

"Argus," she corrected. "The Undying gave the Keeper life with his blood, but her spirit was created from a portion of Kato's spirit. Because of that connection, Kato can call her to him without needing her consent."

"I'm glad he could bring you back to us."

She heard the hesitation in his tone. They were all beholden to the warlord now. It wasn't a comfortable feeling. Although she had reason in the Keeper's memories to want to trust Kato, too many questions still needed answering. She hoped those answers would come before the Keeper was called again. The Blooded Women hadn't made another attempt yet to get her back. Perhaps they were rethinking things now that Kato could interfere. In whatever time she had, she meant to see to other matters that needed attention.

"Naago-ra..." she trailed off when he shook his head.

He smiled, though there was a distinct sadness in his eyes. "You don't have to explain. I know where your heart lies. It was unmistakable when you looked at him the moment before you disappeared last time." He shifted his gaze away. "Deynas-ra is in the back room practicing with his staff. Since we got here, he's been back there either practicing or sitting on the floor with his head in his hands. I haven't seen him eat or sleep. He needs you."

She took his hand, giving it a light squeeze—she hadn't strength for more—and leaned in to kiss him lightly on the lips. "You are dear to us, Naago-ra. You helped bring us back to life." She touched her hand to his chest then. "You carry a fragment of my spirit in you, but you also carry a piece of the heart we share. Never doubt that."

His answering smile was halfhearted. It would take time to make him see the truth of her words.

When she stood, he lifted his violin and started to play another melody, this one sad and sweet. The melody followed her through another room to a closed door. Beyond she could hear the swoosh of the staff cutting through the air. She closed her eyes, seeing with the Keeper's spirit sight. Even through the wood door, she could see his *umahk-ra*, full of sorrow and anger. She watched it move for a time, remembering the fighting forms from her own training days. When his back was to the door, she silently entered.

Deynas wore no shirt. His muscles trembled, glistening with sweat. The room smelled of him, a scent that woke desire and called up reserves of strength in her. She stepped in as he spun and caught the blade with her right hand, trusting the black roots to protect her. He froze, staring at her with his bright blue eyes.

"Argus?"

She nodded and pushed the blade to the side.

For a few seconds, he didn't move or speak at all. He barely seemed to breathe. Then he disarmed the staff and tossed the handle to one side. He reached behind his neck, took off the god's blood pendant, and stepped close to place it around her neck. The stone slid down beneath the cloak.

She slid her fingers into his sweat-damped hair and pulled him close, rising on her toes to kiss him. His arms wrapped around her, drawing her in against him and he kissed her back. She tasted salt on their lips and wondered if it was his sweat or her tears that she tasted. With one leg, she reached back and nudged the door shut.

THE END

ACKNOWLEDGEMENTS

The people who have been most supportive in this journey don't change much, but there are sometimes those who come and go. As always, there are many people in my life who aren't mentioned here for brevity sake. All of you are still very important to me.

I want to offer specific thanks to the following people.

To my mom Linda for your loving support and for helping me brainstorm and refine my ideas.

To Rick and Ann for always being willing to read and give feedback on my books and for being the best of friends.

To Kai for staying by my side and believing in me through some incredibly difficult times.

To Uncle Brian for saving my life when I was very small (not that I've grown much).

To Aradia for knowing I would succeed from the first time we met and being an inspiration in your dedication to your own art.

To Michael for many years of partnership.

To my good friend and fellow author Eldritch Black for being an amazing writing companion for many years. Also to the rest of that writing group, for making so many Thursdays productive and fun.

To my cover artist, Heather, and my interior designer, Brian, thank you both for your fantastic work.

I must also offer thanks to my sixth grade teacher, Mr. Johnson, for being so pleased and excited when I told you I was going to be an author and to my eighth grade algebra teacher, Mr. Siebenlist, for almost letting me flunk because you were so delighted that I was writing books in class rather than notes.

AUTHOR BIO

Nikki started writing her first novel at the age of 12, which she still has tucked in a briefcase in her home office. She now lives in the magnificent Pacific Northwest tending to her sweet horse, two manipulative cats, and a crazy dog. She feeds her imagination by sitting on the ocean in her kayak gazing out across the never-ending water or hanging from a rope in a cave, embraced by darkness and the sound of dripping water. She finds peace through practicing iaido or shooting her longbow.

•

Thank you for taking time to read this novel. Please leave a review if you enjoyed it.

•

For more about me and my work visit me at http://nikkimccormack.com.

•

OTHER NOVELS BY NIKKI MCCORMACK

The Girl and the Clockwork Cat
A young adult steampunk adventure.

The Girl and the Clockwork Conspiracy
The adventure continues.

Forbidden Things, Book One: Dissidents
Forbidden Things, Book Two: Exile
Forbidden Things, Book Three: Apostate
An epic, romantic fantasy.